"We can't relive the past. Do you understand that?"

Hendrick set his jaw. "I'm not asking to go back in time, Mariah. I'm talking about getting you safely to Montana so you can help Luke."

She breathed deep, squared her shoulders and turned to face him. "I owe you an explanation, about last time. Why I left. I shouldn't have run off."

He couldn't agree more, but he had the sense not to say that. Instead, he waited for her.

"It's my work," she finally said. "Helping the orphans is my calling. I couldn't leave them. I'll never stop helping them. Please understand. It's not that I don't care for you. You're a wonderful...friend."

Did he imagine that hesitation? Hope crept into his heart.

She shook her head, as if she knew what he was thinking. "It wouldn't work. If we're going to survive this trip to Montana, you need to understand that there can't be anything between us beyond friendship. Ever."

The sliver of hope turned to cold steel.

Books by Christine Johnson

Love Inspired Historical

Soaring Home
The Matrimony Plan
All Roads Lead Home

CHRISTINE JOHNSON

is a small-town Michigan girl who has lived in every corner of the state's Lower Peninsula. After trying her hand at music and art, she returned to her first love—story. She holds a bachelor's degree in English and a master's degree in library studies from the University of Michigan. She feels blessed to write for Love Inspired and is thrilled to be twice named a finalist for Romance Writers of America's Golden Heart® award. When not at the computer keyboard, she loves to hike and explore God's majestic creation with the love of her life, her husband. She participates in her church's healing prayer ministry and has experienced firsthand the power of prayer. These days, she and her husband, a Great Lakes ship pilot, split their time between northern Michigan and the Florida Keys.

CHRISTINE JOHNSON

All Roads Lead Home

Love Inspired

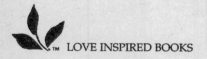

LOVE INSPIRED BOOKS

Recycling programs for this product may not exist in your area.

ISBN-13: 978-0-373-82901-9

ALL ROADS LEAD HOME

Copyright © 2012 by Christine Elizabeth Johnson

www.LoveInspiredBooks.com

Printed in U.S.A.

Dear Reader,

Welcome to Love Inspired!

2012 is a very special year for us. It marks the fifteenth anniversary of Love Inspired Books. Hard to believe that fifteen years ago, we first began publishing our warm and wonderful inspirational romances.

Back in 1997, we offered readers three books a month. Since then we've expanded quite a bit! In addition to the heartwarming contemporary romances of Love Inspired, we have the exciting romantic suspenses of Love Inspired Suspense, and the adventurous historical romances of Love Inspired Historical. Whatever your reading preference, we've got fourteen books a month for you to choose from now!

Throughout the year we'll be celebrating in several different ways. Look for books by bestselling authors who've been writing for us since the beginning, stories by brand-new authors you won't want to miss, special miniseries in all three lines, reissues of top authors, and much, much more.

This is our way of thanking you for reading Love Inspired books. We know our uplifting stories of hope, faith and love touch your hearts as much as they touch ours.

Join us in celebrating fifteen amazing years of inspirational romance!

Blessings,

Melissa Endlich and Tina James

Senior Editors of Love Inspired Books

To Jenna and Kathy
This long journey has been all the more worthwhile
because of you.

Special thanks to the Love Inspired editors,
especially Emily Rodmell,
whose guidance has been invaluable.
You're the best!

* * *

For the Lord seeth not as man seeth;
For man looketh on the outward appearance,
But the Lord looketh on the heart.
—1 *Samuel* 16:7

Chapter One

❧

Pearlman, Michigan
July 1922

"Don't die here," Mariah pleaded.

But her motorcar threatened to do just that as it coughed and slowed to a crawl. She depressed the accelerator to the floor, and the car lurched forward a few feet before slowing again.

"Just one more block." She gripped the wheel and as an afterthought added, "Please."

Mariah Meeks, agent for the Orphaned Children's Society of New York, didn't ordinarily talk to automobiles, but she *had* to get to her brother's church before he left for the day, and she had to do so without anyone noticing she'd returned to Pearlman. That mission died along with her car in the worst possible place—at Simmons Motor Garage.

As the car rolled to an ignoble stop, her pulse rocketed. Had Hendrick seen her? Surely he had. She hazarded a glance at the gleaming whitewashed garage, but no one had come out yet. Maybe he was still angry at her. Her brother Gabe said Hendrick hadn't dated anyone since she left town two Octobers ago.

Her fingers curled around the wheel. Hendrick Simmons. Did he look the same? The same strong loping stride, the same warm brown eyes, the same lock of hair across his brow that she'd always wanted to push away? Her palms sweated. She couldn't breathe. Memories swirled like a summer cyclone.

She tugged at a lock of her dark, springy hair, resisting the urge to tuck it into her mouth. What a mess she'd made of things that October. Her brother Gabe's wedding was supposed to be a joyous time. But then she'd caught the bouquet by accident and saw the look on Hendrick's face. Hope. Desire. Love? But they could never be more than friends. She'd panicked, had left town the next day without telling him why she could never marry. Coward.

He must despise her.

He wouldn't want to fix her car. She tried and tried to restart it, but the engine simply wouldn't turn over. What would she do? She could walk to her brother's church, but she had to have a car to get to Montana. A child's future depended on her getting there soon, and the trains weren't running, thanks to the nationwide rail strike.

Why, God? She looked to the heavens, but He didn't answer.

Gabe would know what to do. Her brother would figure out a way to get her to Montana. She plopped the stifling rolled-brim hat on her head and gathered her handbag.

"Miss Mariah?"

She jumped so high she crushed the crown of her hat on the roof.

"Peter," she gasped at the sight of the grinning teenage boy. "You've grown."

The orphan had always been a beanpole, but he must

have shot up six inches in the two years since the Society placed him with the Simmons family.

"Yes'm, almost a foot," he said with obvious pride.

She squinted. What was that? A few straggling hairs on his upper lip? She rapidly calculated his age. Goodness, he must be nearly seventeen now.

"What brings you to town?" he asked. "I ain't seen you practically since I come to Pearlman."

She stifled the urge to correct his grammar. "I'm just here for a brief visit." She started to open her door, but Peter finished the job and helped her from the car. Clearly, Mrs. Simmons had taught him manners. Judging by his broad grin, he was happy, exactly what she hoped to ensure for all the children she placed—especially Luke, the foster boy her brother Gabe had taken in. That was why she had to talk to Gabe right now. That's why she needed to get to Montana.

She glanced again at the garage. Still no Hendrick. "Are you helping Mr. Simmons at the garage?"

"More'n that. Mr. Hendrick taught me everything about engines. I'm practically running the place now."

"Running it?" She frowned. "Just for the summer, correct? You still plan to finish high school."

"Yes'm, but Mr. Hendrick's so busy at the airfield that he lets me take over here."

The airfield. Of course. She breathed a sigh of relief. That explained why he hadn't come out to greet her. Hendrick had worked on Jack Hunter's aeroplanes from the moment Jack landed in Pearlman. According to Gabe, the two were collaborating to build bigger and better engines for a foolhardy attempt at flying to the North Pole.

"I'm sure he'd wanna see ya," Peter said. "He'll be back anytime now."

Then she must hurry. She darted a glance down the

street in the direction of the airfield. No one in sight yet. "Thank you, Peter, but I need to see my brother. Will you look after my car? I think it's burnt a valve."

"I'll take good care of her, Miss Mariah." He tipped a finger to his grimy cap.

"Thank you, Peter. If you need to reach me, I'll be at the church for an hour or so and then at the parsonage."

He knew that, of course. In tiny Pearlman, everyone knew where everyone stayed, who their relations were and what they were doing. Everyone in town doubtless already knew she was here. Her reappearance would make tongues wag with speculation that the romance between Hendrick and her was back on.

They could talk all they wanted. Romance was out of the question. In fact, she didn't even need to see Hendrick. She'd ask Gabe to talk to him about fixing her car. Hendrick wouldn't be able to refuse his pastor.

She squared her shoulders, quite pleased with her solution, and hurried toward her brother's church, intent on defusing a much more pressing crisis.

The heavy twin-engine plane landed without a hitch and lumbered down the runway.

"Sounds good," Hendrick Simmons said with relief. He'd never understand why Jack Hunter, the plane's owner, allowed his wife to fly test flights. Hendrick would never let his wife face that kind of danger. If he ever got a wife, which hardly seemed likely after Mariah made it clear they could never be more than friends. For now, he was married to his work. He'd developed the high horsepower, air-cooled engines Hunter needed for his new plane.

"Your engines sound better than good." The suave aviator followed the plane's progress down the graded runway. "They'll take Darcy and me to the North Pole."

Hendrick scowled. "You're taking Darcy? After what happened on your transatlantic attempt, I'd think you'd want to stick with the flight school."

Jack Hunter didn't look fazed by the reminder of the failed flight. "Darcy wouldn't have it any other way. You know her."

Hendrick did know Jack's wife, Darcy. They'd been friends since childhood. "I wouldn't want my wife doing something that dangerous."

Jack laughed. "Wait until you meet the right woman. She'll change your mind. You'll do anything to make her happy."

"Even risk her life?" Hendrick shook his head. "No woman is going to change my mind. I'm looking for someone nice and quiet. The headstrong ones are too much trouble."

"That they are, but worth every minute. I wouldn't be here if it wasn't for Darcy."

"Do you ever miss being a test pilot for Curtiss Aeroplane and living the bachelor life?"

Hunter shook his head. "Not for one second. And after this flight, we're going to start a family." He looked wistfully toward the plane's cockpit, where his wife sat.

Hendrick swallowed hard. Darcy was his age, Jack only a little older. "I'd sure like that someday."

Hunter clapped Hendrick on the shoulder. "Keep the faith, pal. There's someone out there for you."

Mariah. Only, she didn't want him. And he couldn't see marrying anyone else in Pearlman. Hendrick squinted into the afternoon sun. "Lately I've been thinking I need to get away from Pearlman, try my hand at something else."

"Is that so?" Hunter patted the pockets of his leather jacket. "Then I might have just the opportunity for you." He pulled out a letter, folded and refolded until the seams had worn thin. "Remember Dick Burrows from Curtiss Aeroplane?"

How could he forget? Burrows used to be Jack's mechanic out East, and he'd inspected every repair Hendrick had made to Jack's plane two years ago. The arrogant aeronautical engineer thought he knew everything there was to know about engines, but he couldn't find a single thing wrong with Hendrick's work.

"He's still with Curtiss," Jack said. "A while back he wrote asking if I knew anyone working on air-cooled engines. It looks like Wright Aeronautical might get Lawrance's air-cooled radial motor, and Curtiss wants to build something to rival them, something like your engine."

"My engine?" Excitement bolted through Hendrick. A big-time aviation company wanted his invention to battle their rivals at Wright Aeronautical. They wanted *him*. He wouldn't be a lowly mechanic anymore. He'd be an aeronautical engineer. He swallowed and tried to sound calm. "What're they offering?"

Jack shrugged. "You'll have to talk to them. I can cable Burrows to set up an appointment. You'll need to bring some sketches of your engine to Garden City and explain how it works."

"Garden City's in New York?" Hendrick vaguely recalled Jack came from there.

"Yep. Long Island."

Long Island, New York. Hendrick had never left Pearlman. He'd never had that chance. After Pa's death, he'd supported his mother and kid sister and come to the conclusion that dreams belonged to other men. He'd put his on hold. Maybe now he could dare to try something new. His sister was out of high school, and he'd earn enough at Curtiss to support the family. Real wages, not the ups and downs of running a small-town business.

Hunter was grinning. "Pretty near someone you know."

Mariah. Hendrick's gut knotted up. Like Burrows, it was clear that she thought he was beneath her. Oh, she'd picnicked with him and joined him at church suppers, but when it came to anything serious, he wasn't good enough. She didn't say it right out, but that had to be the reason she'd snubbed him. She was wealthy and college-educated. He was just a mechanic. Well, he'd show her he was much more than that. His engine would bring fame and fortune, enough to impress anyone, even Mariah Meeks. He'd show her exactly what she'd missed out on.

"Send the cable," he said. "Let Burrows know I'm interested."

"Will do." Jack grinned as his wife climbed out of the cockpit. "Gotta run, pal."

Hendrick nodded and watched Hunter hurry across the airfield. Darcy raced toward him, arms opened wide. Their embrace and the way he swung her in a circle tore Hendrick to pieces. Everyone his age was getting married and having children. He wanted a family so bad it hurt.

He couldn't stand to watch any longer so he hopped on his motorbike and tore toward town in a cloud of dust. The wind against his face made him feel free. No responsibilities. No worries. No business to run or family to support. And most of all, for one moment, he could forget the aching emptiness.

Then he saw it: a green-and-black automobile parked beside his garage. He pulled his motorbike to a stop alongside the Overland. That knot in his gut wrenched tighter. It couldn't be. But even before he saw her gloves on the front seat, he knew the car was hers.

Mariah was back.

News travels fast in small towns. Gabe met Mariah before she reached the church. Her little brother looked the same, perhaps a bit filled out in the midsection, but his dark curls still flopped wildly and he still disdained a suit jacket in the summer. Neither the ministry nor marriage had changed him one bit.

"Sis." He enveloped her in a big hug. "Heard you were in town. What brings you here?"

She squeezed tightly, relishing this last moment before she broke the bad news. "I missed you, little brother."

"Then you shouldn't have stayed away so long." He stepped away and assessed her. "You should have let us know you were coming. Felicity will blame me for not telling her in time to set up the guestroom."

"I'm sorry for being so thoughtless." Mariah brushed the dirt from her duster. "I don't want to put you out, especially with Felicity so close to her due date. I'll stay at Terchie's."

Naturally he refused to let her stay in a boardinghouse. "We have five extra rooms. You're staying with us. Did you leave your car there?"

She crossed her arms, pretending to be vexed at his assumption. "How do you know I drove?"

He shook his head. "Even if the trains were running, you'd drive that car of yours." He glanced up and down the street. "Where is it?"

"At the garage," she admitted.

"The garage?" he snorted, unable to hide his mirth. "How's Hendrick?"

"I didn't see him. Peter looked happy, though. He's grown so tall, and I think I saw the beginnings of a mustache."

Gabe chuckled. "Luke asks every day when his will start to grow. They're good friends, you see. I have to give Peter credit for letting a ten-year-old hang around him so much."

Mariah's heart ached at Gabe's words. Two years ago Mariah had facilitated the placement of five Society orphans in Pearlman. Peter and Luke had been the last chosen and had apparently formed a deep bond from that day forward. Normally that would be good, but it would also make any separation that much harder. She sucked in a shuddering breath.

Gabe's brow creased. "You still haven't told me why you're here. Mom is coming in two weeks. You could have joined her if you wanted to be here when the baby's born." He drew a sharp breath. "It's business, isn't it? I didn't think the Society sent agents on follow-up anymore, especially when the reports are all good."

She swallowed hard. "It is Society business, in a way." But she couldn't say more because one Pearlman matron after another stopped to greet her. This was not the place to tell him the bad news. When she had a moment's break from the greetings, she asked if they might talk in private.

He nodded. "Let's go to the church. Florabelle will be gone by now."

Mariah was relieved to hear that. The church secretary was notorious for her gossiping, and this was the sort of news that Florabelle would love to spread.

Gabe extended an arm, always the gentleman, but she preferred to walk on her own. He set an easy pace. They were of a similar middling height, their strides equal. It wasn't like walking with Hendrick. He'd always had to slow down to match her shorter stride.

After a dozen more greetings, they were alone again on the sidewalk. Gabe buried his hands in his pockets, brow furrowed, looking very much like a little boy. She wished she could reassure him, but her news would only bring more worry.

"Lovely day," she said to break the tension.

He mumbled a reply but didn't look up until they reached the church, its solid oaken door darkened from all the hands that had touched it through the years. She reached for the handle, but Gabe stopped her hand.

"Is this about Luke?" he whispered.

She couldn't answer. Not yet. "Let's go inside."

He nodded and pulled open the door. "Whatever it is, God will see us through."

She wished she had that much confidence. Until now, she thought she'd placed total reliance on the Lord, but this news had shaken her. It would devastate Gabe.

Once they'd settled into their respective chairs, Gabe behind his desk and Mariah taking the seat opposite him, he waited expectantly, hands clenched, as if clinging to his new family.

Mariah blinked back tears and tried to dislodge the lump in her throat. The last thing she ever wanted to do was hurt her beloved little brother. She'd always looked after him, mothered him. Then two years ago, he came to Pearlman for his first pastoral appointment and fell in love with Felicity. Their romance had been rocky, for she barely gave him the time of day at first, but Felicity had a tender soul, and Gabe was one of the few people who saw it.

Shortly after, Mariah arrived to arrange the placement of five orphans into foster homes. All had been snapped up except Luke, whose darker coloring challenged deeply rooted prejudice. Gabe took in the traumatized little boy, and Mariah raised him for three months until Gabe and Felicity married. In that time she lost her heart to the little boy, and that's what made this news so difficult to bear.

She squeezed her hands together to stop the shaking and took a deep breath. "There's a little problem concerning Luke."

Gabe frowned. "We haven't gotten far in the adoption process. I thought that was due to the paperwork and investigations. Have you heard something else?" He leaned forward. "I'll do anything to make Luke my legal son."

"It's not about the adoption."

"Then what is it?"

She fought the bile rising in her throat. How she wished she didn't have to tell him this, but there was no way around it. "Luke's father has returned." The words fell between them like stones. "He wants Luke back."

All the life went out of Gabe. "His father?"

She tried to temper the pain. "Perhaps I should say that a man who claims to be Luke's father wants him back."

"Claims?" Gabe pressed his hands against the top of the desk. "Is he Luke's father or not?"

"That's what I intend to find out, and that's why I have to go to Montana."

"Montana? What on earth does Montana have to do with this?"

"The man who says he's Luke's father lives in Montana."

Gabe paused, processing what she was trying to tell him. "Why do you think he isn't who he says he is?"

She traced the wood grain of the chair's arm with her fingernail. "His name doesn't quite match the records. The old Detroit office listed the father as Francesco Guillardo. The man says he's Frank Gillard. He claims he anglicized his name."

He sat back heavily. "People do change their names to avoid prejudice. Remember how Luke was received when people heard his full name was Luciano?"

She nodded. How could she forget the gasps of shock, the slurs against the boy's dark skin?

Gabe's long sigh weighed heavily on the hot summer air. "Where in Montana?"

"The western part. A town called Brunley."

He stared off into space. "So far."

Mariah ached for him, for Felicity and even for herself. During those three months she'd stayed with Luke, she'd spent every moment of the day with him, had heard his first words, had wiped his tears after the nightmares. Luke was the closest she would ever get to having a son. "I won't let Frank Gillard take him."

"Mariah! That's kidnapping."

"Is that any worse than abandoning a child?" She stood, too agitated to sit. "That's what Luke's father did two-and-a-half years ago. And whatever happened before they got to the asylum made Luke so afraid of his father that he stopped talking. I'm not about to let that man touch him."

Gabe frowned. "You're making a lot of assumptions."

"Don't tell me you haven't come to the same conclusion."

"That he was abandoned, yes. That's on the record, but you don't know what made Luke stop talking."

She held his gaze. "Did Luke ever tell you anything about that time?"

Gabe shook his head. "He got so upset any time I tried to talk about his parents that I stopped trying. I figured he'd be ours soon, and it wouldn't matter."

"Do we dare ask him again?"

He shook his head. "He can't know a thing. Promise me you won't say a word."

"If you promise to fight." She felt the hot tears rise. "We'll find a way to keep Luke here. We have to."

He stared into space a long time, thinking. At last he hit on something. "Didn't Frank Gillard sign away his parental rights when he left Luke at the orphanage? That is the usual procedure."

Mariah squirmed under the horrible truth. "The termination-of-rights paperwork wasn't done correctly. The agent must have mixed up Luke's paperwork with someone else's because the signature doesn't match the name. Instead of Francesco Guillardo or even Frank Gillard, it's signed Desmond Corliss."

"What?" Gabe shook his head in bewilderment. "How is that possible?"

"I don't know." She bit her lip. Mistakes seldom happened, and, when they did, they hadn't mattered. Until now.

He strode back to the desk. "Show it to me."

She drew the papers from her handbag and laid them on the desk. He pulled them close and sat down, jaw taut as he scanned the pages.

After agonizing minutes, he raised hopeless eyes to her. "You're right."

She couldn't stand to see his despair. "I'm going to do everything in my power to stop him. Everything."

"How?" His voice sounded hollow. Defeated. "We have no proof of wrongdoing other than a child's refusal to talk. That could mean anything, and in a court's eyes, it's useless. You know as well as I that the birth parents have every right to reclaim their children, as long as they haven't signed that right away. We have no way to stop this man from taking Luke."

She couldn't allow it. She wasn't going to let Gabe or Luke down. "I'm going to Montana, and I'll get Mr. Gillard to sign new termination-of-rights papers." She pressed her hand over his. "I promise you I will not rest until Luke is safe."

Gabe slowly shook his head. "I don't see how you can

convince a man who has already asked for his son to sign away his parental rights. I wouldn't sign them if I were in his shoes."

"That's you. You're a good, loving father. You would never have abandoned Luke in the first place. Frank Gillard is another matter. Something's not right about this, Gabe, and I intend to find out what it is. Come with me. Together we can find a way to save Luke."

He sank back in his chair. "I can't go to Montana. Felicity—" He rubbed his eyes to hide the tears, but he couldn't hide the quiver in his voice. "She doesn't want anyone to know, but the pregnancy has been difficult. She started bleeding last week. It stopped, but—"

Mariah gasped and pressed a hand to her mouth.

Gabe stared off into space. "Doc Stevens wants her to carry the baby as long as possible. I'm supposed to ensure that nothing upsets her. Hearing this would be the worst thing for her and the baby. If I left with you, she'd know something was afoot." He turned worried eyes on her. "Promise you won't say a word."

Mariah nodded. "I wouldn't dream of it."

"Did you plan to take Luke with you?"

She shook her head. "Of course not." She gripped her brother's hand. "It'll turn out all right, Gabe. I promise."

He smiled weakly. "First you have to get to Montana. The trains aren't running right now, but you're welcome to stay until they are."

She didn't have the luxury of waiting. "I'm driving my car."

"Your car?" he said incredulously. "The one that's broken down?"

She nodded.

"By yourself? That must be two thousand miles. You can't drive that far alone."

She would not be dissuaded. "I will do whatever it takes to stop that man from uprooting Luke."

Gabe shook his head, signaling he knew when he was defeated—and when his goal matched hers. "I don't know how you're going to manage."

"With God's help."

He let one corner of his mouth lift, just for an instant. "Promise me you'll take someone with you, preferably a mechanic."

She knew exactly whom he had in mind. "Gabriel John, you know full well that I can't travel two thousand miles with a man who's not a relative. I will drive to Montana myself." She whisked the papers into her bag and left his office.

He followed on her heels. "Then take a woman along, but don't go alone."

Her hand stilled on the door handle. A woman might be acceptable. "I'd love to bring a female mechanic. Whom do you suggest?"

He didn't answer, of course. He had no more idea than she did.

"Just what I thought." She yanked open the door and stepped into none other than Hendrick Simmons.

With a gasp, she jerked backward, losing her balance. Hendrick steadied her with a hand to her shoulder, and the touch sent electricity zinging to her toes. *No, no, no.* It couldn't be. The time apart was supposed to erase those crazy feelings.

He quickly pulled his hand away, and she retreated a step to recover her senses.

"Miss Meeks," he said dryly, the tone telling her he was just as unhappy to see her.

She swallowed hard, but the pain wouldn't go away. "What are you doing here?"

He lifted her valise. "Bringing your luggage." But instead of handing it to her, he set it down while his gaze drifted to her face.

She gulped when his warm brown eyes met hers. Why did he still affect her so? His commanding height took her breath away. The sculpted features and strong jaw made her heart flutter. His brown hair curled just a bit at the temple, and she had to resist raising a hand to brush that one stray lock off his brow.

"Hendrick." Gabe ducked around her. "It's good to see you."

Hendrick ripped his gaze away from her. "You, too, Pastor." He pointed to the valise. "Well, I've delivered your sister's bag, so I'll be going."

Mariah couldn't help noticing that Hendrick's speech was more polished and that he'd worn his Sunday-best shirt and trousers. Odd. Peter said he'd been working on Jack Hunter's aeroplane engines.

Gabe cornered Hendrick on the edge of the church steps. Though her brother couldn't drape an arm around the taller man's shoulders, he didn't hesitate to leverage Hendrick by the elbow. "I've got a project I'd like to discuss with you. Why don't you come to supper at the parsonage tonight?" He briefly glanced her way. "Bring your sister along."

"Gabe," Mariah warned. She knew exactly what he was up to, and it was not going to work. Under no circumstances would she drive to Montana with Hendrick Simmons.

"I, um." Hendrick looked from Gabe to her with obvious discomfort. "Supper?"

"And your mother, too. Bring everyone," Gabe added a bit too cheerfully.

The whole Simmons clan? What was her brother up to?

He couldn't suggest that Hendrick travel to Montana with her in front of his mother and sister—not to mention Felicity. There'd be too many questions. But to all appearances, that was exactly what he planned to do. Mariah folded her arms and tapped her foot. She couldn't be any clearer that this was a bad idea, but Hendrick actually looked like he was considering the invitation. She had to put a stop to this crazy idea right now.

"I don't think Mr. Simmons would care to dine with us tonight," she stated. There, she'd given him a way out. Alas, her effort produced the opposite effect.

With a look of defiance, Hendrick turned to Gabe. "I'll be there."

Chapter Two

What had he been thinking? Hendrick sure didn't want to spend the evening with Mariah, but she'd goaded him into accepting the pastor's invitation when she said he wouldn't want to come. No one told Hendrick Simmons what he did or didn't want.

Her jaw had dropped, and that made him feel good for a moment, but then she'd clapped her mouth shut and shot a glare at her brother. She did not want to see him, even for a couple of hours. The realization hurt as much as it had a year and a half ago.

Still, even though he knew it would only hurt more, he couldn't stop looking at her. That wild mossy scent hung about her, not exactly perfume, just entirely her. The curly dark hair, the way her hazel eyes turned greenish in the sunlight and the determined tilt of her chin still turned him inside out. He couldn't look away.

"Everything's settled, then," said Pastor Gabriel. "I'd better get home to tell Felicity we're having guests, or there'll be trouble."

Mariah didn't say a thing, but judging by the set of her mouth, she wasn't pleased.

Gabriel pointed to Mariah's valise. "That your bag, sis? I'll take it so you can stay to chat with Hendrick."

"Why on earth would we need to chat?"

Pastor Gabriel picked up her bag. "Oh, something about your broken car."

She wrestled the valise from her brother. "I can carry my own luggage." She added a glare at Hendrick, as if he somehow had finagled this invitation. "How long will it take to fix my car? I have important business that can't be delayed."

"Me, too," Hendrick countered with equal vigor. "It's not like I don't have important things to do." Like a future with Curtiss Aeroplane.

A flicker of worry crossed her face, and her voice softened. "But you can fix it? I—I don't have much time."

The hint of vulnerability almost made him feel bad for her. Almost. But any sympathy passed the moment she offered to pay extra for speedy repairs.

She had to bring up money. She knew he could never compete with her there. The Meekses were wealthy New Yorkers at the top of society. They hobnobbed with Astors and Vanderbilts. They attended the opera and ballet. He could afford only one good suit and shirt, a shirt that needed pressing if he was to look respectable tonight.

"I won't charge one dime more than I'd charge anyone else. Now, if you'll excuse me, I have to get ready for dinner." He tipped his cap and retreated down the church steps. His sole consolation was the glint of terror that crossed her face when he mentioned supper. At least this meal was going to be as painful for her as it would be for him.

Mariah was going to kill Gabe.

She sat on the bed in one of the parsonage's guestrooms

and yanked a comb through her knotted hair, trying to get it into a semblance of order. The dust and wind on the drive had left it a mess, and there was no time to wash it. She'd changed her gown, but the hair would have to do.

Why she should care was beyond her. Hendrick Simmons shouldn't mean anything to her anymore, but the man still somehow sent her calm, stable world spinning out of control. Even though he despised her.

To be honest, she deserved it after the way she'd treated him. She owed him more of an explanation, and she'd give it, but not at dinner. Above all, she couldn't upset Felicity. Gabe had made that clear.

So why had he invited the Simmons family? The stress of hosting a dinner party couldn't help Felicity's nerves, but when Mariah insisted on cooking, Felicity had coyly informed her that Gabe had hired a housekeeper. Mariah never thought she'd see the day when her brother hired help. For years, he'd decried their family's social status and insisted on living without the trappings of wealth. That's why he'd accepted the pastorate in small town Pearlman. Hiring help must have wounded his pride. Thankfully Felicity had talked some sense into him.

"Luke's home," Felicity called up the stairs.

Mariah smoothed her wrinkled skirt, though the boy wouldn't care one bit what she looked like. Little Luke had spent the day with the Highbottoms, who had a farm and five very energetic children, including one of the orphans Mariah had brought here. After all that running around, he'd be tired and cranky.

She rose and set the comb on the vanity. Would he remember her? She'd never forget their three months together, but he'd been so young, a terrified little boy who would only speak to Gabe's dog.

Mariah dabbed away a tear with her handkerchief. This

emotion was silly. She had to put on a cheerful face for Luke. He couldn't suspect that danger lurked in his future.

Before descending, she offered up a prayer, asking the Lord to watch over and protect Luke. As always, prayer calmed her. Somehow God would see this through. He always did.

She took one last glance in the mirror and headed downstairs. Before she reached the bottom step, a war whoop rang out from the kitchen, and the door banged open as Luke barreled into the living room.

"Aunt Mariah, Aunt Mariah." Dressed like a member of Buffalo Bill's Wild West Show with his child-size Indian headdress, he jumped up and down, waving his toy tomahawk. "I'm Geronimo."

"I see that. And what a fierce chief you are," she said as she gave the boy a hug.

He submitted for a few seconds, but quickly squirmed free, and she had to remember that he was ten now and too old for hugging and kissing.

"My, you've grown tall," she said.

"Five whole inches just this year," he confirmed proudly. "Daddy says it's the most anyone in the family ever grew in half a year."

Oh, dear. He called Gabe Daddy. That would make the transition harder if she failed.

She forced a smile. "I'm sure he's right."

"It's time to change your clothes for dinner," Felicity urged, pointing Luke toward the stairs. "Neither Geronimo nor Buffalo Bill are invited tonight. And do wash off the war paint."

"Aw, Mom," Luke protested.

Arguing with a child couldn't be good for Felicity. Mariah motioned Felicity to sit down while she addressed

Luke at eye level. "It's a special pow-wow tonight, and Geronimo will want to look his best."

His eyes lit up. "A pow-wow?"

She nodded.

Convinced, he tromped off to his room to change.

"You're good with children," Felicity said after Mariah sat beside her. "One day you'll have some of your own."

Mariah couldn't tell Felicity that was beyond even prayer, and she certainly didn't want to discuss it, so she diverted the conversation. "Luke is doing so well."

"He gets a little more independent every day." Felicity sighed. "And he's so bright, especially with his letters. He's reading *Tom Sawyer* all by himself."

"How does he feel about getting a new brother or sister?"

Felicity smiled softly and rubbed her large belly. "I'm not sure he understands, but he trusts us." She laughed. "He thinks we're going to pick one out, like at the store."

Mariah chuckled, though part of her ached.

"I can't wait for the adoption to come through. Then we'll be a whole family, the way it was meant to be. And I owe it all to you." She squeezed Mariah's hand.

"Me?" Mariah tried to hide her alarm behind a smile.

"Yes, you're the one who brought Luke here. You're the one who showered him with love. He wouldn't be the wonderful little boy he is today without you. I'm so glad you decided to visit."

Mariah felt sick. What if she failed? What if Frank Gillard took Luke away from this safe and loving home into a life of terror? She couldn't live with herself.

"Mariah?" Felicity looked concerned. "Are you all right? You look pale."

"I'm fine," Mariah assured her. "Just a bit tired after the drive. I think I'll go outside and get some fresh air."

She hurried onto the porch and tried to shut the door on the tangle of her emotions. Tears wouldn't help Luke. Neither would worry. She needed to act, and quickly, but Gabe was right. She needed someone to go with her to Montana. It just couldn't be Hendrick Simmons.

Lord, send courage. And a good mechanic.

After the awkwardness with Hendrick at the church, Mariah should have realized that dinner would be no better. Normally, she had nerves of steel, but tonight her stomach tumbled and rolled. She tried not to look at him, but that could hardly be avoided since Felicity had placed him directly across the table from her. His sister Anna's presence did little to alleviate the tension. Their mother had declined the invitation, which removed only one matchmaker from the mix. Gabe and Felicity kept the conversation centered on Hendrick.

"I understand you've developed a new aeroplane motor for Jack Hunter," Felicity said pleasantly. "Isn't that wonderful?"

Though her remark was directed toward Hendrick, her smile was meant for Mariah. No doubt she intended to call attention to Hendrick's good points, but Mariah was already all too aware of them. How handsome he looked in his suit and freshly pressed shirt! His damp hair still smelled of soap, and the little curls at his temple sprang loose from his neatly combed locks. He sat pallbearer stiff, so uncomfortable that she could have giggled if she wasn't worried that she'd inadvertently say something that would alert Felicity to her Montana mission.

Speaking of her sister-in-law, she was staring at Mariah as if she expected her to say something. What had Felicity been talking about? Mariah combed her memory. Oh, yes, something about engines.

"A new motor?" Mariah hazarded.

Hendrick shifted in his chair and ran a finger underneath his collar. "Yep...uh, *yes*," he corrected, "two motors, actually." His eyes darted ever so quickly toward Mariah and just as quickly away. "For their North Pole flight."

Mariah heard the displeasure in his voice. In this case, she happened to agree with him. The risk had to be outweighed by gain. "I can't imagine what they hope to accomplish."

Anna perked up. "They're going to be the first to fly across the Pole. Won't it be grand? I wish I was going along."

"You're not going to go anywhere near the North Pole," Hendrick stated emphatically.

Mariah smothered a smile. His grammar might have improved since the last time she'd seen him, but he was just as protective.

"You're no fun at all," Anna whined. "You're worse than Ma." She tossed her mousy brown hair, which was mercifully no longer pulled into tight braids. "I want to do things, like Mariah."

"Me?" Mariah was startled by Anna's observation. She'd never considered herself particularly adventurous.

"Yes, you drive anywhere you want, whenever you want." Anna's eyes shone.

"That's not quite true," Mariah cautioned. "I only drive when I have a purpose."

"But you drove here," Anna insisted, "and that's just for a visit."

Mariah bit her tongue when she realized how close she'd come to giving away the secret. She tried to recover. "True, but visiting my brother and sister-in-law is a wonderful purpose."

"I agree." Felicity lifted her water glass. "To safe travels."

Gabe quickly seconded his wife's toast, clinked her glass with his and followed that with a kiss. "My wife is uncommonly beautiful tonight."

Felicity blushed. "Now, is that any way for a pastor to talk at the dinner table?"

Gabe didn't back down. "It is when he loves her as much as I love you."

Mariah smiled to herself as they kissed again. Two years had not dimmed their love. As she turned again to her dinner plate, she noticed Hendrick watching her, an odd expression on his face, but the minute he realized she'd seen him he looked away.

Gabe looked only at Felicity. "And I love you even more for giving me a baby."

Luke, who hadn't followed most of the adult conversation, suddenly picked up that one word. "Where is it?" He wiggled around in his chair as if expecting to see a baby behind him. "At the pow-wow?"

Mariah stifled a laugh. "A pow-wow is a gathering of family and friends. No baby."

"Oh." Luke turned back around. "Is that all?" He picked up his fork and resumed mashing his peas before turning his questions on her. "Do you have a baby, Aunt Mariah?"

She started. "No, I don't. I'm not married."

"Luke," Felicity scolded, "it's not polite to ask personal questions. Remember our rules for the dining room table."

He hung his head. "Yes, Mom."

"I'm sorry, dear," Felicity said, her expression so concerned that it was almost as if Gabe had told her Mariah couldn't have children. But she knew she could trust her brother to keep her secret.

"That's all right," Mariah said, though she couldn't suppress the waves of embarrassment. "Children can't help being curious."

Felicity heaved a sigh. "I suppose you're right. Children can be a challenge. Pets, too. What do you think, Gabe?" She looked to her husband, who gave his blessing. "Mariah, dear, we wanted to talk to you about the home I'm starting."

Mariah blinked. "Home?"

"An animal haven for abandoned and unwanted pets," Felicity explained. "I wanted to have it here in the parsonage, but the church trustees put their foot down." She sighed. "I think Daddy had a lot to do with that. He and Mother are not much for pets." She looked at Gabe, who smiled his agreement.

The simple gesture raised an uncontrollable envy deep in Mariah's heart. Mom and Dad were like that, so closely allied in their minds and hearts that they could communicate with just a gesture, and now Gabe and Felicity appeared to be the same. Her older brothers had married happily as well. Only she walked alone.

Felicity bubbled on, "Remember my idea to start a home for orphans? I'd like to combine that with the animal haven, but we'd need a large house. The Elder house, behind the church, just came on the market. It would make the perfect parsonage, and then this house could be the orphanage."

Mariah did recall that Felicity had proposed an orphanage two summers ago, but she'd thought that idea had passed. Clearly not. Felicity looked so pleased that Mariah couldn't bring herself to explain how difficult it would be to start a private orphanage.

"All the paperwork has been approved, and now we're ready to hire a director," Felicity said pointedly. "Someone who loves children and animals. Think how perfect it would be. The children would learn the responsibility of caring for a pet and in return would receive unconditional love. But we need a director, and with the baby coming soon—" she sighed "—I can't take it on."

As if Mariah didn't understand the offer, Gabe reaffirmed it. "What do you think, sis? You'd be perfect."

Mariah concentrated on the china pattern with its delicate roses and gilded edge. She couldn't leave her job. The orphans depended on her. She also couldn't live so close to Hendrick. Yet Felicity had such hope that she'd accept. Mariah didn't want to upset her.

"God has called me to the Society," she said carefully, "but I'll give it prayerful consideration."

"You would still be working with orphans," Felicity argued.

Mariah could see she wasn't going to get out of this easily. "It's not a decision to be made lightly."

"I know." Felicity sighed. "But it would set my mind at ease to have someone in charge before the baby arrives."

Mariah knew when she'd been backed into a corner. She wasn't as certain how to get out of it.

Luckily, Luke came to her rescue. "Is the deliveryman going to bring my baby brother?"

All the adults chuckled.

"No, Luke." Felicity leaned over and kissed him on the forehead. "I promise the baby will arrive soon, but not before dessert."

"Dessert?" He squealed with delight when the housekeeper brought out chocolate cake, and the business with the baby was forgotten. "My favorite." He pulled himself tight to the table as a slice of cake was placed before him.

Everyone was distracted for long, precious minutes, but after the last bite was eaten, the adults settled in the parlor with its brocaded wingback chairs and polished wood floors. Luke went outside to play with the dog, and conversation inevitably turned to adult topics.

"Tell me, Mariah," Gabe began from his perch beside Felicity on the sofa, "how is Mr. Isaacs?"

Mariah shifted so she wouldn't see Hendrick in the other wingback chair. Naturally, Gabe would inquire about his dear friend and director of the Orphaned Children's Society, but this conversation was likely headed back to the job offer Mariah couldn't possibly accept.

"A bit weary of government interference, I'm afraid," she said, hoping the hint would dissuade Felicity.

"That hasn't changed, then."

"I'm afraid it's gotten worse. It's difficult to keep a private agency running these days."

Instead of discouraging Felicity, her remark had just the opposite effect. "Then you should come here. You'd be the perfect director for our home."

"Am I being railroaded?" Mariah shook her head with a laugh. "The truth is, I love my work. It's where I belong." And though she liked Pearlman, with its cozy streets and tight-knit community, the town had one big problem, currently seated in the other wingback chair.

"How many children does the Society handle each month now?" Gabe asked.

Mariah hesitated. That's why the Detroit office had closed. "A handful."

"Exactly. It used to be dozens." Gabe's brow puckered. "I can't believe there are fewer children in need. They must be going to the state institutions."

"Children belong with their families," Hendrick stated.

Mariah was so surprised by the passion in his voice that she couldn't think of a thing to say.

"Agreed," Gabe said. "That's why Mariah's going to Montana, to protect a child."

Mariah's jaw dropped. The room got deathly quiet. Hendrick, Anna and Felicity all looked stunned. Why had Gabe said that when he'd made her promise not to tell Felicity? She stared at her brother until she realized that he hadn't mentioned Luke. His statement had been vague. She could be going to help any child.

Felicity recovered first. "I didn't realize the Society placed children that far west."

Mariah knew her cheeks were glowing but she hoped Felicity would just think she was warm. "They've sent children to many Western states." That was true, though none had gone that far west in years.

Hendrick looked like he was gagging. He kept pulling at his collar until he managed to ask in a strangled voice, "You're driving to Montana by yourself?"

"She might think she's going by herself," said Gabe, "but as her brother, I insist she take someone with her."

"I'll go," Anna instantly volunteered.

"Wait," Mariah cried. This was rapidly spinning out of control.

No one paid her the slightest attention.

Hendrick glared at his sister. "Mariah doesn't need to look after a girl."

"I'm not a girl," Anna said hotly. "I'm nineteen."

"And know nothing about the world," he added.

A thought crept into Mariah's head. Perhaps taking Anna along would satisfy Gabe. She did enjoy the girl's company. How much trouble could she be? Certainly less than Hendrick.

"I think it's a splendid idea," Mariah said.

Anna beamed. "See?"

"That's solved," said Gabe. "Now all you need is a mechanic." He looked right at Hendrick. "I can think of no one better."

Hendrick gulped. "The garage—"

"That's right." Mariah capitalized on his excuse. "He has a business to run."

"It'll be in fine hands with Peter," Gabe said.

Hendrick shook his head. "He's a boy."

Felicity glowed with the thrill of matchmaking. "He did a wonderful job fixing Daddy's car. I'm sure he can handle anything that would come up while you're gone. I think it's the perfect combination." She smiled broadly at each of them.

Mariah cringed. "But it will take at least two weeks to get there, and another two weeks back. Surely Hendrick can't be gone that long."

Felicity waved a hand. "The trains will be running by the time you're ready to come back."

Gabe increased the pressure. "What do you say, Hendrick?"

Mariah fumed. Apparently, she had no say in this. "He's busy."

Hendrick opened his mouth as if to protest, glanced at her and then changed his mind. "If Ma says Anna can go, then I'll *have* to go, too. I can't let anything happen to my only sister." He emphasized the point by glaring at Mariah.

No. No. No. She couldn't spend all that time with Hendrick, talking to him, seeing him, sitting an arm's length apart. It would be intolerable.

Felicity clapped her hands. "It's the perfect solution. Just perfect. Hendrick can make any repairs and ensure that you arrive safely. Well, then, it's settled."

It was not. But Mariah couldn't say a word to change their minds. Anna bounced around the room like a rubber ball. Felicity and Gabe looked so pleased. Luke could come into the house at any moment. All she could do for now was accept that she would be driving west with Hendrick and Anna Simmons.

Until she figured out a way to get out of this little mess.

Chapter Three

Hendrick cornered his sister the moment they'd walked out of sight of the parsonage. "Why did you volunteer to go on that trip?"

Anna tossed her head and wormed past him. "It's time I got out of this town and saw the world. Pearlman is so limited. I want more. I want to experience everything."

What had gotten into Anna? She'd always been the quiet and shy type, until… "Did Mariah put you up to this?"

Anna laughed so loudly that everyone else on the street looked to see what was so humorous. "That's what's bothering you, isn't it? That it's Mariah."

Hendrick choked back more than a little irritation. "That has nothing to do with it. I wouldn't let you make a trip like that with *any* woman."

Anna skipped ahead. "Well, you don't have the final say, do you? It's up to Ma. You said so yourself."

Hendrick charged after her. She scooted along, face lifted to the sun, and only by virtue of his long legs did he catch her. "Ma won't give her permission."

"Yes, she will."

It felt like they were kids again, sparring over a toy or

a game. Then Pa died, and Hendrick had taken over as head of the family. Anna had listened and obeyed him for years—until Mariah set foot in Pearlman.

"Ma wants me to be happy," Anna was saying, "and seeing the world will make me happy. I certainly don't need you along, and neither does Mariah."

Hendrick felt the slap of those words, but he refused to let her childish emotions change his mind. "Anyone driving that far needs a mechanic along. Two thousand miles on bad roads will break apart an automobile. Neither one of you can do more than change a tire."

Anna huffed. "Then we'll find someone who does, but the last thing I need is an overprotective big brother tagging along. We'll find someone else. Even Peter."

"Peter? He's too young for a trip like that." Hendrick wasn't about to entrust his only sister to a sixteen-year-old. "Besides, I thought you hated him." They'd reached the house. The sun hung low, just above the trees. Ma would be reading her Bible and saying her prayers. Peter was probably building something with the Erector Set that Hendrick had given him last Christmas.

"I don't hate him. I just don't love him." She wrinkled her nose. "He's two years younger than me." Anna stopped in the front doorway. "Promise you won't go?"

He set his jaw. No way would he let Mariah—or any woman—drive west alone. "Let's see first if Ma gives you permission."

The door opened, and Ma stepped outside. "Give you permission for what?" Her cheeks rounded above her embracing smile. Ma was the most optimistic person Hendrick knew, despite losing Pa.

Hendrick didn't wait for Anna to wrap Ma around her little finger. "Mariah Meeks is driving her car to Montana, and Anna wants to go along. I say it's a foolish idea."

Of course Anna disagreed. "No, it's not. It'll be such fun, Ma. I'll see the world. Oh, please, let me go."

Hendrick hated to disappoint his sister, but he had to stick a pin in her plan. "It's dangerous. The car will break down. If they're far from a town, they could die of thirst before they get help."

"We'll bring water," Anna countered.

"There could be wolves or bears or cougars," he added.

"Then we'll bring a rifle."

Ma looked from one to the other as he brought up every possible catastrophe and Anna refuted each one.

"You might run into outlaws and rumrunners," he pleaded. "It's not safe for two women." He nearly choked calling his kid sister a woman.

Ma smiled softly and touched his arm. "It's good of you to worry about your sister's welfare, but she's grown up now and needs to spread her wings."

"But Ma."

Anna grinned in triumph.

Ma clucked softly. "We can't protect our loved ones from everything."

Her eyes misted, and he knew she was thinking of Pa. A lump rose in his throat as he recalled finding his father crushed beneath a truck, his spilled blood already dark. He'd been dead for hours, and none of them knew. For years Hendrick wished he'd come home from school earlier, that he'd skipped classes that day, that he'd listened to his pa's advice to quit school after he graduated from the eighth grade. If he had, he might have been there. He might have saved his father. At least Pa wouldn't have died alone.

"I have to protect Anna from unnecessary risk," he countered.

Ma nodded. "That's why you must go, too."

"But—"

"The garage will be in fine hands with Peter. Plus Mr. Thompson said he'd help out anytime you wanted to take a holiday."

Hendrick recalled Pa's working partner, now retired, extending that offer. "I think he meant he'd help for a couple days. This could be a month."

Ma patted his arm. "Everything will be fine, Hendrick. Go, with my blessing."

Had all the women in his life gone crazy? Suddenly they wanted to run all over the country and thought nothing of the risk.

"But what if something happens?" he said, not quite able to spell out the possibility that they could be killed in a wreck. "We're all you have. Except Peter, of course, but that's not quite the same." Peter was just a foster son. He could leave at any time. Hendrick and Anna were blood. Nothing could break blood ties. That's why a man needed his own children.

"Peter will take good care of me." Ma patted his arm again. "You two will be in the Lord's care, and that's all the assurance any of us have. Wherever you go, I know God will be with you."

Ma's words reminded Hendrick that he hadn't told her about the possible job with Curtiss Aeroplane. Rather than escort two women to Montana, he should be headed to New York to present his engine design to a company that could pay a lot of money for the right to produce it. If ever he had a way out of this foolish trip to Montana, this was it.

He licked his lips. "What if I go to New York?"

"New York?" Ma's brows puckered. "I thought you wanted to help Mariah drive to Montana."

He struggled not to show any emotion at the mention

of Mariah's name. Ma still harbored hope they'd get back together, no matter how many times he told her it was over. "I've got a chance to sell my engine design to Curtiss Aeroplane. Jack Hunter is having his old mechanic put in a word for me, but I need to go to New York to present the plans to their engineers."

"Is that what you truly want, Hendrick?"

He did. Or at least he thought he did. "Yes, Ma."

She bit her lip, and her eyes filled with tears. "Then pursue your dream, dear. Don't let anyone stop you."

"I'll take care of you, Ma. They'll pay more than I earn here at the garage, and Peter can help out around the house."

"I understand."

Anna caught her breath. "Does that mean you're not going with us to Montana?"

Hendrick felt the tug of responsibility. Judging by her muted reaction, Ma didn't want him to take the Curtiss job, but doing so would ensure that Anna stayed safely at home. She would hate him, but she'd be safe. "That means I need you to stay here with Ma."

"Stay here?" Anna's eyes filled with angry tears. "How could you? You did this just to ruin my life. I hate you. I hate you." Then she ran inside and slammed her bedroom door.

Hendrick watched in silence, his gut a tangled knot.

Ma touched his arm. "Don't fret, dear. She doesn't mean it."

"I know." And he did know, but it still hurt. "It's tough being the one in charge."

Ma softly murmured a protest. "God's the one who's in charge. Pray on your decision, Hendrick. He'll give you the guidance you need."

Trouble was, Hendrick couldn't hear the answers above the din of everyone's conflicting needs.

"I'm going to take a walk," he grumbled and headed out to find some peace.

Mariah held her tongue until Felicity took Luke upstairs for bed.

"I'd like to see the river," she announced to her brother, rising from her chair. "Will you show me the way?"

Of course she remembered how to get to the river, but she needed to talk to Gabe away from the parsonage.

She silently followed him across the expansive backyard. Any wind had vanished, and the evening descended with a golden haze and the croak of bullfrogs. Once Gabe closed the backyard gate behind them, she let loose. "How could you? You know Hendrick and I had a falling-out. Traveling with me for a month is the last thing he'd want to do."

Gabriel whistled a few notes. "Seems to me he said he'd go."

"Naturally he did, once you forced him. What could he say? You certainly manipulated that little scenario your way." Every word only made her angrier. The air was thick and cloying. The last bit of daylight barely filtered through the trees. She felt trapped.

"*I* manipulated *him?*" He tsked audibly. "Seems to me Hendrick Simmons is a grown man with a mind of his own. He made a decision. The fact that I happen to agree with him doesn't make me manipulative."

Normally, Mariah kept her emotions in check, but Gabe and Hendrick had sent them catapulting out of control. "Why can't you accept that I can do this myself? The fewer people involved, the better. You said so yourself."

"Hendrick's a good, honest man. You can't deny that."

She couldn't.

"I trust him to keep the secret."

"And Anna?" Mariah pointed out. "Do you feel the same way about her?" Even as she said the words, she recalled that Anna had been infatuated with Gabe when he first arrived. A shy girl then, she'd pined for him and must have suffered when Gabe chose Felicity.

"She's a good girl," Gabe said softly, "and has grown up a lot since you last saw her. Yes, I have faith in her."

Mariah sighed. He was not going to let her out of this. "You know how difficult this will be."

"I know, sis, but you'll manage. You always do."

They'd reached the river, flowing gently at this season. To the left, mostly out of sight, a footbridge crossed to the other side. In the low light, the water below looked black and endless, but once they'd climbed down to the water's edge, it turned silky green.

"I'm afraid, Gabe," she whispered as they made their way to the rocky sandbar that was exposed this time of year. She wasn't just afraid for Luke or all the problems that might happen on the trip, but for her heart. The old longing had returned with a fierceness she hadn't expected, but a life with Hendrick could never be. One impossible obstacle still loomed between them, and his remarks tonight confirmed that it was still there. He wanted children of his own. Children she could never give him.

Gabe hugged her shoulders. "I know."

Her shoes scrunched against the stones, sinking in slightly as they made their way to the center of the sandbar. They both looked downstream. For years she'd watched over Gabe, making sure he was all right. Now their roles were reversed. He was trying to take care of her. She bit her lip to stem the tide of emotion.

"It'll turn out all right," Gabe said with another brisk hug. "It always does for those who love the Lord."

The corner of her mouth twitched at that reminder. "Are you preaching to me?"

He bent and picked up a stone. "I've been teaching Luke how to skip stones. He can beat me now." He let the stone fly. It bounced once, twice, three times before sinking beneath the surface. "Are we stones that sink to the bottom or twigs that float on the surface? Do we succumb to trouble or are we carried wherever the water flows?"

"I'd like to think we're boats, able to navigate treacherous waters." Mariah was used to her brother's philosophical musings, but this one deeply touched her soul. "You're afraid, too."

He bowed his head. "Of course. Losing Luke would break my heart, but knowing he'd be beaten down by someone who's supposed to love him would kill me."

He swiped at his face, and she knew he'd lost control of his emotions. She hugged him around the shoulders, as she used to when he was a boy.

"I won't let that happen," she said, softly at first but with growing firmness. "God won't let Frank Gillard take Luke."

"I hope you're right," he gasped, his shoulders shuddering as he gave in to tears.

Behind them, a plank of the bridge creaked, telling her that they were not alone. She turned.

Hendrick Simmons was watching.

"Mariah. Pastor." Hendrick knew she'd seen him.

He'd come to the bridge to think, to let the steady flow of water help him sort things out. Instead, he'd heard the real reason for Mariah's trip west. That changed everything. Someone had threatened to harm Luke, and she was going to Montana to stop him. Now he had to go with her.

"Hendrick," called out Gabriel. "Wait there." He led his reluctant sister up the riverbank, and in minutes they appeared on the bridge. "Nice night, isn't it?"

Mariah hung back.

Hendrick didn't know if he should tell them he'd overheard their conversation. It had been so personal that he felt as if he'd been eavesdropping. He decided to pretend he hadn't.

"Needed to get some air." Hendrick leaned against the rail and watched the river flow. "Water's down for this time of year. Hope we don't have a drought."

"That's something to pray for," Pastor Gabriel said softly. "I'm glad you're going to Montana with my sister."

Mariah didn't say a word. She stood on the other side of her brother, staring straight ahead.

"Ma gave Anna permission to go." He didn't bother saying that he'd thrown a wrench into the plan, since he wouldn't be going to New York now.

"Good," Gabriel said. "Then you two have a lot to talk about. See you at the parsonage, sis."

"Gabe," she cried. "I'll go with you. I might get lost."

Pastor Gabriel laughed and shook his head. "Hendrick knows these woods better than I do. Get her home safely, okay?"

That's precisely what Hendrick intended to do, after he got her to Montana.

The pastor hiked up the path and vanished into the woods, leaving Hendrick alone with Mariah, who watched her brother's departure before turning to him.

"How much did you hear?"

Hendrick heard the accusation in her words. "Enough."

She swallowed, looking more like a frightened girl than

the confident woman he was used to seeing. "Please don't tell anyone." She clutched her arms around her midsection. "Felicity can't know." Her eyes looked haunted, desperate. "Please."

He nodded. "I promise."

Relieved, she collapsed against the bridge railing, and he thought for a moment that she was going to cry. Instinctively, he reached to comfort her, but she flinched, and he backed away, confused.

"I just wanted to say it's all right," he said, struggling to find the right words. "I'll help you all I can."

"I know." She lowered her face so it fell in the shadows. "But we can't relive the past. Do you understand that?"

He set his jaw. "I'm not asking to go back in time, Mariah. I'm talking about getting you safely to Montana so you can help Luke."

She shushed him. "Don't say his name."

He nodded. "I'm sorry."

"It's all right."

They stood in silence for long moments, each staring downstream, headed in the same direction yet miles apart.

He licked his lips. "What can you tell me?"

She continued to watch the river. "We're going to Brunley, near the Rocky Mountains. The rest I'll tell you once we leave Pearlman."

He understood. She couldn't take a chance that anyone would overhear.

She breathed deep, squared her shoulders and turned to face him. "I owe you an explanation."

He frowned. Hadn't she just said she couldn't tell him anything until they were on the road?

"Not about our trip," she clarified, "about last time. Why I left. I shouldn't have run off."

He couldn't agree more, but he had the sense not to say that. Instead, he waited for her.

"It's my work," she finally said. "Helping the orphans is my calling. I couldn't leave them. I'll never stop helping them. Do you understand?"

He didn't. Didn't all women want their own children? Others would step up to help the orphans, but she couldn't let it go.

"It's not that I don't care for you. You're a wonderful... friend."

He steeled his jaw. "You, too." He'd never let her know how much she affected him. "Besides, I have a chance to work at Curtiss Aeroplane. I'll be heading to Garden City as soon as we return."

"Good." She drew a shaky breath. "That is, congratulations."

Did he imagine that hesitation in her voice?

She shook her head, as if she knew what he was thinking. "I'm glad you realize that there can't be anything between us beyond friendship." She stuck out her hand.

He reluctantly grasped it. "Yeah, friends." Her hand felt like cold steel.

Chapter Four

Not because of her. Hendrick recited that over and over as he fixed Mariah's car. He wasn't going on this trip because of some misguided romantic nonsense. He was going to help a little boy. Period.

He repaired the car in a day. Putting the interview with Curtiss Aeroplane on hold wasn't quite that easy.

Jack Hunter gave him a sharp look. "Dick told me the engineers are eager to see your design. If you wait too long, they'll change their minds or find another designer, and the opportunity will be gone."

Hendrick couldn't tell him why he had to go to Montana. He'd promised, and Hendrick never broke his promises. "It's just a few weeks."

Jack's wife, Darcy, who had been silent until then, chimed in. "Of course Hendrick has to go with Mariah. Jack, you'd do the same. After all, you followed me here rather than start up that Buffalo flight school."

Jack groused, "That's not the same thing."

"It's exactly the same. A woman has a way of convincing the man who loves her."

Hendrick felt the heat creep up his neck. "This has

nothing to do with Mariah. I need to take care of my sister. That's all."

"If you say so." Darcy laughed as she leaned against the lower wing of the plane.

Jack rolled his eyes. "Show me a woman who isn't a matchmaker. Sorry about that."

"Sorry to disappoint you, Darcy, but we've already decided to stay friends."

She shrugged, as if his revelation meant nothing. "You can't blame me for trying."

Jack sighed. "I'll ask Dick to see if they'll delay the interview a month. No guarantees."

"Understood." Hendrick knew the cost. He would lose his one chance to strike out on his own.

"Don't worry," Darcy said sympathetically, "if Curtiss wants the engine badly enough, they'll wait."

He hoped she was right.

On Friday morning, Mariah paced in front of the parlor windows, waiting for her car to arrive. Maybe she should have gone to the garage and gotten it herself, but Hendrick assured Gabe he'd drive it to the parsonage.

"Do you think he's forgotten?" she asked Felicity, after checking the time. "They're ten minutes late."

Felicity chuckled. "I'm sure he hasn't. Give them time."

"I hope you're right." Mariah tugged on a lock of hair.

The fact that Felicity couldn't know the reason for her trip made this parting more difficult. Mariah had to bury any misgivings and pretend the drive would progress without a hitch, but she knew Gabe was right. A host of problems could derail her effort.

By the time Hendrick parked the Overland in front of the parsonage, her anxiety level had escalated. It got even worse when he unfolded his lean frame from the driver's seat. The sun accentuated his broad shoulders and muscular arms. She would have to be close to that, to him, every day for the next month.

"Doesn't Hendrick look handsome?" Felicity said.

Mariah did not need her sister-in-law's observations. The sight of him made her tremble. "He's changed."

Felicity nodded, a knowing smile on her lips. "He studied the last two years and received his high school diploma. Jack Hunter taught him drafting so he could make blueprints for his engine designs. Jack says he's brilliant and could go far."

Mariah couldn't take another minute of Felicity's glowing accolades. She grabbed her valise. "It's time to go."

"I'll fetch Gabe and Luke." Felicity headed for the kitchen.

Mariah wished she could leave without the heart-tugging farewells, but Felicity would have none of it. While her sister-in-law vanished into the kitchen, Mariah carried her valise onto the porch.

"Mariah, Mariah!" Anna leaned out the backseat window. "Can you believe we're actually going? I can hardly wait. Will we see Lake Michigan? And Chicago? Hendrick says it's a huge city with buildings so tall you can't see the tops."

Anna rattled off her questions so quickly that Mariah had no hope of answering, so she nodded and smiled and let Hendrick take her valise. Their hands brushed, and the same electricity coursed through her. Hopefully, he didn't notice.

"Sis." Gabe hefted a small crate down the porch steps. "Thought you'd sneak away, did you?"

"What on earth are you carrying?"

"Provisions. Tins of food, matches, a hatchet, everything you'll need for camping."

"But I already have supplies and a tent." Mariah pointed to the half-full backseat. "There's no room for more."

"I'll make it fit." Hendrick lifted the heavy crate from Gabe's arms like it weighed no more than a sheet of paper.

My, he was strong. Mariah fanned her suddenly hot face.

Hendrick unpacked the crate and somehow wedged the contents into the backseat without forcing Anna out.

Meanwhile, Gabe pulled her aside. "My prayers go with you." He held her face in his hands. "Find the truth."

His eyes looked tired, and the lines around his mouth had deepened.

She hugged him. "I won't fail you."

The dreaded round of farewells began when Felicity and Luke joined them in the yard. Mariah managed to say goodbye without shedding a tear.

"When are you coming back, Aunt Mariah?" Luke solemnly asked.

"Soon," she said, praying that her return would not be to take him west.

Gabe gave her a bear hug. "Godspeed, sis. May He guide your every step." Though he didn't say more, both knew where they wanted the Lord to guide her.

"I'll let you know where you can reach us when we arrive." She pretended to smile even while choking back tears. "Call or cable if the baby comes early."

"Of course."

Then she had to walk away. How she loved them all. They stood together, Gabe's hand on Luke's shoulder, confirming to the world that Luke was his son. Felicity waved, and Mariah lifted a hand in response before heading to the driver's-side door.

She reached for the handle at the same time as Hendrick. Their hands met, generating another jolt of electricity.

"Thank you," she said stiffly, "but it's not necessary to open the door for me."

He flushed. "Uh, I thought…that is, I assumed…"

"Thought what?"

Felicity laughed and motioned her to the passenger seat. Apparently, she wasn't supposed to drive. But this was her car. She always drove. Why must she turn over control simply because a man was in the car? She started to protest but then decided, in the interest of peace, to relinquish the wheel.

"For now," she explained. "We will share driving."

Before Hendrick could protest, she walked around the car to the passenger side, but he'd scrambled to get there before her and, by virtue of his long legs, managed to pull the door open just before she arrived.

Anna groaned. "I hope you're not going to be like this the whole way."

"I can't imagine what you mean." Mariah took her seat with regal formality.

"Goodbye," Felicity called out again as Hendrick got into the car.

At last they were ready to go. Hendrick set the spark and throttle levers in preparation for starting the car.

Mariah pushed the throttle back a bit. "It doesn't need that much."

Hendrick glared at her. "I think I know how to start a car."

She crossed her arms. "I think I know my car better than anyone else."

Anna groaned again. "What is wrong with you two?"

Neither of them bothered to answer the preposterous question. Hendrick started the car, and Mariah stared straight ahead. His elbow practically butted into her side. No more than six inches separated them on the seat. She couldn't last two thousand miles that way. At the next stop, she'd drive and insist that Hendrick sit in the back.

She plastered herself against the door and kept her gaze straight ahead while they drove through Pearlman and past Hendrick's garage. Mrs. Simmons waved to them from her yard.

"Goodbye, Mama," Anna called out.

"God be with you," she called back, and Mariah hoped she didn't know the true reason for their trip.

She glanced at Hendrick. "Does she...?"

He must have understood, because he shook his head.

Soon they left town, driving up the little rise before passing through a tunnel of ancient maples that had somehow missed the lumberman's ax. On this warm July morning, the dappled shade created an oasis of coolness in the midst of the hot fields.

"Isn't this wonderful?" Anna mused, her chin on the back of the front seat between Mariah and Hendrick. "Hendrick comes here all the time. It's his favorite spot in the whole world."

Anna pointed out every barn and unusual tree. Ordinarily the chatter would have driven Mariah to tears, but today it passed the miles and ensured that she didn't have to talk to Hendrick. Though they couldn't go much over thirty miles an hour on the rutted road, within a couple hours they reached the West Michigan Pike, the highway that ran along the shore of Lake Michigan.

"Can we stop to see the lake?" Anna queried from the backseat.

"May we," Hendrick corrected.

Mariah lifted an eyebrow. Hendrick Simmons correcting grammar?

"*May* we stop?" Anna sighed.

Mariah hated to waste time on sightseeing, but she couldn't deny Anna this little pleasure. She asked Hendrick to pull over at the first place he could park. When he finally stopped the car on a grassy spot alongside the beach, the view startled her. Lake Michigan wasn't like any lake she'd ever seen. Why, it stretched unbroken to the horizon, exactly like the ocean.

"It doesn't smell like the ocean, though." She sniffed the air. "No salty odor."

No one listened to her musings. Anna raced to the shore, where she peeled off her shoes and stockings. Within seconds, she'd waded into the crashing surf. The waves rolled over her feet and dampened the hem of her skirt.

"You're getting wet," Mariah called out, but Anna either didn't hear or didn't care.

"Sounds good to me." Hendrick kicked off his shoes and socks and followed his sister.

Anna laughed, running out when each wave ebbed and racing back to shore when the next one arrived. Her giggles were infectious, and, since everyone else was taking a break, Mariah removed her shoes and stockings, too.

The sand blazed beneath her feet, and she gingerly hopped to the water's edge. The wet sand cooled her blistered soles. When a wave rolled over her feet, the icy water made her shriek. "It's freezing."

"It's wonderful." Anna ran down the shore, splashing water with every step.

Within minutes, Mariah grew accustomed to the chill water—or perhaps numb to it. She walked a few steps, but the sand gave way beneath her feet, making her stagger. The wash of the waves tugged at her feet, burying them deeper in the soft, pebbly sand.

"It's like quicksand," she exclaimed.

Hendrick bent over laughing.

"It's not funny. My feet keep sinking, and my skirt is getting wet. I can hardly walk."

"Hold still." In an instant he swept her off her feet and into his arms. "There, you're safe now."

Safe? He was holding her. *Holding her.* Goodness, he'd lifted her as easily as if she were a child. His heart thudded against her side. His shoulders loomed at eye level. He smelled so masculine that she couldn't think straight. She wanted to lay her head on his shoulder, to sink into his arms and stay there forever.

"Put me down," she squawked, terrified at the rush of emotion. She couldn't fall for him again. She couldn't.

He didn't listen. Instead of setting her on her feet, he carried her toward the car.

"What are you doing?" she cried. "I told you to put me down."

But he didn't. He just kept walking, carrying her away from the shore. She had no choice but to hold on.

"I know how to walk."

"I know, but the sand's hot," he explained when they reached her abandoned shoes. He gently set her down and smoothed the collar of her middy shirt before turning to call for his sister. "Anna, it's time to go."

Mariah sat, embarrassed by her reaction to him. "I could have walked."

He sat beside her. "I didn't want you to burn your feet."

She grabbed a stocking. "How could they burn when they're blocks of ice?" To demonstrate that she hadn't been affected by the way he held her, she tried to pull the stocking over one of her damp, sandy feet. It went nowhere.

"Here, let me help." He scrunched up the other stocking

so it would fit easily over her toes. "Brush off the sand, and I'll slip this on."

She yanked it away from him. "I think I can put on my own stockings." But the gritty sand clung to her feet as if it had been glued on.

"I'd be glad to help," he said again.

"I don't need help." She yanked on the stockings, even though they bunched in the wrong places and she hadn't gotten all the sand off her feet. She shoved on her shoes and stood. "There, see?" She strode toward the car, the sand rubbing against her toes with every step.

Hendrick hurried after her. "Let me get the door."

She'd had quite enough of his help. She was an independent, fully capable woman, not an invalid.

"I'm driving," she stated, whipping open the driver's-side door.

He halted, either surprised or dismayed.

She didn't care. They'd had a deal. No romance. He'd broken it. This was the last time she'd let down her guard around Hendrick Simmons.

Didn't she feel a thing? Hendrick watched Mariah, confused by her reaction. When he first picked her up, she'd clung to him and even laid her head against his shoulder, but then she'd tensed, as if she realized she wasn't supposed to enjoy being carried by him. Then she got all defensive when he was just trying to help and stomped off to the car, insisting she had to drive. She didn't even wait for him to open the door.

He would never understand women.

They ate lunch in silence and reached Chicago that afternoon. Anna hung her head out the window and gawked at the buildings.

"That one has ten stories," Anna cried out as they entered downtown. "And that one, oh, my." She drank in the traffic signs and policemen at the street corners, the elevated railway and the crowds of people. "Thousands must live here. How do they know each other?"

"They don't," Hendrick said. "Cities have lots of people, but they're all strangers. I'd rather live where everyone knows each other."

"Like Pearlman," Mariah said tartly as she slowed the car for an intersection.

"What's wrong with Pearlman?" Though he planned to move to Garden City if his interview with Curtiss went well, he rose to his hometown's defense.

"I didn't say anything was wrong. Pearlman's a lovely town. Gabe adores living there."

"It's a good place to raise a family," Hendrick said softly.

She visibly tensed.

So that was it. The woman who helped place orphans didn't want children of her own. Of course. That's what she'd tried to tell him at the bridge, that her career came first. What a shame. She'd be a wonderful mother. He'd seen her with Luke, especially, but also with Peter and the other orphans she'd placed. She was a natural parent. Maybe she didn't want children now, but given time, was there any hope she might change her mind?

He'd test his theory. "I definitely want children."

She hesitated long enough that he knew he'd struck a nerve. "Children are a blessing, but I'm busy with the Society. Those are the children in my life."

"I want to wait, too," Anna chimed in.

He'd forgotten that his sister was there or he would never have brought up such a personal subject.

"First I'm going to see the world," Anna babbled on.

"Look at these buildings. They're monstrous. Now I can tell everyone I've been to Chicago. Is New York like this?"

"It is, only bigger," Mariah said quickly, apparently eager to change the topic.

"Bigger?" Anna cried. "I want to go there."

Mariah launched into descriptions of streets and buildings and department stores until he wished they'd be quiet.

"Do you go to parties and dances?" Anna asked Mariah.

"Some, but my college studies took most of my time."

College. Hendrick stewed. Only the rich could afford college. Anna could never attend, so why bring it up?

"What did you study?" Anna said. "I'd do something exciting like classics and explore Greek ruins."

He gritted his teeth. Maybe, if Curtiss offered enough for his engine design, he could afford to send her to teacher's college, but no point in a degree for something frivolous, like classics.

"We should fill the fuel tank and get oil before leaving the city," he said to change the topic.

Some blocks later, Mariah pulled the car into a filling station. The hulking attendant smirked when he saw Mariah in the driver's seat. Humiliation coiled in Hendrick's gut and spread quickly to his fists. Just because he wasn't driving didn't make him less of a man.

"Please fill the tank," Mariah told the attendant, oblivious to the slight.

"Yes, ma'am." The man spoke politely to her, but he snickered when he stepped to the fuel pump.

Hendrick sprang out of the car, unable to take any more of this. "I'll check the oil." He slammed the door and whipped the hood open.

"What's wrong with you?" Mariah followed him. "The attendant can do that."

He would not dignify her question with a reply. "You're low a quart."

"You don't have to snap at me."

She didn't understand. For a woman who worked with people all the time, she should realize that a man needed to be a man. Instead, she always had to be in charge. He grabbed a rag from the car and wiped his hands.

"I'm a mechanic," he stated to the smirking attendant.

Mariah followed his gaze, and her confident smile fell. "Oh, I see," said the attendant.

Her demeanor softened, became more open, the way she'd been at the Founder's Day picnic two years ago. That day she'd laughed and chattered and eagerly taken in every word he said. That day he'd thought she cared for him. They grew closer and closer over the following months until the day of Felicity and Gabriel's wedding. Then suddenly, a wall went up between them and she only wanted to be friends.

Apparently, that's all she'd ever want.

He reached for the passenger-side door, but she stopped him with an electric touch to the arm.

"Thank you, Hendrick, for letting me practice driving, but I think you'd better take over now."

The knot in his gut loosened when he spotted the attendant and realized she'd said that for his sake. Maybe, somewhere deep, deep inside, she still cared for him.

She rummaged in her bag and shoved a roll of bills into his hand. He stared at the thick wad. It must total fifty dollars.

"Take it," she whispered as the attendant approached.

He didn't have time to protest.

"That's $1.40." The burly attendant looked from him to Mariah.

She smiled and returned to the passenger seat.

Fine, rather than make a fuss, he'd pay, but not from her funds. He withdrew the $1.40 from his wallet, leaving a little over $15 for the trip. Once the attendant left, he stuck Mariah's bills into his pants pocket where they couldn't fall out. As soon as they were alone, he'd give it back.

Chapter Five

❧

Tourist parks proved few and far between on their route, so Hendrick selected a flat, grassy spot between corn-fields to camp. The women weren't sure the area afforded enough privacy, since the corn wasn't yet waist high, but a little exploration of the area yielded a more secluded spot where a creek trickled under drooping willows.

"This will do," Mariah stated.

Hendrick eyed the terrain. He'd maneuvered the car between the cultivated fields on a rutted old path, but there wasn't room to turn the car around. He'd have to back it out.

"Hope it doesn't rain," he said as he put down the top.

"Me, too." Mariah grabbed the topmost bag from the backseat. "I haven't tested the tent for watertightness."

She strained under the weight of the canvas bag, so Hendrick tried to relieve her of the burden. "I'll unload. You ladies rest."

"Rest?" Mariah refused to let go. "All we've done is rest." She carried the bag to the tree and set it down. "Where's Anna?"

Hendrick heaved a sigh. "I'd better go find her." It was

just like his sister to run off when there was work to be done.

Mariah's throaty chuckle eased the tension. "Give her some time. It's not as if she could go that far."

True, but the cornfields and hayfields weren't tall enough to hide someone. The only place to disappear was down by the creek. "She should have told us where she was going."

Mariah smiled softly. "She's just excited to be on her first trip away from home."

It was his first trip, too, but he didn't go running off at the first opportunity. Besides, Anna was his responsibility. If anything happened, Ma would never recover. She doted on Anna. Since they couldn't afford new clothes very often, Ma got the old fabric and scraps of lace from Mrs. Fox's dressmaking shop to make Anna's dresses. In his opinion, his sister was spoiled, but Ma said she deserved a few niceties in life.

Money. It all came down to that. If he sold his engine design to Curtiss and became an aeronautical engineer, he'd be able to afford anything his mother and sister desired. He'd have as much money as...as Mariah. Hendrick stuck a hand in his pocket and encountered the roll of bills. Her bills. He should have given the money back right after they left the filling station. He'd do so now.

Naturally, she refused to take it. "Use it to pay for fuel and oil."

"But I should be paying."

She waved that idea away. "I'm on agency business. The Society is paying."

"Not for Anna and me."

"You're here at my request. If you don't want to handle the money, I will, but I'd prefer you do it."

She trusted him. Despite their differences, she had faith

in him. He ran a thumb over the edge of the bills before sticking them back in his pocket.

Meanwhile, she'd grabbed another bag from the car.

"I'll take that," he offered.

She strode past him with a laugh. "Get your own."

Her joy was infectious, and he smiled as he hefted the next bag onto his shoulder. It rattled and clanked. Must be the pans and tins of food she'd packed. It weighed plenty, more than she could lift. He paraded past her with a grin of triumph.

"Set that one under the tree closest to the stream," she commanded as she tugged the canvas tent out of its sack.

"Yes, ma'am." He snapped to attention, imitating the salute used by soldiers who'd returned from the Great War. He'd tried to enlist, but the local board denied his application, saying he had to support his mother and sister.

Mariah waited until he set down the last sack before instructing him to put the car's roof back up. "It does look like rain."

Other than a couple puffy clouds, the sky was clear. Apparently, she wanted to keep him busy, and he, the foot soldier, was at her command.

While he refastened the roof, she spread the tent in a nice grassy dip in the ground. If it did rain, he thought, they'd be soaked.

"You might want to pick a different spot."

"What's wrong with here?" she snapped, her breathing heavy. She tugged the canvas over the pole. "I happen to like a soft, grassy place to lie down. I suppose you prefer rocks?"

"Fine. Suit yourself." If the rain arrived, as she suspected, she'd be sorry.

He finished raising the car roof, and she was still struggling with the tent. Only one end would stay up. She'd set one pole, leave it balancing and then race to the other side. By then, the first pole would topple over.

"I can help," he said.

"Don't need it."

Yet over and over her efforts yielded the same result. The scene looked like it came from a Charlie Chaplin film. Hendrick bit his lip to stifle a laugh, but he couldn't hold back the guffaw forever. When both poles fell down and the whole thing caved in, the laughter erupted, each wave making his sides ache even more.

"Do you think you can do any better?" She threw a pole to the ground in disgust. Hands on hips, she positively glared, but he couldn't stop laughing. "Well, you're no help. Where is Anna? Maybe she can hold herself together long enough to get this tent up."

His sister dropped from the nearby willow and took one of the poles. "What do I do?"

Instead of answering Anna, Mariah focused her wrath on him. "Hendrick, stop laughing and hold up the other pole. I'll start pounding in the stakes."

My, she was bossy. He'd always considered her directness a virtue. She knew what needed to be done and did it. But sometimes she could be wrong. The ground outside her little patch of green grass was rock hard. She'd have some time of it trying to pound in those stakes.

Nonetheless, he obediently took up his pole and watched while she pulled the corner line taut and attempted to hammer the stake into the ground. It pierced the soil no more than half an inch when she gave up and moved to the next one. But as soon as she pulled the line tight, the first stake came loose. With a growl of frustration, she mopped her brow with the back of her hand.

"The ground's so hard," she muttered. "I can't get it in."

Hendrick wanted to help. Perspiration ran down her

forehead, and her hair curled around her face in damp little tendrils that begged to be touched. But she would only yell at him and insist that she didn't need his help. So he watched her try and try without success.

Finally, he couldn't stand it anymore. "I'd be glad to give it a go."

Naturally she scowled at him. "Did I ask for your help?"

He wanted to rip the mallet from her hands and get the job done. Why did she have to be so stubborn?

Then Anna giggled. She tried to hold back, so it came out in a snort, but she couldn't maintain control for long and a second later burst out laughing.

Mariah frowned, but apparently Anna's laughter didn't irk her as much as his because before long she started to giggle, too. Her prickly-porcupine attitude eased, and she handed him the mallet. "See if you can make any headway."

They traded places, and in minutes he had the tent up and ready for their blankets and clothing.

"Which bag has the other tent?" he asked.

Mariah swiped damp hair from her brow. "I, uh, didn't count on company."

No second tent. He couldn't very well sleep with the women. That left only one option.

"I'll take the car." He'd have to sleep sitting up or curled into a ball, but it was the only option that kept him out of the weather.

Mariah's lips formed a perfect rosebud. Her cheeks glowed from the exertion. "I'm sorry I didn't think to bring another tent. Thank you." She tugged at a curl, the hat long ago discarded and her bobbed hair flying out in every direction. "We can take turns."

But of course they couldn't. He wouldn't let the women get all cramped in the car.

"We'll get another tent at the first outfitter," she said.

"Don't waste your money." He was still too aware of the wad of bills in his pocket, not to mention the hole in his heart. "The car will be fine."

After supper, Mariah conscripted Anna to help her scrub the dirty dishes in the creek while Hendrick checked the car's tires. Camping reminded her of family trips to the Catskills. Dad would rent a cabin for a couple weeks each summer. He wanted his children to know how to survive in the wilderness, so he took them out on short expeditions, teaching them how to build a fire, how to tell which plants were edible and how to fish. Gabe loved it, but she whined about the damp and the dirt and finally talked Dad into letting her skip the trips. Now she wished she'd stuck with it.

"Isn't it beautiful?" Anna exclaimed after handing Mariah the last pan. She stretched and spun around to take it all in.

Mariah didn't consider an Illinois roadside beautiful. High clouds streaked the sky, but the grass and corn didn't provide much of a view. Forty feet away, Hendrick bent over the rear tire on the far side of the car. He couldn't possibly hear what they were saying. That gave her a chance to ask Anna something that had been bothering her since they left, something that the girl's disappearance that afternoon had highlighted.

"Anna?" Mariah touched the girl's arm to capture her attention. "Could I ask a favor of you?"

The girl stopped spinning. "Of me?"

There was no easy way to say this. "I don't have anything against your brother. He's a fine and honorable man. It's purely about propriety. As a single woman..." She let her voice trail off for emphasis. "I shouldn't be alone with an unmarried man, especially after dark. Could you ensure we're never alone together?"

Anna shrugged her shoulders. "If you want."

"Thank you," Mariah breathed, relieved that Anna had agreed so readily. There'd be no repeat of the episode at the beach, no teasing of her emotions and no chance he'd fall in love with her again.

With that worry gone, she could enjoy the sunset. Mariah stacked the dried dishes and carried them back to the campsite where Anna helped her put them back in the canvas bag. Then the three of them settled on the grass. At first they chatted about what they'd seen that day, but as the sun streaked the undersides of the clouds pink, all conversation stopped. Anna swatted at a cloud of gnats while Hendrick pulled out a stalk of wheatlike grass and nibbled on the end. Mariah remembered doing that as a child. How long had it been since she saw the world with fresh eyes? Even while caring for Luke two summers ago, she'd bustled about doing chores, never stopping to experience his world.

She plucked a stalk of grass and tasted its tender, sweet end, rich with the promise of summer. God's golden sunlight had seeped into the earth where the plants drank it up. Tonight that light shimmered in the air and streaked the sky in hues of pink and red and violet.

"Nothing can top the Lord's paintbrush," she said softly.

Anna murmured agreement, but Hendrick gave her a look that swept over her like gale-driven waves. Both pain and longing and something else. Was it hope or despair?

This trip must be difficult for him. His presence certainly upset *her* composure. Suddenly, she had to consider his feelings. It wasn't just what she wanted. He was there, always there, within arm's reach. And his thoughts were so transparent. She hoped he didn't read her so easily.

He tossed away his stalk of grass. "What are you going to do once we get to Montana?"

"Get Mr. Gillard to sign the termination-of-parental-rights papers." The memory of Luke playing Geronimo made her voice catch. "I can't risk Luke's happiness."

Anna rolled onto her stomach, chin propped on her hands. "Who is Mr. Gillard, and what does he have to do with Luke?"

Mariah realized that she'd never filled in Anna and Hendrick. They were far from Felicity and Luke now. She took a deep breath. "Frank Gillard claims he's Luke's father, and says he wants his son back."

Her eyes widened, the pupils black in the declining light. "You don't think he really is Luke's father?"

"I'm not sure. That's what I need to find out."

"How are you going to do that?" With the setting sun behind him, Hendrick looked as stoic as an Indian, his expression veiled in darkness.

"I'll ask around Brunley, see what people know about him and what he knows about Luke. If he's truly Luke's father, he'll know things no one else would know."

"Like what?" asked Anna. "Does Luke have a peculiar birthmark? I read a novel once where the true princess was found because she had a birthmark shaped like a heart."

She shook her head. Luke didn't have any birthmarks.

Anna vibrated with excitement. "Is Luke the heir to a fortune?"

"More likely Frank Gillard is hiding something."

Hendrick frowned. "Like what?"

"I don't know exactly, but I have a gut feeling he's not who he says he is. Tell me why, after two-and-a-half years without one word of correspondence, he would suddenly want Luke? Is he even Luke's father? I don't know what's going on, but I intend to find out." She took a deep breath.

"That's where I need your help. I don't want Mr. Gillard to know our purpose right away, not until I discover his true character."

Anna sat up. "You want us to play parts, like actors and actresses."

"Not exactly. Just don't tell anyone why we're there."

Hendrick's expression darkened with every word. "Then what are we supposed to tell them?"

"That we're tourists come to see the Rocky Mountains," she said. "We're on our way to Glacier National Park to see the sights."

"But we're not going to the park, are we?" Hendrick said.

The words pricked her conscience. "We will make a point of seeing the park, but first we need to learn if Mr. Gillard is really Luke's father."

"What do you mean *if* he's Luke's father?" Hendrick stirred. "How would he know where to ask for Luke if he wasn't his father? And why? You just said Luke isn't heir to a fortune."

"True, but Frank Gillard isn't the name listed as the father on the agency paperwork. It's Francesco Guillardo. Mr. Gillard claims he anglicized his name, but I'm not so sure. If I can prove he's not really Luke's father, then Luke won't have to leave Gabe and Felicity."

"And if you can't prove that?"

A flutter of nerves started deep in Mariah's gut. "Then I'll have to convince him to sign the termination-of-rights papers."

Hendrick shook his head, and for the first time her resolve weakened. How would she accomplish that? Gabe was right. No real father would willingly give up his son. Except Frank Gillard had already done so once. If she could just discover what made him walk away then, she'd be able to convince him to walk away now.

Mariah rubbed her throbbing temples. "I place my trust in the Lord. He will help us."

He reached out and grasped her hand tightly, as if afraid to let her go. "I'll help you, too."

To relieve her headache, Mariah washed her hair in the creek. The cool water rinsed away the tension, and even after toweling dry, the coolness remained. Unfortunately, it could not remove the feel of Hendrick's touch. That moment when he'd looked in her eyes and committed to helping her had brought such strength…and such confusion. Was he helping her for Luke's sake or because he still hoped for a relationship that could never be?

She could know for certain if she told him the real reason she'd left two Octobers ago. Tell him she could never have children, and every tender feeling he had for her would vanish. But she couldn't bear to do that— couldn't stand the thought of his regard for her changing if he knew her secret. So she would stay silent and pray that Hendrick did not fall in love with her again.

The moonlight silvered the hushed landscape, and for long moments, she drank in the stillness before heading back to their camp. Hendrick sat by the dying embers of their cook fire, his chiseled features even more dramatic in the light. The oranges and yellows flickered across his cheeks, lightly stubbled at the end of the day. Such a man could steal into her heart if she let him. She could not.

He looked up when she approached. "Feel better?" he asked.

"A bit."

Tiny glowing sparks rose between them before dying in the night air. He poked at the fire with a stick. They hadn't been able to scavenge much wood, so the last embers would soon die.

"I'm sorry," he whispered.

Her heart lurched. "Why?"

"For not giving your plan credit. I shouldn't have questioned it."

She had to look away, at the tent, the cornfield dusted in moonlight, anywhere but at Hendrick. "Thank you."

He drew in a shuddering breath. "I meant what I said. I will help you."

She hugged her arms, suddenly chilled. "I know."

Their gazes met across the thin trail of smoke.

The corner of his mouth twitched, but he made no move toward her. "Be careful. Please."

She knew what he meant. Frank Gillard might be dangerous. Hendrick worried about her, yet she also knew from the way he took care of his mother and sister that he'd do everything in his power to protect her. The thought brought a lump to her throat.

"I guess I'd better get some sleep," she said, motioning to the tent. "Anna's waiting."

The flashlight glowed inside the canvas. She'd probably heard every word they'd said.

"Good night, Hendrick."

He nodded and poked at the embers. "Good night."

Mariah made her way to the tent, pulled aside the flap and ducked inside, away from the rush of emotion that Hendrick always managed to bring on.

"He likes you, you know." Anna sat in the middle of the tent, the bedrolls unopened.

Mariah felt the heat flood her cheeks. How ridiculous. She could not complete this mission if she came apart whenever she thought of Hendrick. "I am not interested in romance," she said in as flat a tone as she could muster.

"Not interested in romance?" Anna wrinkled her nose. "Why not? Everyone wants romance. Marriage can wait, but romance?" She hugged her knees and sighed. "Everyone loves romance."

This was not what Mariah wanted to talk about, even in general. She'd nip the conversation off with a little taste of reality. "When you're a bit older you'll realize that romance is fleeting. Marriage requires much deeper love." She wrestled with the knot on one of the bedrolls. The sooner they fell asleep, the better.

Anna didn't touch the other bedroll. Instead, she propped her head on her knees. "What is love?"

The knot began to give a little, and Mariah worked a finger into the center and pulled. "Thinking only of the other person."

"It would be wonderful to have a man think only of me."

The loop widened but didn't release the knot. "Love is mutual, Anna. You must think only of him, too."

"I know, but that's the easy part."

Mariah stared at the girl. "It is?"

"Of course. If he's handsome and kind, I wouldn't be able to get him out of my mind."

Ah, the passions of youth. Mariah stifled a smile as the knot gave way. "That's not exactly what I meant. Love requires sacrifice." She unfurled the bedroll and laid out one set of blankets.

"Sacrifice?" Anna wrinkled her nose. "I thought love was all about giving."

"So it is. You must be willing to give up everything." Mariah tackled the second bedroll, and Anna scooted on top of the first set of blankets.

"Everything?" She shrugged. "I don't have much, so

it'd be easy, but you have a lot. Who would you give up everything for?"

"For whom," Mariah began, but when Anna groaned, she realized the girl didn't need a schoolteacher. She truly wanted to know. It was also an opportunity to clear up any misconceptions about Mariah and Hendrick. "If I ever married, and I do mean *if,* I'd choose a widower with children."

"A widower? Who would want an old man?"

"An old woman, perhaps." Mariah laughed as she spread out the second bedroll. "Thirty-one is pretty old for marriage."

"No, it's not."

But Mariah had talked enough. "Time for bed. We need to save the dry cells in case we need the light for an emergency."

Anna sighed and turned off the flashlight.

That left Mariah in blackness. The night air was still warm, so she lay on her side on top of the blankets and closed her eyes to listen. Leaves rustled, insects chirped and Hendrick coughed.

With a sick feeling, she realized that he'd heard every word.

Chapter Six

Marry a widower!

Mariah's words irritated Hendrick more and more as they passed through Iowa and into South Dakota. Two flat tires and a nagging problem with blown fuses only made things worse.

He should be pleased. Getting involved with her again was like putting a bad battery back into a car. It was bound to fail. Still, he couldn't forget that moment on the beach, when she'd curled into his arms and he'd felt her heart beating against his. That moment should have meant something. Obviously, it didn't.

He groaned and shifted his weight behind the wheel. The tedium left too much time to notice the way she smelled, the curve of her neck and the way her curls just brushed her cheek.

"Are you all right?" Mariah asked.

"Fine," he snapped. "Just wish we'd pass another car."

The plains and rolling hills yielded few travelers. In fact, on this day, they hadn't seen a single other automobile.

"You'd think we'd see *someone*," Anna complained.

"It's so boring, all the same. Grass, grass and more grass. At least yesterday we met the old couple in that Mash."

"Nash. A Nash 681." Hendrick had tired of his sister's whining days ago. "And they weren't old. They couldn't be more than forty."

"As I said, old."

Mariah laughed. "I guess that makes me middle-aged."

He liked to hear her laugh. Most of the time, a frown creased her brow. Probably thinking about how to thwart Luke's father. Whatever she came up with, she'd have a tough time making it work.

"You aren't old," Anna said.

"Older than your brother, I think."

Was that what bothered her? Age didn't have anything to do with how a person felt about someone. Besides, they weren't that many years apart.

"He's twenty-seven," Anna chirped.

"Almost twenty-eight." He glanced briefly at Mariah, trying to judge her reaction.

"Keep your eyes on the road," she said. "We don't want to have a wreck in this wilderness."

He bit back the urge to snap at her constant harping. Instead, he accelerated. A moment later, the car hit a bump, sending the women flying. She glared at him. He eased off the accelerator just a bit.

"What's that?" Anna screeched, and he slammed on the brakes. The car slid to a halt in a cloud of dust.

"What?" He looked around once the dust cleared but didn't see anything.

Anna's attention was riveted to their right. "Something popped out of the ground next to the road."

"Something?" He leaned around Mariah and peered at the dirt and grass.

"A little head." Anna hung out the side, pointing to the grass.

"Good grief." Hendrick settled back behind the wheel. He would kill his sister before this trip was over. "Little? I thought you saw a rock in the road or a huge animal, something dangerous."

Mariah relaxed, a faint smile on her lips.

"It looked strange," Anna said, indignantly, "like a muskrat."

"A muskrat?" Hendrick couldn't believe his sister's vivid imagination. "Muskrats live in lakes and rivers. There's not a drop of water out here."

"There's another one," Anna cried, springing out of the car so fast she left the door hanging open. "And another and another. They're everywhere." She ran into the meadow to hunt down the creatures.

Mariah followed at a much more leisurely pace. Since the ladies were already out, Hendrick decided to stretch his legs, too.

It didn't take long for him to spot one of the critters, like an overgrown weasel. "What is it? A gopher?"

Mariah shaded her eyes. "I believe we've spotted a prairie dog. Soon there'll be hundreds." She fanned her face. "My, it's hot. Let's get going again so we'll have some breeze to cool us."

Hendrick was all for that. He sweated just standing still. "Come back, Anna. Time to go."

At the sound of his voice, the prairie dogs shrieked and ducked back into the ground.

"Do we have to? I want to see one up close, but you keep startling them, and they disappear."

"Yes, we must," Mariah said firmly.

Apparently, hers was the voice of authority, for Anna grudgingly obeyed. They all piled back into the car and headed down the road, but within a few hundred feet, a cloud of steam brought their progress to a halt.

The engine had overheated.

Hendrick hopped out, hoping he could solve the problem with a little water. As he unlatched the right-hand hood, Mariah started to get out. He did not need a supervisor right now.

"How far to the next town?" he asked to occupy her.

"Why? The car's just a little low on water, isn't it?"

He grimaced at the scorched smell. They'd run it way down. "How much water do we have with us?"

Instead of answering, she pulled out the map. One finger traced their route while she gnawed on her lip. He adored the way she could lose herself in thought. At those moments she didn't try to control everything.

After careful examination, she said, "Rapid City is sixty miles or so. Or we could go back to Kadoka."

"Is that the closest?"

She puckered her lower lip. "There might be a hamlet or village closer. This map doesn't show every town."

Great. They were stuck in the wilderness, probably without water. He walked to the back of the vehicle and saw a trail of water that ended several paces before their current position. The cooling system was bone-dry.

He crawled under the car to check the hoses. Sure enough, the lower hose had split where it clamped to the radiator. He cut off the damage and reclamped. That would get them to Kadoka, if they could refill the radiator. He scooted out from under the car.

Mariah's eyes met his. "What's the verdict?"

He wiped his hands on a rag. "We're out of water."

"Out?" Something caught Mariah's attention. "Anna, don't go too far."

Hendrick spotted his sister running after the prairie

dogs again. Good. At least she wouldn't be within earshot. He closed the hood but didn't latch it. "I don't remember seeing any containers of water in the car."

Mariah's cheeks flushed pink. Combined with her damp ringlets, the effect left him breathless.

"We have a canteen." She rummaged in the back and came up with the tin container. From the sound of the swishing liquid, there wasn't much left.

"Put it back. We're not using our drinking water for the engine."

She blotted her brow with a plain cotton handkerchief, as unadorned as everything Mariah wore. "Then we need to find water."

Practical advice. The only trouble was he hadn't seen a river in miles. Hendrick looked to the north, the south, the east, the west and all points in between. The land was dry, the grass yellow and odd craggy rocks loomed low in the distance. "Where exactly?"

Mariah pulled out the map again. "I'll find the nearest river."

"I don't suppose your map shows creeks and ponds?"

She bit her lip. "It's not that detailed. In fact, there's not supposed to be a road here."

"What?" Hendrick ripped the map from her hands. "Where are we?"

She pointed to a blank spot beside an area marked Badlands. "But we're on the correct road. That nice couple we met said to take the right fork to go to Montana."

Hendrick didn't remember that. "Which fork? We passed a dozen."

"The first one, I assumed. That's the one I took."

Hendrick scrubbed his damp hair. That meant they were lost in the wilderness with a dead car and insufficient water. Things couldn't get much worse.

She removed her hat and mopped her forehead. "This car is too hot with the roof up. What I wouldn't give for a shade tree."

Shade would solve only part of the problem. He needed to find water. That small amount in the canteen wouldn't last the three of them long in this heat, never mind the car. "How far to the nearest river on that map of yours?"

For the tiniest instant, she looked panicky. "Too far. Oh, Hendrick, I'm sorry. I've gotten you and Anna into a mess."

Tears threatened to fall, something he hadn't expected from Mariah Meeks. He fought the urge to console her and focused on finding a solution. While he thought, he watched Anna chase the critters from mound to mound. That was it. "Seems to me those prairie dogs must be getting water from somewhere. Those rocks over there might have some pools of water under them. I'll check and be right back."

She lifted worried eyes. "Be careful. We don't need you hurt or lost."

Her concern touched him. He smiled to assure her. "I'll keep the car in view."

"I'll go with you." She started to get out of the car.

He stopped her. "No. You stay here in case another car comes past."

Though she nodded agreement, she shoved the canteen at him. "At least take the water. It must be a hundred degrees."

"No, you keep it." He couldn't take the last ounce of water from her. "It's equally hot here, and I'll be moving."

"But what will you put the water in? Take it. We'll make do in the shade of the car." She held out the canteen again.

Her argument made sense, but he wasn't taking the last of the water. He climbed into the backseat and rummaged through their belongings until he found a tin drinking cup. He emptied the canteen into it. "You take this." He handed her the cup and kept the canteen. "If I find water, I want to get as much as I can."

She nodded but held the cup toward him. "Take one sip before you go."

He knew she wouldn't let him leave without taking that sip, so he pretended to drink and then set the cup on the floorboard, out of the sun. The heat was already sapping his energy, but he wouldn't let her see how much it bothered him. "I won't go far."

"Be careful. Please." She grasped his hand for just an instant, but it was long enough to buoy his strength. With her support, he could do anything.

When Anna left with Hendrick to search for water, Mariah wished she could tag along. That childhood feeling of being left behind reared up from the dark recesses of her memory. With five brothers, four of them older, she had always been the odd one out at playtime. No one wanted a girl around.

Today, sitting in the shade of the automobile watching Hendrick and Anna head across the vast field, Mariah whispered, "I want to go, too," to absolutely no one. She could see down the arrow-straight road for miles, and no other car or truck or buggy was in sight.

After what seemed like hours, but was in reality only forty-five minutes according to her watch, she rose to stretch her legs. Hendrick and Anna's distorted figures stood far in the distance. If she wasn't mistaken, they appeared to be headed back.

"Helloooo," she called out, waving one arm.

If they heard her, they didn't answer. A prairie dog stopped, head held high, to watch.

She smiled at him. "Sorry I disturbed you."

The creature scolded her before popping back into its hole.

She waited for it to reappear, but the spot remained empty. Nearby, another prairie dog appeared, considering her carefully.

"See many strangers?" she asked it.

The animal cocked its head. No wonder Anna had been enchanted. She looked up and noticed that Hendrick and his sister were much closer now.

She cupped her hands around her mouth and called out, "Did you find water?"

Hendrick shook his head. He loped toward her, his long legs erasing the distance quickly.

Dry. Mariah's spirits sank. Without water they'd die of thirst.

"Nothing?" she asked when he reached the road.

"A big gulch."

"No river at the bottom?"

He shook his head. "You'd think there'd be one, but there wasn't a drop in sight. Might as well be a desert."

"What are we going to do?"

"Set up camp." He walked to the car and pulled out the tent bag. "We'll use it for shade. After dusk, when it's cooler, we'll walk to Kadoka."

"That's ten miles." If she was right about where they were located. "Can we make it?"

"With God's grace." He glanced at Anna, who, feet dragging, had finally reached them.

Mariah didn't want to frighten her. "Of course He'll see us through." She forced a smile. "I'm sorry my car has been so much trouble."

Hendrick shrugged. "It's a car. They break."

"Mariah, you should have seen that place," Anna said

breathlessly. "Gorges as far as you can see and big craggy rocks."

Mariah had clearly misinterpreted Anna's expression.

"They're like little mountains," Anna was saying, "as big as you've ever seen and in lots of colors. You'd be astonished. The ground just goes along and then all of sudden, it's gone. If I wasn't watching my step, I would have fallen right over the edge."

Mariah sighed, the most enthusiasm she could muster. "You make me wish I'd seen it. If only you'd found water. Maybe we're not looking in the right places."

Hendrick's jaw tightened. "It's July."

Mariah surveyed the dry grasses and barren terrain. Of course. Any spring runoff would be long gone by now. Her speculation had been thoughtless. The best thing they could do for now was stay out of the sun. "Let's set up the tent."

The rest of the afternoon, they sat in the shade of the canvas and swatted flies. At first Anna chattered about all she'd seen. Then they told humorous stories about growing up. Then even that felt like too much. Everyone knew the last precious cup of water sat in the car. They'd agreed to take one sip each just before sundown and then head toward town. With luck another car would pass before then.

None did.

By the time the sun hung low and the air cooled to a tolerable temperature, Mariah was so parched and tired that walking was the last thing she wanted to do.

"I guess it's time." She sighed.

Hendrick nodded. "One sip of water each, then we go."

Their situation was dire. If they didn't reach town tonight, they'd succumb to thirst. As if to emphasize the point, lightning flashed across the darkening sky. A bank of purple clouds loomed to the southwest.

"Heat lightning," said Hendrick, following her gaze. "It'll pass."

She wasn't so sure. That looked more like a storm to her. "Maybe we'd better wait. No garage would be open by the time we arrive anyway. We'll start out immediately after it passes and spend the night at a hotel." She touched his arm without thinking, and the electricity crackled between them.

He jerked away. "If you insist. After all, it's your car and your mission."

She did not need an argument now. "I'm sorry. We're all a bit cranky from the heat. If you think it's safe, we'll leave now."

The fight went out of him. "Sorry. You're probably right."

Of course she was, but she had the sense not to point that out. "All right. Let's unroll the side windows. We'll wait out the storm in the car."

The storm swept over without one drop of rain or crack of thunder. Hendrick could have rubbed it in her face, but instead he suggested they get some sleep and rise early for the walk to town. That made more sense than anything she'd suggested.

She and Anna crept into the tent and soon drifted off to a fitful sleep. Thunder rumbled and wolves howled. She tried to fend them off, and then…she awoke with a start. What had awakened her? Must have been the dreams, but then she heard it. A low rumble, like an animal's growl. She shivered and looked to Anna, who didn't make a sound.

Again the low rumbling, closer this time. Mariah pulled the blanket tight around her shoulders, though that could offer no protection should a wolf or coyote consider her worth eating.

"Anna," she hissed.

The girl murmured and stirred but didn't awaken.

Mariah felt a bit foolish. Here she was a grown woman looking to a nineteen-year-old girl for protection. She lifted the tent flap a few inches and spotted the car. It would be safer in there, except for the very different danger inside.

"Anna," she whispered again, "wake up." She didn't want to shake her, but she would if she had to.

"Mmm-hmm," the girl murmured without waking.

How could anyone sleep so soundly? Mariah supposed that she had, too, at that age.

A light tapping sound on the canvas set her already frayed nerves on edge. What if the animal was nuzzling the side of the tent? She scooted toward the center and felt around for the flashlight. She could crack it over the beast's head if necessary.

The tapping sound increased. Next she'd hear its claws ripping through the canvas.

"Hendrick," she cried, getting to her knees. "Anna, wake up."

This time she shook the girl, and Anna groggily asked what she was doing.

"There's a wild animal outside."

The tapping sound had increased in frequency, almost like... Oh, dear. Ashamed, she sat back on her heels. Rain. It was raining.

"Did you see it?" Anna asked, sounding much more awake.

"I, uh..." Mariah hated to admit how foolish she'd been, but she didn't want to actually lie. "I think it's probably gone now that the rain has begun."

The clouds let loose torrents, banging the tent like a drum.

"Ugh," Anna cried. "It's leaking right down my neck."

Sure enough, the canvas had soaked up all the water it could hold and was now allowing the rain to stream unhindered into the tent. Mariah's blanket was already damp.

"We need to get to the car. We'll have some shelter in there." It had to be better than the tent, which was filling with water. She wrapped the wet blanket around her shoulders, and Anna did the same with hers. "On the count of three we'll dash for the car. One, two, three."

They threw aside the tent flaps and crawled into the muddy grass. Anna hopped to her feet and raced to the car before Mariah had even cleared the tent. The deluge soaked through the blanket to the skin in moments.

In the flashes from distant lightning, she saw Hendrick doing something with the canvas roof of the car. Oh, dear, that was leaking, too.

"Aren't you coming?" Anna asked from the backseat.

"What's the use?" Rainwater streamed down her face. The blanket was wet through and through. The ground had turned to muck, which oozed between her toes.

"Hurry," Hendrick said, opening the passenger-side door for her.

"It's too late." She pushed the door shut. "What are you doing to the car?"

"Nothing. I'm collecting water." He held empty tins to the edge of the roof, where the rainwater streamed off.

Of course. Here he was being practical while she fussed over getting wet. "Let me help."

He shook his head. "Get in the car in case it starts to hail or the lightning gets worse."

"I think it's almost over." Indeed, the rain had eased slightly.

When a flash of lightning lit the landscape, Mariah spotted the canteen leaning against the front tire. She held it up to a stream flowing off the adjacent set of roof supports. Most of the liquid missed the narrow opening, but over time she got enough inside to fill it.

"Drink," Hendrick said, positioning his mouth under the stream.

She did as instructed, delighting in the cool liquid. Water had never tasted so good. Anna followed suit on the other side of the car.

Mariah laughed. "It's wonderful, the best I've ever tasted."

Anna giggled and coughed. Even Hendrick chuckled.

"You should laugh more often," she said.

He mumbled something indiscernible and set aside the last tin. "I think we have enough water for the radiator to get to the next town." He opened the passenger-side door. "Let's wait out the rest of the storm in the car." Then he extended his hand to assist her.

Her heart, caught off guard, leapt. After all their disagreements, he wanted to help her. He thought first of her. Tears rose as she placed her hand in his.

In the backseat, Anna groaned. "Just get in. I'm getting soaked."

Mariah and Hendrick both laughed.

"We probably have enough water to half-fill the radiator," Hendrick announced.

"Just from this rain?" Mariah gave a little awkward laugh as if she wasn't quite comfortable. "I didn't realize it was coming down that hard."

"What do you mean you didn't realize it was coming down that hard?" Anna mimicked from the backseat. "We got soaked *inside* the tent."

"True, but…" Mariah's voice trailed off.

"But it's hard to tell in the dark," he finished for her.

"Exactly."

Though he couldn't see her smile, he could hear it in her voice.

"We did it," she mused, still sounding pleased. "We got the water we needed."

He felt her settling in beside him. "Should be enough."

"Do you think the problem can be repaired easily?"

"Already made a temporary repair, but we should get a new hose down the road. All we have to do is add the water. I'll check the hose and water in the next town while you refill our canteen."

"That would be wonderful." She sighed. "Today's trouble put us a bit behind schedule. I'd hoped to get to Brunley around midmonth."

"That's pretty ambitious, isn't it? How far do we have to go?" Hendrick asked, though he knew the answer. Too far.

"Probably another eight hundred miles, but I'd have to look at a map to know the exact distance."

They couldn't leave until morning, so for a long, long time they sat quietly as the rain turned to drizzle and then stopped altogether. A break appeared in the clouds, allowing them a peek at the blanket of stars above. Then another break opened and another. Before long, the clouds disappeared entirely and the moon's glow lit the landscape.

"There's Cygnus," he said softly.

She leaned forward to look. "I don't see it."

He pointed toward the constellation. "Remember two summers ago when we saw the shooting stars?" It had been a wonderful night, though she had seemed unusually quiet. He had thought she was thinking about how she'd miss living at the parsonage after her brother married, but she wouldn't tell him her thoughts.

Tonight she was just as quiet. "I didn't see them at first. You had to point them out."

He remembered the thrill that had shot through him when he held her in his arms and guided her sight toward the spectacle. She'd felt so natural against his shoulder, like she was meant to be part of him. That was the first time he'd wanted to kiss her. No, that wasn't true. He'd wanted to kiss her the moment he laid eyes on her, but that night had offered his first real chance. Her attention was on the stars, and he'd breathed in her excitement until he convinced himself she felt the same way he did. But then she pulled away, the moment passed and he never got up the courage to try to kiss her again.

Tonight was no different. She kept to her side of the front seat. The narrow gap between them might as well have been one of those Badlands chasms.

"There must have been thirty or forty shooting stars that night," he mused.

In the backseat, Anna murmured before her breathing deepened.

"Shh," Mariah said softly, "she's sleeping."

At last they were alone. The thought made him nervous. What could he say that wouldn't frighten her off? His tongue was tied, and he could do no more than stare at the stars.

"And there's the Big Dipper." Mariah leaned toward him to point out his window.

"You're right," he said, his voice husky.

"And by following the two end stars of the cup, I can find Polaris, the North Star." She ducked low to look out the windshield.

He bent down, too, and lightly brushed against her

hair, still damp. "Your hair is wet. You'll catch cold." He couldn't believe he'd been so thoughtless. "There's a dry blanket in the back." He swiveled around to rummage for it, but she restrained him.

"Don't wake Anna. I'm fine. Just a little cool."

He saw her hand on the dash, silvered by the moonlight. Without considering her reaction, he touched it and, feeling how chilled it was, wrapped his large hand around her small one. "You're cold."

She shook her head. "Just my fingers." But she didn't pull away.

"Cold fingers must mean cold toes."

"They are a bit cold," she admitted, "but it's refreshing after today's heat."

"Here." He pulled off his outer shirt. The thin cotton had dried while they were talking. "Wrap it around your feet."

"No, they're muddy," she protested, trying to shove the shirt back at him.

"Shh, you'll wake Anna."

She clucked her tongue and shook her head. "Hendrick Simmons, stop being so chivalrous."

Chivalrous. The word puffed up his pride enough for him to think that despite her protests to the contrary, she might admire him a little. "Any other man would do the same."

"No, he wouldn't. And I can't take it. Now put your shirt back on. We're in mixed company here."

Hendrick hadn't thought of that. Light fringed the eastern horizon. He certainly didn't want Mariah to see him at less than his best.

She yawned, and her eyelids fluttered, once, twice and then open. "I'm so sleepy."

He kept his disappointment to himself. "Sleep, then."

Moments later, she nodded off, but he couldn't sleep, not with her so close. The moon gilded her features, making her look like a marble statue. How exquisite the curve of her cheeks. How perfect the tilt of her nose. The expressive lips now still. The lashes so long and curled at the ends. The brow so certain. Once upon a time, he thought she cared for him. They'd gone to church suppers together. People talked of them as a couple. Then, on that fateful night, she'd told him they could never be more than friends and walked away.

Now she was back and just as perfect. He leaned closer to see the unblemished porcelain of her complexion. Her lips, so soft, beckoned, but he didn't dare touch them. But her forehead. That wasn't off-limits. Plus, she was asleep. She'd never know.

He bent close, and then softly, with no more than the brush of a feather, he kissed her perfect brow. He brushed a hair from her forehead, and she jumped, eyes wide.

"What are you doing?" She slapped his hand and retreated until her back was plastered against the door.

He'd just ruined everything.

Chapter Seven

~❧~

Mariah had let her guard down for only a few minutes and look what happened. If she hadn't dozed off, if she'd taken the backseat, Hendrick wouldn't have kissed her. True, it wasn't much of a kiss, but he'd started down a path that could not be traveled.

It wouldn't happen again.

They packed up camp at first light and decided to head west since the radiator was holding water. They reached the next town just as it was awakening for the day. The sole filling station didn't have the right size rubber hose, so Hendrick slid under the car to see how his temporary fix had held.

"Let's take a walk," Mariah suggested to Anna, leaving the men to deal with the car.

The two wandered past the shop windows filled with curios and tourist mementos.

Anna pressed her finger to the glass. "Look at that cowgirl hat, just like the one Annie Oakley wore," she read from the sign perched beside it, "complete with Annie's trademark sheriff's pin."

Mariah smiled at the girl's gullible enthusiasm. The hat might bear a passing resemblance to something Miss

Oakley wore, but it was flimsily constructed of straw instead of bull hide or felt, and the drugstore had stamped its name on the hatband.

"Would you like it?" she asked. "You could use a wide-brimmed hat in this heat."

Anna's face fell. "I can't afford it."

The hat cost only seventy-five cents. "I'd be glad to buy it for you."

"You'd do that?"

Anna's amazement touched Mariah. The girl must have received few gifts in her lifetime. Mariah wrapped her arm around Anna's. "Let's go inside."

After they'd made the purchase, they returned to the filling station with Anna sporting her new hat. A stiff breeze had come up, and they both had to hold their hats to keep them from flying away.

"Your brother is going to wonder where we went," Mariah remarked as they made their way down the street. The Overland still sat at the filling station, but neither Hendrick nor the attendant was around. "I hope he didn't go looking for us."

That concern vanished when Hendrick stepped out of the station. Worry creased his brow. "Where were you?"

"Shopping," said Anna. "See my new hat?"

Hendrick, looking stricken, drew Mariah aside. "You shouldn't have done that."

"Nonsense. She's a dear girl who doesn't get much new. Besides, the gift was mine to give."

He wiped his brow. "I wish you hadn't." Beads of perspiration dotted his upper lip.

"The hat cost only seventy-five cents. That won't bankrupt us."

"But I will." He looked like a boy who'd broken his mother's candy dish.

"What do you mean?"

He looked her square in the eye. "The money you gave me for fuel is gone."

"That's not possible." In that moment of shock, she let go of her hat, and it flew off her head.

He lunged and caught it. "I'm afraid it is." He subconsciously crushed the brim.

She motioned for him to hand it back. "We couldn't have spent all the money already."

"No," he said miserably. "I think it fell out of my pocket yesterday when I was fixing the radiator hose."

"Fell out? And you didn't notice until now?" Mariah battled anger and frustration. That money had to get them to Montana and back.

"I'm sorry. I have more than $10 of my own left." He held out the bills and coins.

Her heart lurched. He'd offered her everything he had.

"Keep your money." She clutched her hat and handbag. Her remaining funds might get them to Brunley. Might. "Maybe we should go back and check to see if it's still there."

Hendrick eyed the flagpole with its wind-whipped flag. "It's probably gone."

He was right. Between the wind, the thunderstorm and the prairie dogs, they'd never find it.

"Oh, dear." She hovered between panic, anger and fear. "How much for today's fuel and oil?"

"I paid for it already."

She shook her head. That wasn't his responsibility. "I'll pay you back."

"Forget it." He strode to the car and opened the driver's-side door for her—right in front of the attendant and anyone else who cared to watch. "We'd better get going if we're going to make any progress."

Careless, wonderful man. She didn't know whether to bawl him out or admire his steadfast honor. In the end, she settled for letting him take the wheel.

Montana proved flatter and more barren than any of the land they'd traversed so far. For the most part, the towns were tiny, trees scarce and fellow travelers even more infrequent. For hours and hours each day, they traveled alone on an arrow-straight road that vanished into the horizon forward and aft. The few landmarks began to look the same, and Mariah longed for a house, a signpost, anything to vary the landscape.

The emptiness drained her energy and her soul. Prayer became difficult. She couldn't feel God near, as she did at home. Her heart grew heavier, followed by a deep sense of foreboding. Each day she tried to shake it off. Each night it grew worse.

"Look at those colors," Hendrick said one morning as they packed up their camp.

Mariah followed his gaze to the sunrise, layered in rose and purple and tangerine and every color in between.

"Takes your breath away," he said quietly.

She noticed how he saw the little things, details that she dismissed without thinking. To him, a different-colored grasshopper or the gradations of color in a sunrise not only pleased the eye but carried significance. To her, the sky looked ominous.

"What's the saying? Red sky in morning?" she asked.

"Sailor take warning. Lucky we're not sailing."

She laughed feebly but couldn't shake the sense that something bad was about to happen.

"Is it going to storm?" asked Anna while she folded the tent.

"Not now, but that don't—*doesn't*—mean a storm isn't on its way," said Hendrick.

Every once in a while he forgot to speak properly. When it happened, he'd stammer and flush until he got it right. Mariah didn't know why it bothered him so much. The slips came infrequently, and, truth be told, she rather enjoyed the rhythm of his natural speech. It matched the cadence of Pearlman, slow and folksy, relaxing.

"Well, it's fine weather now, so let's get on our way," Mariah said, forcing past her apprehensions. "By my calculations, we should reach Brunley by early afternoon."

"We will?" Anna, who had been complaining about everything the past two days, perked up. "But I don't see a town. All I can see is that bank of clouds way off."

Mariah knew better. "That cloud bank is the Rocky Mountains."

"But I thought we were miles from the mountains."

"We are," Mariah said, "but the Rockies are very tall. They have snow on top in the summer."

"Let's hurry, then," Anna said. "I want to see that."

Soon they were on their way, Mariah at the wheel. Grass or wheat, already yellowed, stretched as far as she could see in every direction. The land undulated in long, low waves. Occasionally, she'd see a speck in the distance: a house or a barn or a cow, perhaps. Or maybe a tree or a shrub.

The Overland's tires swirled up dust from the narrow road. It got in her hair, her ears, her clothing and even her eyes. She had to constantly rub an eye or wipe the grit from her lips. She would not miss that one bit when they reached their destination.

"I hope there's a nice hotel in Brunley." Anna sighed from behind her. "I could use a long bath."

The girl's momentary enthusiasm had dissipated within

the hour. Even the new hat's enchantment had worn off. Mariah couldn't blame her. She'd like a good bath, too, not to mention a soft feather bed. The ground had gotten awfully hard the past couple nights.

Hendrick stared straight ahead, brow drawn. She knew that meant he was thinking, and before long she learned exactly what was bothering him.

"Where do you expect to find Mr. Gillard?"

His question seemingly came out of nowhere, but it was one she'd been considering for miles.

She was not about to admit that she had no idea. "It's a small town. Someone will know him."

"I'd talk to the biggest gossip in town," Anna said. "Mrs. Williams knows everything that's going on in Pearlman."

Poor Gabe, stuck with the town gossip as his church secretary, but Florabelle Williams was not the only gossip in town. Plenty of rumors started from both men and women.

"Where do you suggest I look?" Mariah teased. "At the barbershop?"

Anna laughed at her attempt to level the stereotype, but Hendrick looked offended. "Gossip isn't very Christian."

Mariah felt the rebuke and stopped chuckling. "It was a joke, Hendrick."

"My brother doesn't joke," said Anna.

"I don't believe that for a minute," Mariah said. "I seem to recall a joke or two over the years."

Two summers ago, he'd been so much more relaxed. They'd laughed over the smallest things. Had she changed him that much? She'd thought they were just friends, but maybe that hadn't been the case. A person in love finds joy in everything. Maybe he'd been in love that whole summer.

She pressed her eyes shut against the aching memories. This trip could not be making things better. Hendrick needed to move on, to find a woman who could give him the family he so deeply desired. That would happen if she told him she couldn't have children, but she couldn't bring herself to do it.

"It's no time to joke," Hendrick said, as if reading her mind. "We're talking about serious things. What do you plan to tell Mr. Gillard when you find him?"

She squirmed. She hadn't exactly come up with the right way to ask Gillard if he'd sign the termination papers. "I'll get to know him first."

He grunted in disbelief. It wouldn't be that easy. She knew that, but until she faced Gillard and saw who he was, she wouldn't know how to proceed.

They fell into silence. Low rolling hill after low rolling hill passed by, the monotony endless. Here a fence post. There a herd of cattle looking at them as if they'd never seen a motorcar before. No other travelers.

Then out of the blue Hendrick said, "I think you were supposed to turn right back there."

"What?"

"Right. You were supposed to turn right at that intersection."

What was he talking about? "I didn't see any intersection, unless you mean that cattle trail we crossed. That's not an intersection."

He held up the map. "According to this, we needed to turn right." The paper crinkled when he touched his finger to it.

She shook her head. "If it's on the map, it's a major intersection, not a path. Besides, we haven't gone far enough."

"Then why is this road getting narrower?"

Mariah hated when he was right. The terrain was changing, getting hillier, with scrubby low trees just tall enough to block the view.

"If we made a wrong turn," Mariah said, "we'll just turn around and go back."

"This road could go clear to the Pacific Ocean," he countered.

"I don't think so. Look at the map. There aren't many roads across the mountains. None this far north. We might end up in Canada, but not at the coast."

"Suppose we run out of gas?" Anna asked eagerly.

Mariah lifted an eyebrow at her peculiar reaction. "Why do you sound so excited by the prospect?"

"Because interesting things happen to people in danger."

"We're not in danger," Hendrick said. "You got that from a dime-store novel."

"What if I did?"

Mariah understood well the thrill of those adventurous stories. They portrayed glamorous worlds filled with danger and forbidden romance. She'd read a few in her day.

"I'll bet the heroine meets a handsome hero when her car runs out of fuel," she said, playing along.

Anna squealed. "Wouldn't that be wonderful?"

The ladies laughed, but the conversation came to an abrupt halt when the road ended at a two-story brick building surrounded by scrub trees.

She applied the brake to stop her car.

"I wonder where we are."

"Beson Creek School." Hendrick pointed to the sign above the doorway.

Mariah peered at the building. "A school way out here. Imagine that."

The big building certainly looked like a school. It even had a bell near the broad porch. But it included far more outbuildings than any school she'd ever seen, a half dozen in all, ranging from privy-size to almost as big as the school building itself. A split-rail fence lined the drive and enclosed the schoolyard. No one was outside right now except a young dark-haired girl who sat on the stoop staring at her dusty shoes, seemingly oblivious to the motorcar's approach. If not for the size and number of buildings, Mariah would think the place a homestead and the girl dawdling away the time after doing her chores.

She cut the engine. This misstep afforded the perfect opportunity to get directions to Brunley and perhaps learn a bit about Mr. Frank Gillard. There had to be an adult inside.

"I'm going to look for the person in charge." Mariah got out of the car, followed by Hendrick and Anna.

When the doors slammed shut, the girl glanced at them. Terror flashed across her face for an instant but turned quickly to hope. She sprang from her perch and ran across the yard toward Mariah, arms outstretched.

"Mamaaaaaa," she cried, her voice bouncing with each step.

What on earth? Mariah instinctively braced herself. Hendrick stared at the girl and then at her. He couldn't possibly think she was this girl's mother. "I have no idea what she means."

"I think she thinks you're her ma."

"That's obvious," Mariah hissed. But none of the orphans had ever made that mistake. She smiled at the little girl. "I'm sorry, dear."

The girl halted, disappointment crushing her joy. She blinked rapidly and averted her gaze, the black hair falling over her tan face. The poor girl must be waiting for her mother, or maybe she had lost her mama. She might be an orphan. Mariah's heart went out to her. As hard as she tried to shackle her emotions, she inwardly wept for every child who'd lost a parent.

"There, there." Mariah reached to embrace the girl, but she darted away, skittish as a fawn. "This must be an Indian orphanage and school."

Hendrick knelt before the rail-thin girl, who couldn't be more than six or seven years of age.

"My name's Hendrick. What's yours?"

The girl's fingers crept into her mouth.

With a bang, the school's front door opened, and a pudgy, balding man strode out. "Constance," he barked, "here." He pointed at the step, and the little girl reluctantly returned to her perch and tugged the skirt of her ill-fitting brown uniform over her knees.

The man, satisfied with the girl's obedience, crossed the grounds to meet them. He extended a hand to Hendrick. "Allow me to introduce myself. Mr. Layton Sowich, director of the Beson Creek School."

Hendrick limply shook the man's hand while his gaze drifted to the girl. "Why isn't she in class?"

Sowich's expression tightened behind thick lenses that magnified his owlish eyes. Clearly he thought Hendrick was questioning his methods. If Mariah didn't take over, she'd get no assistance from the man.

"It's a pleasure to meet you, Mr. Sowich," said Mariah. "We are headed for Brunley and apparently took a wrong turn."

"Brunley? It's just up the road, less than a mile. I don't know how you missed it." Sowich tore his attention from Hendrick and settled it on her. "Mrs.?"

"*Miss* Mariah Meeks," she said, shaking the man's hand

firmly. "I'm an agent for the Orphaned Children's Society in New York and would love to learn about your school."

The man's momentary surprise shifted to unease when she asked about the school. "You want to learn about my school? Why? Did someone send you to take away some of the children?"

"No, no," she rushed to explain. "Not at all. We are touring the area." She hesitated at the stretch of the truth. "And investigating a prospective parent."

Hendrick shot her a look of reproach, but her response made Sowich's discomfort vanish.

"Then you're here by accident," the man said with obvious relief.

"Exactly," Mariah said, "but I'm fascinated with schools. I studied education in college. I would love to hear about your mission and curriculum."

Apparently satisfied that she was no threat, Sowich smiled broadly and with a flush of pride told her about their progressive agenda. "With the buffalo exterminated, the Indians need to acculturate by acquiring new trades. Unfortunately, all prior attempts have failed, with catastrophic results. We believe introducing new industries to the children will produce more lasting effects. Shall I show you around?"

The entire time Mr. Sowich talked, Mariah watched Hendrick's expression turn to stone. Something the man said had bothered him immensely, but Mariah found it a sensible and responsible program to address a terrible situation.

"I'd love to hear more," she told Mr. Sowich. "Anna? Hendrick?"

Anna agreed, but Hendrick hung back, saying he wanted to check the car. Mariah joined Mr. Sowich for the tour. With any luck, he would know where she could find Frank Gillard and how to approach him. This misstep could yet prove fruitful.

Hendrick watched Mariah get sucked into Sowich's fancy talk. Oh, he could throw around big words, but he was nothing more than the director of a boarding school. Why couldn't Mariah see that? Why did she get that look of excitement, that glow in her eyes and that quickness in her step?

The man stepped right by little Constance as if she wasn't there. What good was all that fancy language without caring about the children?

Once the others went inside, the girl lifted her eyes, chin still resting on her knees. Hendrick nodded at her, and she ducked her face again, as if she'd been told she wasn't to talk to anyone. Hendrick recognized punishment when he saw it. He'd endured his share of sitting in a corner because he couldn't seem to sit still in class. There was so much to do, so many things to explore, and he couldn't stand to spend all that time with books and letters and figures. Years later, after he'd had to run a business on his own, he realized the importance of book learning, but at the time it had been torture.

"I'm going to check the oil level and the water," he called out to the girl. "Do you want to watch?"

She furtively glanced at the front door of the school.

"They'll be busy for a long time," he said, opening the hood, "but you can watch from there if you want. I'll explain. This is where I add more oil to the engine." He removed the filler cap and hazarded a glance at the girl.

She was peeking at him through her fingers.

He checked the oil level. "Could use another quart. Engines need lots of oil. It keeps all the parts moving." She still sat on the porch, but she'd dropped her hands to watch him. Curious black eyes followed his every move. Maybe there weren't any cars in these parts. "Have you ever seen a car?"

She nodded.

"This is an Overland, a solid touring car." He checked the water, which was low again. "Do you have a well or water pump here?"

The girl pointed across the yard.

Hendrick squinted into the sun and finally spied the hand pump. There wasn't a bucket, though. Most everyone in Pearlman had indoor plumbing now, but a few of the outlying farms still used an outdoor hand pump.

"Where's the bucket?" he asked.

The girl pointed in the same direction, so he walked over to investigate.

"There's no bucket here."

The girl sucked in her lower lip, checked the closed door once more and ran over to him. She motioned for him to follow her to the back of a small outbuilding. There he saw an outdoor laundry, with huge tubs and paddles for boiling the wash. Several tin buckets sat on the ground. A regular school wouldn't need a laundry. This was a boarding school. Or Mariah could be right—maybe this was an orphanage.

"Where are the workers?" he asked, looking for the adults. None were around. They must be busy inside.

The girl looked at him blankly.

"The workers," he repeated, "like the women who do the laundry." He pointed at the tubs.

She shook her head and turned a finger to her own chest.

He stared. It couldn't be. "You do laundry? You can't even reach into the tub."

She nodded proudly and grabbed a wooden paddle

before racing to the other side of the tub where she climbed a stool. She pantomimed stirring the wash and then looked to him for praise.

Clearly she was proud of her work, but to Hendrick she looked too young and thin for manual labor. "But aren't you studying? Don't you go to school?"

She nodded, though tears formed in her round eyes. "Wanna go home." Her lower lip quivered.

Hendrick's heart broke. "Where is home?"

She shook her head, and a sniffle escaped.

She didn't know. She was too young to know.

He took the paddle and set it aside before lifting her to the ground. Even in that brief moment, he felt her silent sobs. He had to help her. Mariah believed Constance was an orphan, but what if she wasn't? What if this *was* just a boarding school? Constance had mistaken Mariah for her mama. She begged to go home. Hendrick wanted to help, but first he needed to calm her down.

He knelt and took her hands in his. She wouldn't look at him, so he hummed a bar of the hymn he used to sing to Anna when she couldn't sleep and Ma was too tired or too sick to tend her.

The girl stopped crying and listened. Her dark eyes, swimming with tears, watched his every move. He brushed a tear from her cheek with his rough thumb, but she didn't seem to mind that he had workingman's hands.

When he finished a verse, he whispered in the same soft voice, "How old are you, Constance?"

She held up four fingers on one hand and two on the other. Six.

"Do you know where your home is?" he asked.

Her face fell as she shook her head. "Mama know."

"Is your mama…alive?"

She nodded vigorously. "Mama work Missa Lawd."

So he was right. Constance wasn't an orphan. He would look for this Mr. Lord, and then talk to Constance's mother.

He drank in the girl's dark, trusting eyes. "I promise I will find your mama and get you home."

She threw her arms around his neck with a sob, and he patted the thin little back. He didn't know quite how he'd do it, but he'd find a way. He had to.

"There you are, Hendrick." It was Mariah, and judging by the frown on her face, she wasn't happy.

He patted the girl one last time and sent her scurrying back to her perch on the porch.

Mariah waited until the girl was gone before speaking. "You shouldn't promise things you can't deliver."

"But they're making her do laundry."

"Mr. Sowich says the children are taught basic industries."

"She's only six," he protested, though he knew his sister had helped their mother do the wash when she was that young. "And she's not just helping. She said she does the laundry herself."

Mariah looked incredulous. "Do you really believe that? Mr. Sowich explained that all the children participate, and the teachers supervise."

Mr. Sowich. Mr. Sowich. Mariah seemed to believe everything the man said. Hendrick crossed his arms, knowing he couldn't say a thing to change her mind.

Mariah sighed. "Please try to understand. The children are sent here by their parents, who hope to give them a better life. Constance is just homesick. It will pass."

All Hendrick knew was that Constance was hurting, and he had to help. He'd find her mother. Maybe if she knew how much her daughter suffered, she'd take her home.

* * *

Mariah understood Hendrick's desire to make the little girl happy, but this wasn't their fight. Mr. Sowich had explained the program in full. Indian families sent their children to the school so they could learn how to integrate into American society. By the 1880s, disease and starvation had wiped out most of the Blackfeet tribe. Two winters ago, after a year of drought, the tribe's cattle herd had been decimated. The remnant struggled to overcome poverty.

Government cattle hadn't solved the problem for more than an enterprising few. The new reservation superintendent, Frank Campbell, had a five-year plan for resurrecting agriculture on the reservation, but, according to Sowich, true success would never be achieved until the Indians learned how to live in the white man's world. The next generation was the key.

He'd emphasized that even though living away from her home was difficult, it was necessary for the future of the tribes. Eventually Constance would adapt and be better able to lead her family and her tribe to prosperity.

Moreover, Mariah had seen no sign of neglect or mistreatment. Yes, Constance was homesick, but that would pass.

"We must respect the family's wishes," she insisted as they returned to the car. "They sent Constance here."

Hendrick didn't answer, a sure sign that he disagreed.

Anna ambled to the car with Mr. Sowich. "I'd like that," she told the school's director, "if my brother will let me."

"Let you do what?" Hendrick growled.

"Mr. Sowich said I could help in the classroom. It'll help me decide if I want to be a teacher."

Hendrick studied his sister's determination and nodded curtly, but Mariah could tell that he disapproved. Anna, however, either didn't notice or didn't care. She readily agreed to come back to the school at the first opportunity.

"It's just a mile from town," Mr. Sowich said. "You can walk here."

Mariah did need to verify the directions to town. "Back down this road to the intersection and then turn left?"

Hendrick could have added that he'd already told her to make that turn, but he didn't say a word.

"That's correct," Mr. Sowich confirmed. "Brunley's a small reservation town. You won't find many whites, I'm afraid."

Mariah's hackles rose at the prejudicial tone, completely inappropriate for the director of an Indian school. But she couldn't change his attitude in a minute, and she did need to ask him about Frank Gillard. No small part of her wondered why an Italian immigrant would settle in a reservation town.

"Thank you, Mr. Sowich." She paused, unsure how to phrase this. "I wonder if you happen to know a Mr. Frank Gillard."

Sowich stiffened ever so slightly. "It's a small town. Everyone knows everyone. Why do you ask?"

She couldn't give away her mission, even to a fairly respectable man. "A small matter of personal business."

If anything, his expression grew tenser. "Personal business, you say? If you don't mind a little advice, I'd act with caution, Miss Meeks."

"Why?" What had Frank Gillard done to inspire such concern? "Is he—" she hunted for a respectable word "—in trouble with the law?"

"Not at all, not at all," Sowich said hastily—perhaps too hastily. "I simply meant that it would behoove you to act with due caution. Given your education, you must understand the need for prudence when dealing with a man you've never met. Don't rush into any, uh, *business*."

Mariah processed his words with growing alarm. The man seemed to know exactly why she wanted to see Gillard. How? Had the Society's director, Mr. Isaacs, cabled ahead? If so, how much did Sowich know about her mission, and how much had he communicated to Gillard?

"Are you friends?" she asked.

Sowich shivered, though the day was scorching hot. "I wouldn't say that. In fact, we seldom talk."

Then how had he learned about her mission? "But..." She raised a finger, attempting to hold Sowich's attention as he backed away, but he was rapidly backpedaling out of range.

"Good day, Miss Meeks. I wish I could talk longer, but I must get back to my charges." Without waiting for her response, he hustled back to the school and yanked Constance inside after him.

Chapter Eight

Brunley amounted to little more than a cluster of bleached, ramshackle buildings in the midst of rolling prairie. The squared facades and dusty streets looked as if they belonged in a town from half a century ago. Mariah suspected that few strangers graced its streets except the curious few who stepped off the train on their way to visit the national park.

A group of Indians on the mercantile porch watched Mariah's car pull into town and slow to a stop. Wind swirled the dust into miniature cyclones, and a horse-drawn wagon waited outside a feed store. The purple mountains still loomed in the distance, their snow-dusted peaks not yet visible. If God had touched the mountains with beauty, He must have run short by the time He got to Brunley, and man did nothing to enhance the starkness.

Hendrick whistled. "Lucky there's a filling station."

So there was. Its fuel pump squatted beneath a wooden canopy, looking so rusted and clogged with dust that she doubted it worked. Mariah looked up and down the main street and saw only two motorcars, a dusty Model T and a shiny blue Packard, both parked alongside bleached wooden buildings. Other than those, transportation appeared relegated to horse travel. Hitching posts stood in front of every business, though only a few were occupied. Brunley was clearly a sleepy little town.

"Let's see if they have any gasoline," she said. Hendrick drove up to the pump, and, after several minutes, out sauntered a tall, lean Indian wearing a stylish fedora over his braided black hair.

As with every other man they'd encountered on this trip, his gaze slipped past her and landed on Hendrick.

"What'll it be?" The Indian spoke perfect English and, upon closer examination, had startling green eyes that betrayed at least some white blood.

"A fill and a quart of oil." Hendrick hopped out of the car. "I'm going to check the cooling system. We're still using too much water. I don't suppose you'd have any inch-and-three-quarter hose?"

Mariah started to leave a five-dollar bill on the seat for Hendrick, but changed her mind and gave it to Anna. "Pay for the gasoline and whatever else your brother needs for the car. I'm going to the mercantile for supplies. I'll also ask about the hotel."

"All right," the girl said dreamily, her chin propped on the back of the driver's seat where she had a good view of the tall and admittedly striking station attendant.

"I'll return here when I'm done."

Anna barely nodded her head.

Mariah left the girl and crossed the street to the mercantile. White heat shimmered off the ground, and dust clogged the air. She'd never been the nervous sort, but she had to admit to a bit of flip-flopping in her stomach today. How would she find Frank Gillard, and what would she say to him when she did? Mr. Sowich's warning rang in her ears. Until this moment, she'd thought she had a plan. Now she knew wasn't so sure.

Mouth dry, she ascended the mercantile steps. The Indians silently watched, one occasionally spitting tobacco juice into a clay pot at his feet.

"Hot day," she commented with a smile.

They did not reply. Maybe they didn't understand English. For the first time in years, she felt out of her element. She could dash into a tenement or wrest a youth from a sweatshop, but she knew nothing about Blackfeet culture.

"I need to get supplies," she needlessly explained before darting inside.

The door slipped silently closed behind her without the familiar tinkle of a bell. Once her eyes adjusted to the dim light, she examined the sparse goods. The store's shelves held a few tins of canned meat, some filthy muslin and rolls of commercial flypaper. Judging by the fly population in the building, some of those rolls could be put to good use. A goodly quantity of dust had blown in, and the plank floor had been worn into dips and furrows. The boards creaked with every step as she surveyed the paltry offerings.

"What kin I do for ye?" asked a pink-faced white man in a soiled canvas apron. Sweat poured down his chubby cheeks and stained the underarms of his grayed shirt. Tufts of wheaten hair curled upward like pigs' tails. "Pickles are on sale ta-day." He pointed to a barrel of slimy pickles well past their prime.

"No, thank you." Mariah turned from the acrid odor. "Do you have any fresh bread?" A fruitless inquiry, judging by the shelves, but worth a try.

"The missus don't bake in this heat. Maybe tomorrow."

"Of course," she said, trying to keep the frustration from her voice. Town after town had offered little more than tinned meat and the occasional shriveled potato. How she longed for fresh peas, which would be in season in Pearlman, or even overripe strawberries. She sighed. The Lord always provided for their needs, not necessarily for their wishes. "Perhaps some crackers, then."

"One pound or two?"

She hesitated. The hotel might offer a restaurant, but that would soon prove too costly for her dwindling funds. "Two."

While the clerk packaged the crackers, she selected several tins of potted meat, beans and prunes. A pound of coffee, ground, rounded out her supplies. Not fine fare, but they wouldn't starve.

She looked through the store. No one else was inside. That gave her the chance to ask the clerk about Mr. Gillard. While the man calculated the total, she gathered her courage. An innocuous question was always the best start. "Could you direct me to the hotel?"

"Nex' block down," he said with a wave of the hand. "Can't miss it."

Considering she'd missed the entire town earlier, that was not a given. "Do you know if meals are served there?"

The clerk's hand paused in the midst of calculations and his small eyes narrowed to dots. "Do ya mean ya won't be wanting these supplies?"

"On the contrary," she assured him. "We expect to tour the park and will want provisions."

"Right." He resumed calculating without bothering to answer her question. "That'll be $10.72."

"Ten dollars?" She surveyed the small quantity of goods. They would cost little more than two dollars in New York, less in Pearlman.

He scowled. "If you don't like the price, you can take yer business elsewhere."

"There's another general store in town?" She couldn't imagine a town this size supported more than one.

"Nah." He grinned, revealing yellowed teeth, probably from tobacco, which seemed to be the only commodity in great supply.

"Then why did you suggest I go elsewhere?" The clerk was clearly taking advantage of her. She could argue the price, but since this was the only store in town, he held the upper hand. "Oh, never mind." She pulled the money from her handbag and noted how low her supply had dipped. She needed to wire for money today. "Is there a place where I can send a cable?"

"Sure is," flowed a smooth masculine voice from directly behind her. "A block down the street."

Mariah whirled around to see a muscular man of perhaps forty dressed in a fine brocade vest, denim trousers and shiny boots. He took off his cowboy hat, revealing a head of wavy chestnut-colored hair, slightly crimped by the brim.

"Ma'am." He pressed the hat to his chest. "It'd be my pleasure to escort you there."

Mariah had to admit he was good-looking and well dressed for a cowboy, but definitely not her type. He hovered a tad too close, too eager to please.

"No, thank you. I have a car." She nodded and turned back to the clerk. "What did you say? Ten dollars?"

His Adam's apple bobbed with a hard swallow. "No, ma'am, $6.72," he spluttered.

Mariah frowned. She was sure he'd said ten, but she wouldn't argue with the more reasonable price.

"Are you sure, Drivett?" asked the man behind her.

The clerk paled and with shaking hands pored over his tally sheet. "Seems I made a bit of an error here." He ran a finger over his calculations. "Yep, here 'tis. My two looked like a six. Total's really $2.72."

"Two seventy-two?" Mariah repeated. Given the clerk's abrupt about-face, the man in the brocade vest must be more than an ordinary cowboy.

"Thas what I said." The man cowered, wiping his mouth repeatedly. "Take it or leave it."

She'd take it. Mariah handed him three dollars. He fumbled in his cash register drawer and with a shaking hand dropped the change into her hand.

"Thank you." Now was her last chance to broach her most pressing question. Despite the cowboy hovering at her back, she couldn't let this opportunity slip. One or the other might have the answer. "I don't suppose you know a Mr. Frank Gillard?"

If at all possible, the man got even paler. "M-m-mister Gillard?" He licked his lips, eyes darting past her. "I fergot. Them canned plums is on sale fer ten cents." He dug two quarters from the register and offered them to her.

She didn't take the money. Judging by the clerk's reaction, the cowboy must be Frank Gillard. But how could that be? He looked less Italian than she did.

"Donate the change to the Beson Creek Indian School," she instructed before turning to face Gillard.

The man was grinning. His steel-gray eyes raked her from head to toe.

"Mr. Frank Gillard, at your service."

Mariah searched his features, but she couldn't find the slightest resemblance to Luke. There must be a mistake. This couldn't possibly be Luke's father.

"Uh," she said, her brain whirling. What on earth was she supposed to say to him? She couldn't come right out and announce that she was from the Orphaned Children's Society. That would put him on high alert. She couldn't betray her mission if she hoped to discover the truth about this man.

"Miss?" He extended a hand. His nails were manicured, and he wore a heavy perfume that made her feel like sneezing.

She wiggled her nose to arrest the impulse. "Sir." She grasped his hand, expecting a handshake, but instead he raised her hand to his lips.

"Call me Frank, please."

Frank? The familiarity shocked her. "Is it usual to call strangers by their Christian names in Montana?"

One side of his mouth lifted in a wry grin, the controlled response of a man of power and influence. "Forgive me, but we don't see many women in Brunley, certainly none as beautiful as you."

Mariah cringed. Beautiful she was not. Plain and practical, yes, but definitely not beautiful.

"Then there must be no women here at all," she said dryly.

He laughed. "And intelligent, too." He nodded toward her hand. "Not to mention unmarried."

Mariah instinctively glanced at his hands. No rings. If he was Luke's father, he'd never remarried—or didn't wear a wedding band.

"Beautiful, unmarried women are particularly rare in these parts," he continued, "especially when they're alone."

"I'm not alone." Mariah turned back to the counter, suddenly uncomfortable. She'd wanted to find Frank Gillard, but she hadn't expected to face him right away. Now that he stood before her, she couldn't think of a way to ask him what she needed to know.

"I'm glad to hear it," he said, standing beside her. "A woman like you shouldn't be alone here."

Was that a threat? She glanced at his face, but those steely eyes didn't give away a thing. She took a deep breath as Gillard directed the clerk to package her purchases.

"Have the lady's purchases sent to…where are you staying?"

"The hotel next block down, but I can certainly carry them that far."

"Nonsense. I'll walk you to the Mountain View Hotel, and you can tell me more about yourself along the way." He extended an arm, expecting her to take it.

She did not. "I must return to my friends first. Hendrick and Anna will wonder what's taking me so long."

He frowned at Hendrick's name. "Your fiancé?"

She hesitated. If she said he was her fiancé, Gillard would stop trying to attract her, which he was very clearly attempting to do. But Hendrick wouldn't know she'd said that, and besides it wasn't the slightest bit true.

"No," she admitted. "They're just friends. We hope to see the park."

"So you shall," he said, taking her hand without permission. "Miss…?"

Clearly he wanted to know her name, but she couldn't tell him her last name. If he knew her brother was taking care of Luke, he'd recognize the surname.

She forced a smile. "In the spirit of Brunley, you may call me Mariah."

He laughed and kissed her hand again. "Pleased to meet you, Miss Mariah. Shall we leave this dark establishment for the brightness of the open air?" He swept a hand toward the door, but that was hardly necessary seeing as he'd never released her hand. "To the Mountain View?"

She shook her head. "I need to get my automobile. It's at the filling station."

"Ah, this friend Hendrick is your driver."

She blushed as he pushed open the door. "No. I drive my own car."

"A woman of means and daring." The oily-smooth smile returned as he escorted her onto the porch. "You said you needed to send a wire?"

Not with Gillard looking over her shoulder. "It can wait."

"Good. Do you have any plans for supper, Miss Mariah?"

She hesitated. After the long drive she really wanted a bath, but dining with Gillard might produce valuable information.

"I'll take your silence as a no," he said. "I hope I'm not too bold, but would you care to dine tonight at my ranch?"

"*Your* ranch? Aren't you a cowboy?"

He roared with laughter, and the Indians on the porch joined him.

"What did I say that was so humorous?" she asked.

He patted her hand. "I own a ranch, High Plains. I'd love to have you—and your friends, of course—for supper."

Gillard owned a ranch? But two-and-a-half years ago, he'd been too destitute to support his child. Something was not right, and the ranch would be the best place to discover what that something was.

She offered the biggest smile she could manage. "We'd be delighted."

Hendrick was a little annoyed at his sister's brazen interest in the tall Indian, but Mariah would soon take care of business, and they'd leave this town forever. He watched Mariah cross the dusty expanse, nod at the Indians on the mercantile porch and disappear inside.

Brunley was no Pearlman. Hendrick missed the tidy yards and familiar faces. He longed for the honks of a horn when customers drove past. He wished he could tear apart an engine instead of worry about two women who wished he wasn't there. As far as he could see, the town had only a couple of cars. Not enough work for a mechanic. Not enough to keep anyone busy, apparently. Few seemed to be working.

The Packard backed away from the building and motored down the street. It turned the corner and parked alongside the mercantile. A man in a fancy vest and cowboy hat stepped out and bounded up the mercantile steps. One of the Indians touched a finger to his tattered hat, but no one said a word. The place was quiet. Dry and quiet.

"Dollar twenty," the Indian said. "We can order the radiator hose, if you want."

Hendrick dragged his attention from the unmoving mercantile door and handed the man the five-dollar bill Anna had given him. "Yes, order it."

"Be back with your change." The Indian headed for the dim interior, and Hendrick followed.

Maybe the man could tell him about Frank Gillard. This whole quest of Mariah's worried him. If she was right about there being something suspicious at work, the man would fight her, maybe even fight dirty. But maybe she was wrong, and Gillard was an honest man who deserved his son. For Mariah and Luke's sake, Hendrick hoped he was.

The Indian looked up from the cashbox, his expression unreadable. "Four-eighty in change."

"That's $3.80." Hendrick handed the man one of the dollar bills.

The Indian's impassive mask melted in disbelief.

"I'm sure I'm right," Hendrick said. "I'm not great at grammar, but I know my figures."

The Indian shook his head. "Not many would give that dollar back."

"It's nothing. Could happen to anyone." Hendrick looked around the small shop. No cars in the work bays, but the place was filled with engines and parts. "Nice garage. Do you get much business?"

The Indian shrugged. "A little here and there."

Hendrick knew a straight shooter when he saw one. This man could be a much-needed ally in a strange town. He stuck out his hand. "My name's Hendrick Simmons. I'm a mechanic back East."

The man shook his hand. "Joshua Talltree."

"Joshua? What a peculiar name for an Indian."

"We don't all use Indian names, especially with whites. Besides, I'm mixed-blood."

Hendrick nodded, a bit embarrassed that he'd measured the man by common prejudice. "Sorry. I should have known better."

"Happens all the time. I get used to it." A playful grin flitted across Talltree's lips. "Sometimes I have fun with it, use it to my advantage, especially with pretty ladies." He nodded toward the door where Anna lingered, trying to look interested in the Mobiloil sign hanging from the canopy.

"Hey, that's my little sister."

Talltree looked appropriately abashed. "Guess it's my turn to be sorry."

"Apology accepted." Anyone could make that mistake. He was just a little protective of his only sister. "Do you have a sister?"

"No. Wouldn't mind one, though. Brothers are tough."

Hendrick wouldn't know, except for Peter, who was just

a foster brother and had been around for only two years. Thinking of Peter reminded him of Constance. "Do you know anything about the Beson Creek School?"

Talltree's guard went back up. "Why?"

"We went there by mistake. I met a little girl named Constance. She says her mother works for a Mr. Lord. Have you heard of anyone by that name?"

Talltree shook his head. "Most of the children there come from other tribes, far away. She's probably not from here."

Hendrick's heart sank. Maybe Mariah was right, and he shouldn't have made a promise he might not be able to keep. He looked around the garage, wishing he could fix something, anything. His mind was at its clearest when he was tinkering away at an engine. "Too bad you don't have any repairs. I'm dying to get my hands dirty."

Talltree brightened. "You don't say. We've been trying to convert our hand-pumper to a powered fire engine. We have the water pump but we can't get an engine together that'll push the water through the hose with any pressure."

"What size motor are you trying?" Hendrick flung a dozen questions at Talltree, and before long the men were plotting out how to solve the problem.

"It'd be a lot easier to get a new fire engine," Talltree finally said with exasperation, "but the government never seems to have the money for one."

"That's government for you. Guess we'll have to build it ourselves." Hendrick sketched a diagram on the scrap of paper Talltree provided. Within minutes he'd laid out how they could construct the fire engine. He'd need to find a solid motor and work from there. "I'd prefer six cylinders." He looked at the blue Packard. "Wonder what we'd get from a twin-six, like the engine in that Packard. That would pump some water. Know where I might get one?"

Talltree snorted after glancing at the car. "Not from that car. I'll ask Judge Weiss. He owns this station and most of Brunley. He should be on his way back from Great Falls. Expect him day after tomorrow."

"Great. I'll talk to him then." Hendrick stuck out his hand again, and the Indian, after a surprised pause, shook it.

Hendrick looked out the station's front windows and saw Mariah leave the mercantile empty-handed. She swiveled as if waiting for someone. That someone turned out to be the fancy-dressed man from the Packard, who took her hand and assisted her down the mercantile steps. She looked up at the man and smiled. Smiled! The gesture sent a bolt of pain straight to his heart.

"Who is that man?" he asked.

Talltree's lips pressed into a frown. "Frank Gillard."

"Gillard?" Of all the people she could meet, it had to be him.

"I'd steer clear of that man, if I were you."

Hendrick's gut wrenched. "Why?"

Talltree wouldn't answer, and that was all Hendrick needed to know. He took off toward Mariah at a run.

Chapter Nine

"Is that your friend?" Gillard's lips curled in bemusement.

Mariah watched in dismay as Hendrick steamed across the street, fists clenched and jaw set. *Please don't ruin this. Please.* One wrong word, and Gillard would know she was an agent of the Orphaned Children's Society with more than passing connection to Luke.

"Hendrick," she cried. "Meet Mr. Frank Gillard. He's a ranch owner here."

He scowled. "Mr. Gillard." His tone left no doubt he didn't like the man.

She did not need a showdown in the middle of the street. The Indians had gathered at the mercantile rail. Even the attendant at the filling station watched to see what would happen. She pasted on a smile.

"Hendrick Simmons is the friend I told you about," she said to Gillard with exaggerated cheerfulness. "He and his sister, Anna, traveled with me." If Hendrick had an ounce of sense, he'd realize she wasn't acting like herself.

"Mr. Simmons." Gillard extended his hand. "Pleased to meet you."

Hendrick did not shake hands. Instead he turned to her.

"Didn't you get any supplies? I thought that's why you went to the store."

"They're being sent to the hotel." She thought it best not to mention that Gillard had arranged it. "Is the car all set?"

He nodded, still eyeing Gillard with distrust.

She could not let Hendrick ruin her plan, which he was bound to do if he kept up this rude behavior, but she also needed him to join her. Another man's presence would keep Gillard's attentions in check. If she could just get a moment alone to explain the situation to Hendrick, he would work with her. She was sure of it.

"I'd like to invite your entire party to dine at my ranch tonight," Gillard explained to Hendrick. "Miss Mariah agreed."

"Isn't that wonderful?" She shot Hendrick a piercing glare, trying to tell him to go along with the invitation and she would explain everything later. "We'll follow Mr. Gillard in my car."

"Nonsense, Mr. Simmons can drive your car." Gillard laid a proprietary hand on her arm. "I don't want to miss out on one enchanting moment with you."

Hendrick looked like he was going to gag. "That's not proper."

Mariah knew Hendrick was right, and she shouldn't accept Gillard's suggestion, but she might learn something important if Hendrick and Anna weren't present.

Gillard wasted no time rectifying the situation. "Your girlfriend can join us. Miss Anna, is it? Where is she?"

Where indeed? Mariah looked around and spotted the girl lingering behind the filling station attendant. "Anna?" She waved her over.

The girl came at a snail's pace, dragging her feet the

entire way. Though Hendrick still looked displeased, he had no grounds to protest.

"We're dining at Mr. Gillard's ranch tonight. You'll ride with us," Mariah explained when Anna finally arrived. "And Hendrick will follow with my car."

Gillard gallantly offered his arm to Anna. She looked back longingly at the attendant before accepting Gillard's escort.

Their departure gave Mariah the time she needed to explain. "I need you to help me tonight."

Hendrick's facial muscles tightened. "What are you thinking? Going to his house for supper? I thought you hated him."

"It's a chance to find out what sort of man he really is. This Frank Gillard is nothing like the man who dropped Luke off at the orphanage. He's well-to-do and well-spoken."

"A model father, then?"

She brushed off the sarcasm. "That's not my point. I'm saying he doesn't fit the agency record. He can't possibly be Luke's father, unless a whole lot has happened in two-and-a-half years. This dinner gives me the opportunity to get some answers, and I need your help to do it."

Hendrick's frown deepened. "Joshua Talltree said—"

"I don't care what anyone said." Mariah did not have time for debate. Gillard would be back in seconds. "I need to do this." She panicked as Gillard rounded the corner of the building and headed toward her. "Please, Hendrick. You promised you would help."

His jaw worked as he glanced toward Gillard, fast approaching. "It's dangerous." Only he said it too loudly.

"What's dangerous?" Gillard asked.

"Nothing," Mariah said hastily. She shot Hendrick a glare, pleading for him to hold his tongue.

His gaze raked her to the soul, and she closed her eyes, waiting for him to ruin her plan.

Instead he said, "She's right. It's nothing."

Relief surged through her. Hendrick would help.

Gillard's ranch lay seventeen miles from town and could be reached only by dirt trails. By the time they arrived, Hendrick was coated in dust and fuming at Mariah. She'd cut him off, hadn't given him a chance to tell her what Talltree had said about Gillard and then pranced off with the man in his car.

It didn't get any better in the house. Gillard gave them a tour of his palace, and she followed like a puppy dog while he boasted about his expensive china and Indian art.

"That's a Sioux chief's headdress." Gillard pointed to the dramatic beaded and feathered war bonnet hanging on the living room wall. It looked like it had been part of a Wild West show, not something actually worn in war. "I got it for practically nothing."

Hendrick watched Gillard's every move. After Talltree's warning, Hendrick suspected Gillard was every bit as bad as Mariah had anticipated and possibly worse. The man fawned over her. He barely acknowledged anyone else. Most women would find the attention thrilling, and judging by the way she laughed at his bad jokes and encouraged him to tell her about every object, she did, too. By the time they reached the dining room, Hendrick wished he'd insisted Mariah stay in town.

Gillard frowned at the empty table. "One moment, please." He rang a silver bell sitting on the sideboard.

Within seconds, an Indian woman remarkably close to Mariah's height and build appeared through the other door.

"Set three more places for dinner," Gillard instructed tersely without ever looking at her.

Hendrick didn't miss the implicit social hierarchy. The woman, her black hair coiled into a knot at the back of her head, nodded without a word, eyes averted, as if afraid to directly address her employer. Dressed in a plain brown skirt, reminiscent of the Beson Creek School uniform, she blended into the background, in Gillard's eyes less important than his prized art collection.

After the woman left, Gillard took Mariah's hand. "Let's continue the tour."

He led them through every downstairs room on the way to the guest bedrooms in the east wing. The house was enormous. There must be room for ten or more to sleep, yet other than the servants, only one man lived here, king of his private domain.

At the head of the east hallway, Gillard pressed Mariah's hand to his lips yet again. Hendrick clenched his fists to keep from ripping it away.

"If you'd like to freshen up before dinner," Gillard told her, "I've had a pitcher of water and a washbasin brought to this bedroom." He opened the door to escort her inside, but Anna squirted past him.

"Look at it, Mariah. Just look. The furniture. The bed."

Hendrick didn't fail to notice the combination of lustful hunger and disappointment flash across Gillard's face before the artificial smile returned.

"It's nothing, just a little haven from the trials of frontier life." Gillard focused entirely on Mariah. "I'm sure you're dusty from so much travel. If you'd like a bath, just ring, and one of the servants will draw the water for you. When you're ready, please join me in the dining room."

Thankfully, the man did not enter the room. He bid Mariah farewell with a slight bow, and then on his way back to the main part of the house he muttered to Hendrick, "There's a servant's washroom at the end of the hall."

A servant's washroom. Hendrick's frayed temper threatened to break.

"I'm sure he didn't mean anything by it," Mariah said softly after Gillard was gone. She hadn't left Hendrick's side. In fact, she closed the bedroom door behind her to give them a moment alone in the hallway. "It's probably the only room he had available."

He glanced at the five closed doors. "Why are you making excuses for him?"

"I'm not making excuses. I'm simply trying to find a reasonable explanation. We *are* unexpected guests, after all."

"You're giving him the benefit of the doubt?"

"Exactly. It's the right thing to do." She spoke calmly, but red dotted her cheeks.

She was more flustered by this man than she was letting on. Hadn't she heard Sowich's warning? Maybe she'd take heed once she knew Talltree said the same thing.

"Joshua Talltree knows Frank Gillard."

"Talltree?" She stood far too close, and the shimmer of her hazel eyes threatened to distract him. "You mentioned his name before." Her gaze softened, embracing him in ways that made him wish they could start all over again.

"Talltree," he breathed, gathering his wits. There was nothing between them. She'd made that perfectly clear. He squeezed his fists until they ached. "He's the attendant at the filling station."

"Ah. Anna was fascinated by him, wasn't she?"

"This isn't about Anna." He tried to regain focus. Her gentle smile made his thoughts scatter. He looked away. "This is about your friend, Mr. Gillard."

"He's not my friend."

"Is that so? It sure looked like it."

Her eyes flashed with anger. "There's no reason to be jealous."

"I'm not jealous. I'm concerned about your reputation, a lot more than you are."

"I am perfectly in control," she said quietly, even as her gaze drifted from him. "Now, what did Mr. Talltree tell you?"

"To steer clear of Gillard." The words hung between them like fog.

"I see."

But he could tell by the tone of her voice that she didn't see. She didn't even believe him. He had to make her understand the danger she was in. "What do you think he's going to do when he learns what you really want?"

She stared at the wall over his right shoulder.

"I gather you didn't tell him yet," he said.

"I…" Her voice trailed off as if she wasn't sure she should tell him something. "Trust me, Hendrick. Things aren't always what they appear to be."

He placed a hand on the wall to each side of her. "What are you doing, Mariah?" He wanted to wrestle her from this place before something awful happened, but she would hate him for it. Once Mariah set her mind to something, no one could change it.

Her gaze flickered over his face. "For some reason he is trying to win me over. If I play along with it for tonight, I might learn the truth about him—why he wants Luke, why he doesn't fit the description in the agency record, who he really is. I might even be able to persuade him to give up his pursuit of Luke. Please, Hendrick, for tonight, just follow along with what I do."

He didn't like it, but he'd never been able to refuse her. "Tonight only, but if he hurts you…"

She lightly cupped his jaw. "I know you'll be there for me."

Her light hazel eyes, the smell of her, the softness of her skin. They were so close. He leaned closer, whispered softly inches from her lips. "I will."

With the flutter of a smile, she turned and darted into the bedroom, leaving him alone in an empty hallway.

Mariah had come so close to letting him kiss her. Back in the safety of the bedroom, she pressed her back against the closed door and tried to stop the trembling in her limbs. Being so near Hendrick was overwhelming, like sitting in a room filled with fragrant roses.

"Mariah, Mariah, you have to see this!" Anna tugged at her hands until she opened her eyes.

The bedroom's opulence rivaled that of a presidential mansion or a royal palace. Burgundy velvet curtains hung around the four-poster bed and at each window, tied back with matching satin cords. Rose-colored satin tufted chairs and polished mahogany furnishings completed the elegant room. But none of that was what had thrilled Anna.

"Look," the girl cried, throwing open the armoire doors. "Just look at these clothes." She pulled out a crepe de chine bathing robe and tossed it on the fainting couch, followed by one in rose-colored silk and another in pale yellow. When she came to a lacy negligee, Mariah had to put a stop to this.

"Anna, these are not your things. Put them back."

"But they're so beautiful." She donned a lacy boudoir cap. Her pigtails stuck out of each side like two ropes or bellpulls.

Mariah had to stifle a giggle and pretend to be angry with the poor girl, who had probably never seen such beautiful things.

"Put them back," Mariah said softly. "They belong to someone else."

"Who would they belong to?" Anna asked. "Not that Indian woman. She wouldn't wear anything this nice."

"I believe she's the housekeeper."

"Then who? I didn't see any other women."

It was a good question, one that could have only one answer. "Perhaps Mr. Gillard kept his late wife's clothing."

"Eww, these are from a dead person?" Anna hastily tucked the negligee back in the armoire.

"I believe she died years ago." At least before Luke came to the Detroit mission.

"Hmm. She must have been your size. They look like they'd fit." Anna ran a hand over the rose-colored silk robe. "Are you sure you don't want to try it on?"

"I'm positive." Mariah lifted the yellow bathrobe to hand to Anna. Odd that Gillard would choose to bring these garments west with him. What destitute man saves his wife's clothing and gives away his son? It didn't make sense. Moreover, they were expensive, of the highest quality, certainly not something a poor man would own or keep. Nothing about Frank Gillard made sense.

Mariah put the yellow robe away herself and saw the one thing Anna hadn't noted. Every single item in the armoire was lingerie. Why would a single man have a closet filled with only sleepwear?

She gasped at the possibilities. He must have a lady friend. Who occasionally stayed overnight and... She didn't care to imagine the rest. But there were so many items in the armoire—dozens—certainly more than one woman would want. What if many women passed through? What if...? She clutched a hand to her throat. She'd heard the West had once been filled with bordellos.

What if some still existed? What if Frank Gillard made his fortune from prostitution?

She sank to the fainting couch.

"Mariah? Why are your cheeks so red?"

She pressed her hands to her flaming face. Anna was still an innocent, and Mariah was making some pretty big assumptions that she didn't dare spell out. "I'm just hot," she murmured. "Could you get me a cold cloth?"

While Anna soaked a cloth in the water basin, Mariah looked again at the armoire's contents. All lingerie. If she was right about Gillard's source of wealth and if she could get the law to act, she could put Frank Gillard behind bars long enough for Luke to grow up in Pearlman.

Anna handed her the damp cloth, and Mariah buried her face in the coolness. Somehow tonight she needed to find the answers that would spare Luke. As Hendrick said, soon enough Frank Gillard would discover her real purpose.

"Lord, lead me on the right path," she whispered.

"What did you say?" asked Anna.

Mariah forced a weak smile. "Let's go to dinner."

Where she wouldn't be able to eat a thing.

Chapter Ten

Supper proved as opulent as everything else in Gillard's home. The opening course, a beef consommé, had already been served by the time Mariah arrived in the dining room. Freshly baked dinner rolls enticed with their yeasty aroma. Her mouth watered. How long had it been since she tasted fresh bread?

Gillard, of course, presided at the head of the aristocratically long table. He seated Mariah to his left and Anna to his right. Hendrick did not look pleased that he'd been relegated to the chair beside his sister. Though their party amounted to only four, the entire twelve places had been set in shimmering bone china and sterling flatware.

"Are you expecting more guests?" Mariah asked. Gillard wasn't the type to allow his staff to dine with him. She wondered if the mysterious lady friend or friends would appear.

"Not tonight." He picked up his napkin with a flourish.

"Then why set the table for twelve?"

His chestnut hair, now parted down the middle in the style of film actor Rudolph Valentino, gleamed with brilliantine. "It's more beautiful that way, don't you think? And impressive. Do you like my collections? "

She murmured an assent. Gillard had definitely tried to impress her with his wealth.

"You've probably never seen such fine furnishings." He said it to her but mostly looked at Anna and Hendrick.

"Oh, Mariah's rich," Anna blurted out, much to Mariah's dismay.

"Is that so?"

Was it her imagination or did Gillard sit up a little straighter?

"I'm not rich," she hastily explained, "though my parents have done well." She shot Anna a look telling her to be quiet. This conversation was supposed to answer her questions about Gillard, not the other way around, and when she considered his collections, she couldn't help wondering how he'd acquired so much so quickly. Two-and-a-half years was a terribly short time to amass a fortune, except through illegal activities.

Anna thankfully understood the hint and kept quiet. Hendrick was another matter. While Gillard had changed into an expensive gray suit, Hendrick still wore his traveling clothes, which were naturally worse for wear. Judging by his scowl, he thought Gillard was intentionally trying to demean him. She'd have a battle placating Hendrick while trying to weasel information out of Gillard.

Gillard rang the bell, and a male servant appeared, also an American Indian and dressed in starched serving attire. In his gloved hands he bore a bottle of wine.

Wine? Mariah stared. Spirits were prohibited throughout the country. True, some people refused to accept the law. Speakeasies operated everywhere, but she was surprised that Gillard would flaunt the law in front of people he'd just met.

He waited for the servant to pour a small amount in his

wineglass and then sniffed it. "This will do. It's a French Cabernet, acquired before Prohibition, naturally."

Mariah had to admit his explanation made sense. People could keep liquor purchased before the Eighteenth Amendment took effect, but what if he was stretching the truth? What if his liquor was bootleg? What if he made his fortune rumrunning?

Gillard set the glass in front of her. "I've been saving it for a special occasion and can think of nothing more special. Will you do me the honor of approving the wine?"

Anna stared, her mouth agape. Hendrick's eyes narrowed as if to say that he'd been right. But she could use this if she could prove Gillard did more than keep a bottle or two of wine acquired before Prohibition began. If he smuggled liquor into the state from Canada, federal agents would be glad to lock him in prison. All she had to do was prove it, and that meant she couldn't appear to condemn the fact that he owned a bottle of wine.

Though she did not lift her hands from her lap, she smiled at him very graciously. "I'm sorry, Mr. Gillard. Please enjoy the wine, but for personal reasons I don't drink spirits."

His eyebrows lifted, but he maintained his calm demeanor. "Of course. I should never have made such an assumption." He waved to the servant. "Take it away."

The servant whisked the bottle and the wineglass from the room. Gillard hadn't even offered it to Hendrick or Anna. Though she knew neither would touch it, the fact that Gillard had considered only her opinion told her that Hendrick was right.

"I didn't mean for you to deprive yourself," she chided softly.

"It's no deprivation when my table is graced by a woman as lovely as you."

Again she cringed. Like Hendrick and Anna, she still wore her traveling clothes. It had been too hot to wear her duster, so the dust and grime had permeated every seam of her suit and coated every strand of hair. On the best days, her appearance was serviceable. Today, she looked a fright.

After everyone finished the consommé, Gillard rang for the next course to be delivered. Half a dozen male servants, all American Indian and all dressed in the same uniform as the wine steward, appeared from the kitchen carrying covered plates of beef, quail and rabbit. Fresh vegetables had been in short supply at the mercantile, but not here. Potatoes, carrots, pickled beets and even peas filled separate dishes in quantities that would feed a table of twelve. The excess reminded her of the great houses back East. She had dined in many of them with her parents, but never grew accustomed to the extravagance and waste.

Mariah sipped from her Waterford crystal water glass while the dishes were placed on the table. Everything in this house reeked of ostentatious wealth, doubtless gained by illicit means. Gambling, prostitution, rumrunning or all of them? She needed to know, if she was to keep Luke safe.

"Some states were temperate before national prohibition," she began casually.

"Like Michigan," Hendrick added. "We've been dry since 1916."

Gillard twirled a fork between his thumb and index finger. "Interesting. You're from Michigan, then?"

Mariah paled. Did he know Luke was staying in Michigan? Would he make the connection?

"No," she said quickly, "I'm not."

"Then how do you know each other?" Gillard asked. "You are friends."

He was not supposed to be asking the questions, yet somehow he'd put her on the defensive. She took a deep breath and smiled.

"We know each other through mutual acquaintances." She then slipped quickly to her point, before he could waylay her again. "I'm surprised Montana isn't as progressive as Michigan."

He smirked. "Perhaps we are. That depends on your definition of *progressive*. Consider the programs we've instituted to civilize the Indians. Without our help, they'd be wiped out by now."

Mariah shivered at the blatant prejudice. Though there was likely some fragment of truth behind his statement, he hadn't mentioned that the settlers were the ones who'd brought the diseases and starvation that had reduced the Indians to this state.

"What do you mean, wiped out?" Anna asked. "They're not going to die, are they?"

Gillard looked as if he was surprised she was there. "Only if they refuse to listen to us." He returned his focus to Mariah. "Cattle are the solution."

That ushered in a lengthy conversation on cattle ranching. Apparently, his herd ranged freely, even beyond the bounds of his acreage.

"How do you ever find them again?" Anna asked.

"By their brand," Gillard answered. "Some would steal cattle that aren't their own, but no one would dare touch mine. Everyone knows Frank Gillard's mark."

Mariah suspected the punishment for rustling his cattle had been demonstrated on some hapless thief. She shuddered. Her punishment would be just as horrific, maybe more so, if he learned why she was really here. Rustlers only took cattle, whereas she wanted to take his son.

Mariah picked at the beef short ribs, potatoes and beets while Gillard regaled them with tales of cattle drives. When he directed the conversation toward her, she took a bite so she could keep her replies short. Thankfully, Anna had a hundred questions, mostly about the Indians.

"Blackfeet on this side of the Divide, and Flathead on the other," Gillard said with a wave of the hand, "but they're easily controlled now."

"Controlled?" Hendrick leaned forward, eager to challenge.

Mariah tensed, but if Gillard sensed the anger in Hendrick's tone, he ignored it.

"They're a bloodthirsty lot," he said. "Tenderhearted Easterners like to say that we killed off their way of life, but the truth is they did it to themselves. Why, they'd drive whole herds of buffalo over the cliffs to their deaths. Killing is their life." He pointed a table knife at Hendrick. "They scalped hundreds of us before the army got them rounded up on the reservation."

Anna stared in horror. "They don't scalp people anymore, do they?"

"Of course not," Mariah said, sick of these tales. Whether or not these acts had ever happened, they had taken place ages ago and had no bearing on today.

Gillard laughed. "Your friend is right, but don't turn your back on an Indian."

"If they hate us, there's good reason," Hendrick said.

"Because we have the power," said Gillard, "that's why. Even just rulers are hated by their subjects."

For the second time tonight, Mariah wondered if he saw himself as king. He'd certainly established a strict social hierarchy. "*Hate* is a very strong word."

Gillard patted her hand. "You're right, my dear. Perhaps *resent* is a better choice. The fight these days is more between the mixed-bloods and the full-bloods than the Indians and the whites."

She puzzled over his words. "Why would they fight among themselves? That doesn't make any sense."

Gillard leaned back, his elbows propped on the chair's arms. "Each side has a different political agenda. Let's just say it's easier to deal with the mixed-bloods. They understand the need to set up cattle ranches and work with us. The full-bloods refuse to give up their traditions. They accuse us of anything and everything that'll get them sympathy with Indian Affairs. But I can see I'm boring you. I shouldn't be talking politics during a pleasant dinner."

"I'm not bored," she insisted. "In fact, I'm fascinated by politics and make full use of my right to vote."

"Me, too," piped up Anna.

Gillard looked surprised for a second and then burst into laughter. "You are quite the remarkable woman, Miss Mariah."

"And I'm deeply interested in the plight of the Indians. Do I understand correctly that you believe cattle ranching will give the Indians the financial means to better themselves?"

"Absolutely. That and oil."

"Oil?" Mariah blinked. That was the last thing she'd expected to come out of his mouth. "Petroleum?"

"Exactly. Prospectors discovered oil a few years ago in the southern part of the state. Just last year it was found on the Crow reservation. Chances are there's oil here. All that's needed is someone with know-how to tap the reserves."

"The Blackfeet," Hendrick said.

"They don't have the capital," Gillard scoffed.

"It's their land," Anna cried.

Gillard smiled. "Don't worry, Miss Simmons, they'll get their share."

Anna beamed. "Then they can have better schools and even a hospital."

Doubtless, she was thinking of Talltree and the Indian school, but this sort of progress didn't come quickly or without cost. Mariah held her tongue. She didn't know enough of the facts. Arguing with Gillard wouldn't give her what she needed. It was time to make her move.

She cleared her throat. "I'm sorry to change the topic, but you haven't mentioned any family, Mr. Gillard. This is a large house for one man."

His smile faltered. "I had a wife and son once." He paused to take a drink of water. "I lost them. A most horrible death." He covered his eyes with one hand, to all appearances overcome with grief. "I still have nightmares."

"Lost them both?" Mariah asked, perplexed.

"In an accident."

Mariah's mind whirled. Could she have the wrong man? No. The letter was from Gillard. It gave his full name and the address in Brunley, Montana. He said he'd changed his name from Francesco Guillardo and requested that his son, Luciano, be returned. No, she wasn't wrong. Then why was he saying Luke was dead?

"But I thought you wanted—" she began before realizing she'd almost given herself away. She coughed and took a sip of water to hide her terrible mistake.

Gillard didn't let her off the hook. "You thought I wanted what?"

Mariah thought quickly, trying to come up with an appropriate answer. Hendrick looked stricken, and judging by the painful expression on Anna's face, he was squeezing her hand very hard under the table. *Think. Think.*

Gillard waited.

She took another drink and waved her hand to indicate her throat was raw. In truth, it was so constricted she couldn't get a word out.

"Breathe slowly," Gillard said. "Let your throat calm down."

She did as directed until she came up with an idea. "I happened to see the clothing in the guestroom armoire," she began.

He revealed no emotion at her words, so she plunged ahead.

"I'm afraid I leapt to an assumption," she continued. "I thought you already had a fiancée, that you wanted to get married again. Blame it on women's intuition gone awry."

He blinked. Once. Then burst out laughing. "Your women's intuition is absolutely correct." He took her hand and gazed into her eyes. "I do want to remarry."

She had no doubt he had set his sights on her.

What a fraud. Hendrick wanted to grab Mariah and leave that instant, but she wouldn't stand for it. She had this crazy idea she could trick Gillard into saying something incriminating. He'd watched her attempts to worm the truth out of Gillard and how easily he'd deflected every attempt. She was up against a con man well versed in the art of deception.

Now Gillard claimed he wanted to marry her.

"You just met," Hendrick exclaimed. Surely she saw how ludicrous this man's attentions were.

Gillard never let his gaze leave her face. "Do you believe in love at first sight? After today, I do."

Mariah didn't answer. She could have said no. She should have put a stop to it that instant, but she just sat there, cheeks unnaturally flushed.

Though Hendrick had fallen for Mariah the moment he first saw her, he wasn't foolish enough to think that romantic attraction was enough. "It takes more than that for marriage."

Mariah nibbled her lip. "Hendrick's right. Lasting love is built on a stronger foundation. It takes time."

Gillard kissed her hand. "Then we'll give it time."

Hendrick gagged. Mariah couldn't seriously be listening to this.

Gillard had just said his wife and son died. If that was true, then Luke couldn't be his son, and they had no reason to stay there any longer. If false, then he was lying and every bit as rotten as she'd thought he was. Either way, Gillard was not a man to get too close to.

Still, she sat and listened, not saying a word. Didn't she remember that he'd beaten Luke? That Luke was terrified of him? Maybe that man had her turned so far around she couldn't tell backward from forward. Well, he'd straighten her out pronto.

"Then you don't have any children."

Gillard stopped midspeech to stare at him. Mariah looked distraught, but she didn't need to worry. He was just clearing the air.

"I'm saying that because you built an awful big house not knowing if you'd ever have another wife again."

"I had hopes," Gillard said calmly.

"And no other kids, just Luke?"

Mariah gasped and went ashen. She looked like she was about to faint.

What had he done? It took a second for Hendrick to realize how he'd slipped up. He shouldn't have said Luke's name. They weren't supposed to know anything about the boy. They were supposed to be tourists, strangers. Now Gillard knew differently.

The man turned his steely glare on each of them in turn before settling on him. "Who are you, and how do you know about Luke?"

Mariah died a thousand deaths in one instant. Her plan plummeted to earth, shot down. What to say? How to recover her hope of saving Luke? Now Gillard knew she wasn't an innocent stranger. Now he would tell her nothing useful.

She couldn't even swallow. Terror held the clock motionless as Hendrick struggled to find an answer. *Don't give it away,* she pleaded silently, but, of course, he couldn't possibly understand. Only she could salvage this situation, if it could be salvaged. In times of distress, the Bible gave the clearest guidance, but she didn't have time to consult her Bible. She had to remind herself of God's grace and put herself in His hands. That meant telling the truth.

She took a deep breath. "My name is Mariah Meeks, and I am an agent for the Orphaned Children's Society, the mission where you entrusted Luke."

Gillard did not blink. Not one muscle ticked. At least he hadn't reacted to her last name. Maybe he didn't know that Luke was living with her brother.

"He is well, very well," she added.

Slowly, like when the Victrola wound down, he spoke. Each word emphasized. Each word separate. "Then why isn't he here with you?"

He was threatening her. Her. Yet he was the one who'd claimed that his son was dead. He'd denied Luke until Hendrick called him on it. He hadn't answered any of her questions. Oh, no, he could not threaten her. She still had a perfectly reasonable explanation left, the one she'd told Gabe she would use.

She squared her shoulders and looked him straight in the eye. "Before placing any child, we must do a home visit. Since it's been more than two years and Luke was considered abandoned, the visit is necessary." *At least it ought to be necessary.* "I'm sorry for not telling you sooner, but it's essential I get an accurate view of the home situation. Revealing my identity would have tainted the visit."

Mr. Gillard carefully processed each word. After a painfully long pause, he said, "And do you approve of my *home situation?*"

She ignored the sarcasm. "Further investigation is required."

"Because of the wine? It's not only legal, it's gone."

She offered a smile. A little bootleg alcohol would not convince him to sign the papers. She needed more. "The wine is not an issue. I simply need to complete my evaluation. A little more time is all I require."

"Then is it the clothing? My late wife's."

She didn't believe that for a minute. "My condolences."

"Oh, you're upset because I said Luke had died. Let me remind you, Miss Meeks, that you were not playing fair with me, either. I thought you were a beautiful unmarried woman and that you might not want to take on the burden of raising a child. Obviously, I was wrong."

Hendrick cleared his throat, clearly outraged by the man's explanation, but she couldn't let him influence her course of action. She needed to find something substantially wrong with Frank Gillard, and that meant getting back in his good graces.

"I understand," she said. "Rest assured, thus far I've found your home situation more than adequate."

The words did exactly what she'd hoped, easing Gillard's wariness. As she continued to praise his fine china and crystal, he started to relax. When she expressed awe over his Indian art collection, he laughed.

"I'm glad you approve, Miss Meeks." He rose and gave her a little bow. "Please forgive my behavior. You must believe that I'm anxious to bring my son home. I never meant you to think otherwise. I was simply dazzled by your beauty and excellent qualities. Will you forgive me?"

"Of course," she murmured, though the words stuck in her throat.

"I am disappointed, though," he said. "I would have enjoyed courting you."

She forced a tight smile. Despite his charm and good looks, Frank Gillard simply did not attract her. Unlike Hendrick, who could send shivers down her spine with a single glance, Gillard left her cold and empty.

He stepped forward and took her hand, raising it to his lips for a brief kiss. "For you to truly understand where Luke will grow up, you need to see my property. Could you join me on horseback in the morning?"

"I, uh," she stammered, both repulsed by the gesture and recognizing the opportunity it provided.

"Consider it part of the home evaluation." His grin forgave her for not telling him she was an agent from the Orphaned Children's Society. Or was he merely trying to win her over so he could get his son back?

"I, uh," she said again, glancing at Hendrick and Anna.

Hendrick frowned. Anna looked excited.

"Horses?" the girl asked.

Gillard laughed. "Yes, we must take horses. Why don't all of you stay the night? I have plenty of room and few visitors."

Staying overnight would give Mariah a chance to explore those parts of the house Gillard hadn't shown her, perhaps find the incriminating evidence she needed. And tomorrow, Anna and Hendrick could act as chaperones.

"Thank you," she said. "We will."

But Hendrick balked. "We're staying in town."

Mariah needed this opportunity desperately. It might be her only chance to save Luke. She would have welcomed Hendrick's help, but if he were going to let jealousy taint his sense of reason, then she'd do it without him.

"You can return, if you wish." She did not give him a chance to argue. "I'm staying. I need to finish the assessment."

Hendrick's gaze narrowed. "Then I'm staying, too."

Chapter Eleven

What was Mariah thinking? She was walking straight into danger. Gillard looked more and more the predator after her secret came out. Here she was on his turf and at his mercy. Hendrick stared at the woman he thought he knew. Stay in Frank Gillard's house alone? Tell him to leave? What had come over her? He wasn't about to leave her.

"I'll have my housekeeper make up two more rooms." A smile snaked across Gillard's lips. "Glad you saw reason, Mr. Simmons."

On the surface it was a compliment, but beneath the words lurked a hint of superiority. Hendrick knew when he was being put down. He'd taken it from the wealthy Pearlman families all his life. Oh, they didn't come out and say he was beneath them, but he could tell they thought it by the way they talked to him and how they hesitated before shaking hands. Yes, Hendrick's hands were callused, but it was from good, honest labor—something people like Gillard would never know.

Or Mariah. She smiled at the snake. "Thank you for your gracious hospitality."

"My pleasure. Let's retire to the living room." Gillard

wrapped her hand around his arm and led her out of the room. "I hope you find everything to your satisfaction."

"More than satisfying," she purred.

It was nauseating. Hendrick wanted to yank her away from Gillard's clutches, even if he had to drag her, kicking and screaming, from the house, but, of course, he couldn't do that. Instead, he had to watch this disgusting spectacle. She was making a fool of herself, which he intended to point out the moment they were free of the man.

That took far too long. Gillard first called in the housekeeper to order two more rooms readied. He then had coffee served in the living room. After another hour of tedious conversation in which Gillard extolled his accumulated wealth and expressed again his desire to re-create his family, they finally retired to bed.

After Anna settled into her bedroom, Hendrick could finally talk to Mariah. "What do you think you're doing, staying here overnight?" He could barely spit out the words.

"Doing what I came here to do," she said, hand on her bedroom door.

"Can't you tell he's playing up to you so you'll give him Luke?"

She rolled her eyes. "Surely you realize I'm bright enough to see that."

"I was beginning to wonder." But her words did make him feel a bit better. "I don't think he'll tell you anything."

"I know it's unlikely, but I must try." She glanced up and down the hall. "I wonder what's behind these doors."

"I don't know. Bedrooms, I suppose."

"And who might be in them?"

Had she gone mad? "You, me and Anna."

"Exactly." She lowered her voice to a whisper. "But is that all?"

He had to lean close to hear, and her scent flooded his senses, driving away anger and replacing it with painful desire. "What do you mean?"

"Come this way," she whispered, her breath tickling his ear.

She could have told him to jump into an icy creek, and he would have obeyed.

"Mariah." Instinctively, he reached for her hand, but when she stiffened, he let go. "Sorry."

Why did she always make him apologize for doing what any real man would do? She played games with him, one minute leading him close and the next tossing him away. It was driving him crazy. He should have known better than to accompany her on this trip. He should have gone to Curtiss Aeroplane and started a new life far from her. Instead, he'd followed her, and she'd worked her way into his heart, just as before. He wanted to be closer, he wanted...

What did it matter? Once her mission was over, she'd leave him. Again.

"Let's take a walk," she whispered, brushing her fingers across his sleeve. Without waiting for an answer, she glided to the door that opened to the outside.

Like a fool, he followed.

Mariah led Hendrick out of the house and into the night. The feeble light from the house's windows illuminated the patches of wiry grass that dotted the packed dirt yard in front of the house. The night sky spread over them, a half-moon providing enough light so they wouldn't trip. On a less stressful evening, it would be lovely. Tonight, she trembled at what she was about to do.

"What do you think you're doing?" Hendrick asked as soon as they were clear of the house. "Don't you realize this doesn't look good?"

Mariah kept walking. They weren't far enough away yet. Servants or even Gillard might see them leave and follow. She had to be certain no one was listening before speaking freely.

"What doesn't look good?" she said coyly in case anyone did hear them. "Taking a walk with you?"

"You know what I mean. Staying here. Letting that man talk you into things you shouldn't do."

She smiled at his display of bravado and ruffled feathers. Hendrick's guard went up around Gillard. If she'd had any doubt he still felt something for her, she didn't anymore. Though it couldn't lead anywhere, his affection did make her feel cherished. She'd always had that from her parents, but never from a man. Oh, there'd been a male friend here and there through the years, but never anything serious. She'd made sure of that. It wasn't fair to lead a man to think he had hope of a future with her. That's why she'd told Hendrick they could never be more than friends, even though she wished they could.

"Where are you going?" he asked after they'd walked beyond the house's faint glow.

"I think we'll see the stars better if we go a little bit farther."

It was getting difficult to see the ground, so she instinctively reached for his arm. He flinched, and she pulled back.

"Sorry," he whispered, wrapping her hand around his arm and leading her into the black night.

She walked by his side, but not close enough to look like lovers, should anyone in the house be watching.

"Remember that night in South Dakota when you showed me the constellations?" she said evenly.

"Cygnus." His voice cracked just a little, and he placed

his other hand on hers in confirmation of the moment they'd shared.

"And the Pleiades. What's the one that looks like a W?" She halted. They'd walked beyond earshot.

"Cassiopeia the Queen." His voice lowered and roughened. His hand was warm on hers, but he demanded nothing. Unlike that night in South Dakota, he waited.

Such self-control. She'd never given him credit for that. He cared for her, loved her even, but he held back, waiting for her to come to him. Tears rose to her eyes, and she had to blink them back. He deserved a whole woman, a good woman, one who would give him children and raise them and never do what she was about to do.

Wind swept through the shin-high grasses, whooshing and rushing like waves on the ocean. The sun had long since set, but a faint rim of fading gray outlined the mountains to the west. Before long, even that light would vanish, signaling that her work must begin. Until then she could indulge in the moment.

"I want to see those mountains," she whispered, leaning against him. She closed her eyes and breathed in his masculine scent, pretending for one moment that a life together was possible.

His lean yet muscular shoulder trembled ever so slightly. Fear or desire? She longed to know.

"I would take you there," he whispered hoarsely. "You don't need him."

He meant Gillard, who could never compare. If only Hendrick knew how attractive he was. That stray lock. The broad shoulders. His easy gait. Frank Gillard could never top him. Hendrick had character, yet in this moment, it wasn't character that captured her senses. His arms could lift heavy automobile engines or women stumbling on the lakeshore. He'd carried her as if she weighed nothing, and she would remember the feel of his arms the rest of her life.

"I don't like Frank Gillard," she said, still gazing at the stars and leaning against his shoulder.

He shifted slightly but didn't draw away. "You could have fooled me."

"Hopefully, I fooled him. It's an act, Hendrick. I know he's putting on a show to try to win me over. Well, I'm doing the same so he doesn't suspect what I'm doing."

"Working against him to keep Luke away?"

"I need to either find proof he's not Luke's father or get proof he's doing something illegal."

"Like bootleg wine?"

She sighed. "One bottle isn't enough. He had a plausible explanation for everything I found. The wine. The rooms."

"What rooms?"

"Why would a single man need so many bedrooms, not to mention so much staff?"

Hendrick reached an arm around her and held her close. "He wants to impress people?"

"Way out here, so far from everywhere?" She settled into the hollow of his shoulder. "He's earned too much money too quickly." She explained the lingerie she'd found in her bedroom. "What if he's running a bordello?"

She could feel his shock in the tightening of his muscles. "Then I'm not letting you stay here."

"Hush, hush. I don't believe there are any women here now, and the clothing might indeed belong to his late wife or to a lady friend who stays over from time to time. That's the problem. I don't know. That's why I needed to stay tonight, so I could look through the rest of the house."

He spun her around. "You're planning to search the place? Do you know how dangerous that is?"

She held tight. "Of course. But I don't want either you or Anna involved."

He kept shaking his head. "I'm not letting you do this alone. What if he finds you rifling through his stuff? He'll think you're a thief. He's the kind of man who shoots first and asks questions later. You are not searching this house."

She pried his hands off her shoulders. "Yes, I am. I'm a grown woman, and this is my decision."

"I should lock you in your room."

"I'd just climb out the window."

"Then I'll have to stand guard, won't I?"

She loved that he was incensed, that he would protect her no matter the cost, but it wasn't helping her in this instance. She had only tonight. "This is urgent, Hendrick. I can only keep up pretenses for so long before he figures out what's really going on. There are too many questions surrounding Frank Gillard. I can't place Luke in his hands until I know the answers to those questions."

"Then talk to him. Don't snoop."

Mariah tugged at a lock of hair. "Not five minutes ago you said that talking to him was useless. You're right. He's not going to tell me anything useful now that he knows who I am. In the morning he'll probably place a long-distance call to New York to verify that I was indeed sent here to do a home visit."

"What will your boss say? Does he know what you're doing?"

"Yes." She rubbed her arms, suddenly chilled. "Well, at least some of it, but if Gillard calls, Mr. Isaacs will insist Gabe bring Luke here at once. That will devastate all of them. And if Felicity answers the telephone…" She shuddered. "That's why I need to find something against Gillard tonight."

He paused, considering her words. "It's dangerous."

"Anything worthwhile requires risk."

He didn't protest. Instead, he stood silent for so long that she dreaded what he would say, but his words did not condemn, they supported. "I would not want him to have any child's life in his hands. How did he hurt Luke?"

"I'm not sure." She squeezed his hand. "Gabe says Luke won't talk about it, but he starts shaking whenever Gabe asks about his father. Gillard abused him. Emotionally or physically—I don't know."

"Then take me with you," he whispered. "Let me help." He held her again, this time with an intoxicating mix of tenderness and urgency.

She shook her head. "I couldn't live with myself if anything happened to you."

He held her much too close. "And I couldn't live with myself if anything happened to *you*." His breath fluttered across her face, strengthening her and making her more certain of her course, a course that should not include him.

"But your mother, your sister—"

He pressed a finger to her lips, stilling her protest. She could smell the starch in his shirt and feel his overpowering strength. Her head came just to his shoulders, so broad and capable that she couldn't resist laying her cheek against it. She fit perfectly, just like that night in South Dakota. In his arms, the troubles of the world vanished. Only the two of them existed, separate yet one, like twin stars caught in each other's orbit.

He didn't speak. If he'd spoken, it would have ruined everything. No, he splayed his long fingers on the small of her back and oh so gently kissed the top of her head, simultaneously letting her know what he wanted and that he would wait until she was ready. In South Dakota, she'd pulled away. Tonight?

Anything worth having requires risk.

She'd just told him that, but did she truly believe it? Would she risk all on love? In his arms, she felt safe. He rocked her, softly as the grass rippling in the wind, and a great sea of emotion welled from deep within, so strong she couldn't keep it down. On this windblown Montana night she no longer wanted to run. She wanted to risk everything.

His lips brushed her forehead and then her temple. The waves of emotion tossed, their tops windblown, and she lifted her face as if struggling for breath, but it wasn't air she needed. She required something far more nourishing. She needed to know she was loved, and, with the gentlest touch of his lips to hers, he gave her that.

Hendrick ached to kiss Mariah again, but he wasn't foolish enough to think she'd allow more than the one light embrace. Get too serious and she'd run away. Experience had proven that time and again. Even the single kiss was one too many. He risked losing his heart all over again.

So he pulled away. This time he broke the embrace before she was ready.

She blinked and shuddered as if awakening from a sound sleep. "What's wrong?"

Self-preservation. He would not be toyed with this time. He would not expose his heart only to have it crushed. He'd survived a kiss. He could survive anything Mariah threw at him and walk away untouched.

He pointed toward the house. "The last lamp went out at least ten minutes ago."

She peered into the darkness. "Do you think it's been long enough?" Her voice trembled.

"Give it a few more minutes. What is your plan?"

She hesitated.

"You don't have a plan?"

"Of course I have a plan," she snapped. "I want to check the grounds for evidence of smuggling. He must have a cellar or hiding place for the liquor."

"If he keeps it here. Most rumrunners move out the alcohol as quickly as possible. The chances of him keeping it at his house are pretty slim."

"But he might have records—a map, a list of contacts, a ledger. Those would be in his office or study, I'm guessing in the west wing. That's the logical place to start."

That would not be easy. "And where do you plan to find these incriminating documents?"

"In filing cabinets."

"Which would be locked," he pointed out.

"Perhaps, but it's worth checking. And then we move on to the desk."

"Also locked."

"You're trying to talk me out of this," she huffed and took off toward the house.

He caught up to her in seconds. Her quick strides couldn't match his long ones. "And how do you plan to see, Mariah? You can't switch on lights. There's no electricity."

"I know that." She was growing more irritated, a sign he was winning. "We'll bring a lantern."

"And alert the staff?"

She turned on him and stuck a finger in his gut. "Well, then, Mr. Smarty-Pants. What do you propose?"

He carefully removed the finger, rather enjoying this game. "Go back to town."

She whirled away in disgust. "Just what I expected. No imagination. As I said, I can do this myself. I don't need your help, and I certainly wasn't distracted by that kiss."

Oh, yes, she was. Her irritation proved it. He grinned. "Or we could use one of the flashlights from the car."

That stopped her. "Oh." She didn't quite hide her embarrassment at not having thought of such a simple solution. "I suppose you have a set of lock-picking tools, too."

"Not with me." Since Pearlman lacked a locksmith, he'd often been called to unlock cabinets and safes. "But I'll give it a shot with one of your hairpins."

"I don't use hairpins." She resumed her trek, this time toward the car. "But I have a hat pin or two in my valise."

That meant returning to the guest bedroom and possibly attracting attention. Every nerve ending tingled, and his brain was on high alert. "Too risky. We'll get what we can without one."

Locating a flashlight in the car took several minutes. Neither recalled exactly where they'd packed it. Finally, he found it in the sack with the pots and pans.

"Who would put it there?" Mariah asked, or rather accused. "Not I."

Hendrick wasn't about to get into another argument. "It's been at least fifteen minutes. Everyone should be asleep by now."

He felt her tense. "This is it, then." She squeezed his hand.

"This is it."

With that, they crossed to the west-wing entrance.

Mariah's heart pounded like an Indian war drum, relentless and threatening. Surely everyone could hear them open the door. It wasn't locked, but its hinges creaked. She held her breath, waiting for any sign of movement.

At this point, their actions could be explained. They'd gone outside for a breath of air and came in the nearest door. It was perfectly reasonable. Once they reached Gillard's study, no excuse would make sense.

Having Hendrick at her side made her feel better. He

was surprisingly quiet on his feet and acted with more determination than she thought he possessed. Though tall and strong, he held his strength in check, preferring to live by a strict set of morals. She was surprised that he would compromise those by helping her do something that was clearly illegal.

He must care for her deeply. The tenderness of his kiss. The way he looked at her. If only they could have a future together. She shook herself. She had to focus on the task at hand. One mistake, and they'd be caught. Even Hendrick couldn't save her then.

As they crept silently down the hall, she thought her heart would beat through her rib cage and leap out onto the floor. He squeezed her hand, letting her know he was with her. The weak flashlight beam bounced over shadowy objects.

Like the east wing, the west hall was lined with closed doors, five in all, two to a side and one at the end, likely the master bedroom. But which of the other four doors led to the study? Choose the wrong one, and they were doomed. Perhaps Hendrick was right; they shouldn't be doing this. Yet men and women of God *had* deceived evil men for the sake of the good. Rahab misled the king's men in order to spare Joshua's spies. Esther hid her Jewish blood for the sake of her people. Sarah pretended to be Abraham's sister so he wouldn't be killed.

She squeezed Hendrick's hand and pointed to the second door on the left. It faced the front of the house. A businessman would want his study window to face approaching visitors, so he could see them before they saw him. He also would want it next to the master bedroom. That room must be the study.

Hendrick tested the knob. It turned easily. He looked to her for confirmation, and she nodded.

Slowly he opened the door. It glided silently. Then he lifted the flashlight and swept the room. A bedroom. Judging by the feminine pattern on the curtains and the dainty vanity, this, too, was intended for a woman, possibly a future wife.

Hendrick closed the door and pointed to the other room on that side. She nodded, and he began to turn the knob when a terrible thought occurred to her.

She caught his hand and stopped him before he opened the door. What if she was wrong, and the master bedroom adjoined the wife's bedroom?

Heart pounding, she turned to the other side of the hallway. Two doors on that side and one on the end. Which led to Gillard's office and which opened to his bedroom? Mentally she assessed the possibilities. He would have all the family rooms in the west wing. If he was expecting Luke, he'd have set aside a room for him, either next to the wife's room or adjacent to the master bedroom. A man like Gillard would choose the largest room for himself. That would be the end room. They'd already discovered the wife's room. Luke's would be the room adjacent either to the wife's or to the master bedroom. Judging from what she'd seen of Gillard's character, she'd guess adjacent to the wife's room. That left the two doors on the opposite side of the hall. If Gillard were involved in something illegal, he'd keep his office very close. She pointed to the door across the hall from the wife's room.

Hendrick nodded and slowly opened the door. It creaked, and Mariah froze. Hendrick turned off the flashlight. Seconds ticked as she listened. Nothing.

She squeezed Hendrick's hand, and he turned the flashlight back on. The dim beam revealed exactly what she'd hoped. A desk, cabinets, bookshelves. She whisked into the room and pointed to the desk. Her throbbing nerves told her they had precious little time.

Hendrick tried the top drawer. It didn't budge. Locked. The others opened easily but revealed little.

Perspiration drenched Mariah's back. It wasn't just hot inside; it was unbearable.

Luke. Think of Luke.

Lord, where do I look? Show me.

She waited but heard no answer over her ricocheting panic.

Meanwhile, Hendrick was rifling through the cabinet. "I don't know what I'm looking for."

"Shh!" she hissed. Someone would hear them. Someone had probably already heard them. Her heart was in her throat. She wasn't cut out for spying. The task was overwhelming, the terror unbearable.

She motioned to Hendrick that they should leave and whirled around to exit. In the process, her skirt caught some papers on the edge of the desk, and they tumbled to the floor. She gasped and scrambled to gather them while Hendrick shone the light on the mess.

There was no way to know if she had them in the right order, but she did take the time—even though her hands were shaking—to put them all right-side up. They looked like legal documents. Most were about oil leasing, but not all. One was a birth certificate for Luke.

Her hand stilled. This was what she was looking for.

She pulled the flashlight beam over the paper and squinted in the dim light. The birth record listed Francesco Guillardo as the father, but Luke's name was given as Lucian, not Luciano. Still, it was so close that it had to be Luke. She ran her finger along the faded lines. The name of the mother was illegible, but the ethnicity was not.

She gasped.

"What is it?" Hendrick whispered, leaning close.

She shook her head and pressed a finger to her lips to quiet him before she resumed reading the document. The record stated that Luke's mother was American Indian. Just like the servants in the house. Just like the house-keeper. For a second she wondered if that woman was Luke's mother. Impossible. She bore no resemblance to him. No, Luke's mother must be dead, as Gillard said.

Still, her heart stuck in her throat. Gillard had told the Detroit mission that they were Italian, but in truth Luke was part Indian. It didn't change how she felt about him, but she couldn't help remembering the ethnic slurs cast against Luke when he first came to Pearlman. Perhaps Gillard had fibbed so Luke wouldn't face ridicule. Italian was less offensive to some than Indian. Yes, Gillard had lied to the Detroit agents, but he might have done it to spare Luke ridicule.

Hendrick motioned to her to hurry. Though she wanted to take the birth record with her, Gillard would know her purpose at once if she did, so she replaced the papers on the corner of the desk.

Then, before someone caught them, they tiptoed out of the room. The hall was still empty, the house noiseless. Hendrick pulled the door shut, again with the gentle creak, until the latch clicked in place.

Lacking a handkerchief, Mariah wiped her damp face with her sleeve. They only had to get back to the east wing, a simple matter of crossing the vast living room.

They slipped down the hall with the beam of the flash-light to guide them and paused before entering the living room. Hendrick aimed the flickering beam into the room. Furniture cluttered their path. They'd have to weave around it.

She touched his arm and started forward, but the light

blinked out. She heard Hendrick shake it and pound it against his hand. Nothing worked. The dry cells must have died. They would have to reach their rooms in the dark.

After waiting for their eyes to adjust, Mariah saw the chief's headdress rising like a monster in the pale moonlight. The chairs loomed as obstacles. Rugs could trip them. Her pulse still hammered.

Hendrick took her hand, and together they stepped into the room.

"What you do in study?"

The voice froze them. Slowly they turned to see the housekeeper standing in the front entrance.

They could run to the east wing and try to escape that way, but Anna was asleep. They couldn't leave her to Gillard. They also couldn't hope to escape before the housekeeper awakened the whole house.

"What you do?" the woman asked again, her face hidden in the shadows.

Mariah swallowed hard. What if the woman carried a weapon? What if she called Gillard? They were doomed. Oh, to be able to faint at such a moment, but she wasn't the fainting type. Somehow she'd have to explain what she and Hendrick had been doing.

Chapter Twelve

Mariah couldn't think of a single reasonable explanation. She trembled, tongue-tied.

To her surprise, Hendrick took the lead. "We were looking for something to help his son, Luke."

Dear, wonderful Hendrick. She could have thrown her arms around him in thanksgiving if they weren't in such a fix.

The housekeeper wavered, considering his explanation, before pointing to the east wing. "Go."

Mariah caught her breath. Was she letting them go?

That hope died when the housekeeper followed them across the room. What did the woman intend to do? Turn them over to Gillard? Maybe he was waiting in the east wing. Maybe he'd discovered their absence or heard them in his office and sent his housekeeper to corral them.

Mariah clutched Hendrick's hand, and he responded with a reassuring squeeze. Whatever happened, he would protect her to the best of his ability. What a wonderful man. He shouldn't be in this position. Her idea had been ill conceived. If they got out of this alive, she would never do anything so foolish again.

The housekeeper trailed them silently. She did not light

a lamp or speak. Only the whisper of her skirt betrayed her presence. Mariah was not so adept in the dark. Her leg struck the edge of a table. Their shoes clattered on the split-stone floor. She expected Gillard to spring out of the shadows at any moment, but they reached the head of the east hallway without incident.

"Stop," the housekeeper commanded.

They obeyed. Mariah peered into the blackness ahead but couldn't see anyone. Was Gillard there? She strained to hear the slightest sound, tensed and ready to run.

"Thank you, ma'am," Hendrick said out of the blue. "May I ask your name?"

Mariah's jaw dropped. This was not the time for chit-chat. She wrenched on his hand, but he kept talking, out of nervousness, she supposed, though he didn't sound nervous.

"Mine's Hendrick Simmons. I'm a mechanic back in Pearlman, and I'm helping Mr. Talltree fix up a motor for the fire engine."

Mariah yanked again. What was he doing?

"Mrs. Eagle," the woman answered in a softer tone. She then pointed to the door that led outside. "Go."

Go? Outside? Where? Mariah looked to Hendrick.

"Not safe," Mrs. Eagle added.

Mariah breathed easier. The woman was on their side. She was warning them, telling them to leave. Gillard wasn't waiting for them. He wouldn't harm them, at least not yet. But the threat still hung over them. Gillard was dangerous. They should leave.

Hendrick didn't budge. "We can't, not without my sister."

"Take her," Mrs. Eagle said.

"But Mr. Gillard is expecting us to ride with him in the morning," Mariah said, thinking through the situation.

"What will he say when he finds us gone? If we leave in the middle of the night, he'll know something's wrong." And she'd never get the information she needed to save Luke. "I need to stay."

Predictably, Hendrick protested, "Mrs. Eagle just said it's not safe to stay."

"What could happen in broad daylight? We'll be fine."

He didn't accept her assurance. "Would he hurt the ladies?" he asked the housekeeper.

"No," she admitted, "but he no good."

That was what Mariah hoped to prove. "How? I need to know in order to protect Luke."

Mrs. Eagle glanced toward the living room, her fear palpable. "I warn you," she said as she slipped away into the darkness.

Apparently, she was too afraid of Gillard to help, but she also wouldn't stop them. That gave Mariah one more chance to find the evidence she needed. She couldn't return to the office, but she could look over the property for any sign of smuggling and she could ask him more questions.

"I need to stay," she repeated.

Hendrick still held her hand. "Don't. Please."

"I must." Her voice shook a little.

"He'll know we saw the birth record the moment he looks in the office."

She knew that. "He might blame one of the servants."

"I doubt it. I think you're right. He'll call your boss to see if you're who you say you are."

She grabbed onto his arm. "You need to call Mr. Isaacs first."

"How? There aren't any wires running out here."

"Go to town. First thing in the morning. Gillard won't think it odd if you leave. In fact, he'll probably welcome it."

"I'm not leaving you," he growled.

"You must." She was sure of this. "He won't harm us. I'm positive. Besides, I can keep him occupied here, away from telephones, while you place the call to Mr. Isaacs. I'll give you the number in the morning."

"What am I supposed to tell him?" He still sounded reluctant, but at least he was considering her plan.

"That I'm still working on things here. Tell him Gillard might call. Tell him to confirm I've been sent here to investigate and beg him not to promise anything. Above all, don't let him do anything rash, like sending another agent to bring Luke here. Tell him to wait until I call. I'll update him later."

Hendrick shuffled his feet, and she could tell he still wasn't convinced. "Are you sure there's a telephone in town?"

"There must be one in the telegraph office. If not, send a cable. I need you to do this for me, Hendrick." She shook his arm to punctuate the urgency. "Please."

He didn't answer at first, and she could almost see him working through the options.

"Are you going to let Gillard have Luke?"

She sucked in a deep breath. "Not if I can help it." But she was running out of time to figure out how.

To Mariah's relief, Hendrick left at first light.

"What shall it be?" Gillard asked when she and Anna arrived at the dining room. "Breakfast and then a ride, or do you prefer to ride first?"

If he knew about Mariah's snooping last night, he didn't

show it. He gave her the same smooth smile he'd bestowed upon her yesterday.

"Horses first," Anna cried. Her eyes shone. She'd bubbled about the horseback ride from the moment she awoke.

Mariah had a great deal less enthusiasm. She'd ransacked their bedroom last night, looking for any hint of wrongdoing on Gillard's part. Other than the clothing, she'd found nothing.

Neither could she explain the inconsistencies in his story. The birth record said Luke's mother was Indian. The agency record said Italian. Just a few letters' difference. Could there have been a clerical error or a misunderstanding? If Gillard had the birth certificate, he must be Luke's father. Then why lie to the Detroit mission? Why say Luke was Italian? As many times as she asked the question, she could think of only one answer: to spare Luke from prejudice.

If true, that made Gillard a decent man, something she did not want to admit. After all, Luke was terrified of him. Gillard must have harmed or threatened Luke to provoke such a reaction.

In the end, she'd concluded that the only way to get Gillard to sign the termination papers was to unearth the illicit source of his fortune.

Anna tugged on Mariah's hands. "Let's go riding. Please?"

Mariah sighed. "Let me have a cup of coffee first." She needed time to gather her wits.

"Sensible proposition." Gillard led them to the table. "I've had my housekeeper set out some pastries and bread. Help yourself."

As Mariah sipped her coffee, she idly wondered why he never called Mrs. Eagle by name. "Does your housekeeper come from the local Blackfeet tribe?"

"No. She's from the other side of the Divide."

"Why would she come all the way here to work?"

The table had been set for three, as if Gillard knew Hendrick would be leaving. Had he overheard their conversation last night, or had Mrs. Eagle told him?

Gillard leaned back in his chair. "Work is scarce in these parts. Many travel far for a job."

She absently plucked a slice of nut bread from the platter on the center of the table. Gillard revealed little when questioned directly. She'd have to be much more cunning. "I have so much to learn about this area," she said with a sigh that she hoped would allay any suspicions he might have about her questions. "It is a remarkable land, though."

"Wait until you see my property and the mountains."

"The mountains!" Anna perked up. "Are we riding in the mountains?"

"Not today. Today, we'll stay on my land. Nothing too difficult for your first ride, Miss Anna."

He was true to his word. After they saddled up and mounted, he guided them across the rolling hills at a gentle pace. Mariah's only regret was that she hadn't had a chance to look in the outbuildings. She'd try to do that when they returned. For now she enjoyed the warmth, the smell of summer hay and the vast blue sky. The land rolled in great, grassy slopes that increased in size and steepness the closer they got to the mountains.

When the horses needed water, he led them to creeks that flowed between hills. Down there, the scrub bushes grew, but otherwise the land had few trees.

"Why don't the Indians farm?" Mariah stretched her legs while the horses drank. She was not accustomed to riding.

"Too dry." Gillard snapped off a stalk of dry grass. "To succeed, they'd need irrigation, but only one section of the reservation has it in place. Even if they started now, it'd take too long to get a return. Oil leases are their best bet."

That was the second time he'd mentioned oil, and it was all over the paperwork she'd seen on his desk. "If oil is found, then the Indians will profit?" She watched Anna splash around at the creek's edge.

"You're remarkably concerned for their welfare." He looked at her suspiciously. "You'll soon learn to temper that compassion. People here take advantage of tender hearts."

"Compassion is a natural result of Christian living."

He stiffened, and it occurred to her that he might not believe in God. He certainly didn't want to hear about her faith, yet Jesus commissioned Christians to reach out to unbelievers. Could Frank Gillard's heart be turned?

"I prefer to take a more realistic view of life," he said, "but I promise to bring Luke to church, Miss Mariah. I'll do whatever you deem necessary in order to have my son in my life again."

She supposed that was a good start. God could work miracles if only the heart opened to Him. "That would be necessary, of course, as would schooling. The Society is concerned about the child's welfare."

"As am I." He grinned. "Rest assured, I can give Luke anything he wants or desires." He spread his arms. "Look at this land."

The hills stretched on for miles in every direction. "Is this all yours?"

He nodded, mouth quirked up at the corner. "Or soon will be."

"But if farming is out of the question, it must be difficult to succeed here." *And to gain a large fortune.*

"For some, but I have over a thousand head of cattle."

He didn't appear to realize where she was headed. She

took a deep breath and plunged onward. "How impressive."

Pride puffed out his chest. "It's all know-how." He tapped his temple. "Some men know how to work the system. Some—" he paused to let her know he meant Hendrick "—are content to muddle along without taking any risks."

Mariah gritted her teeth. Hendrick had a hundred times more character and intelligence than Frank Gillard. She wouldn't get the information she needed by defending him, though. "Then you made your fortune on cattle, not oil?"

He laughed. "Oil exploration is just getting started. Never fear, Miss Mariah, Luke's comfort is assured. Cattle and oil. That's the secret. My three thousand acres can support a large herd."

"Three thousand! How did you get so much on reservation land?"

A corner of his mouth lifted, wrinkling the sun-dried skin. "The Indians sometimes sell surplus land, but you can't possibly want to know about such dull matters. The most important thing to me is family. I've built a home, so I can bring back Luke."

His voice cracked, and she almost believed him, if not for the fact that he'd initially claimed his son had died. "Yet you left him."

"The worst mistake of my life. I was desperate." He drew in a deep breath. "Let me start a little further back. Times were difficult. I traveled across the country looking for work. I thought I'd find it at the Ford plant in Detroit, but it didn't work out."

That matched the agency report. Mariah's heart beat a little harder as she realized that she could prompt an answer to one of her questions. "Did they discriminate against you because of your ethnicity?"

His mouth quirked, calling her bluff. "My Italian background made no difference."

Oh, he was smooth, but she could play that game, too. "Perhaps that's because you don't look Italian."

"Ah, but I am. Francesco Guillardo, at your service." He bowed. "Some Italians have fair coloring, Miss Mariah. Surely a woman of your education knows that."

She felt her cheeks heat. "But Luke's coloring is dark."

"He got that from his mother."

"Who was also Italian?"

His gaze narrowed. "Is this an interrogation, Miss Meeks?"

"I'm simply clearing up some discrepancies in the paperwork. The Detroit agent's report indicated that your wife had died, that you were Italian and that you'd fallen on hard times."

Grief scoured his face, deepening the lines across his forehead. "It was a difficult time. After my wife died, I fell into such despair that I could barely get through a day. I dragged Luke from place to place, but I couldn't keep a job. We were starving. That kind of life wasn't fair to the boy, so I left him at the orphanage. I'd heard the folks there were kind and good to children. I needed time to pull myself together. I always intended to fetch him once I made my stake." His voice broke, and he swiped at his mouth. "I thought I was doing the right thing at the time."

A trace of doubt wormed into Mariah's heart. What if he was telling the truth? What if it had happened exactly the way he said? What if she'd been wrong from the start? Impossible. Luke feared his father. Gillard had given her no reason why his son would be frightened of him, which meant he still had to be hiding something.

Gillard shook his head. "Maybe I should have tried to

bring Luke with me. It was a hard life at first, scratching for enough to eat."

"But you turned things around," she said, "in only two-and-a-half years."

"Providence smiled on me." He removed his hat and pressed it to his chest, revealing the steel-gray eyes. "And blessed me again by bringing you here."

Mariah felt the shiver deep in her soul. "I am merely doing my job."

"Perhaps it began that way, Miss Mariah, but I have been charmed by your frankness and honesty."

Oh, that man knew how to tempt a woman's heart. She could almost believe he meant what he said. Almost. "Mr. Gillard, I know flattery when I hear it, and none of that will change my decision."

His lips curved upward as he raised his hands. "Guilty as charged. But don't hold it against me that I'm attracted to a beautiful woman like you. That's honest, Miss Mariah." He looked her in the eye. "I do hope to marry, for Luke's sake. He deserves a whole family with a father who loves him."

"He has a father who loves him," she protested, but he must not have understood what she meant.

"Yes, I do, with my whole heart. I'll do anything for him." He took a deep, though shaky, breath. "I'll understand if you want to wait to send him until I marry, but I'd much appreciate if you'd send him now. Two-and-a-half years is a long time. I miss my boy. I'd marry this instant if it meant I could have Luke back, but he deserves a good mother, the best possible. I'd like to find that woman and court her properly. Until then, my housekeeper can look after him."

"And for schooling, will you send him to the Beson Creek School?"

He hesitated, just a second, but didn't confirm Luke's Indian background. "I plan to bring in a tutor."

"Do you think that wise when there's a school nearby?"

His smile was patronizing. "Beson Creek is a boarding school. I certainly don't want to spend more time away from Luke. Considering how far I live from the day school in Cut Bank, a tutor makes perfect sense. Travel during the winter can be difficult. I'd hate for him to miss any lessons. And, of course, if I marry an educated woman, she could help with Luke's education." His hard gray eyes softened. "In short, Miss Mariah, I'll do whatever it takes to bring Luke home."

Though he hadn't admitted Luke's true racial background, he sounded sincere, and that's what worried her. No court would deny him custody. If she didn't find something against him, and soon, Gabe and Felicity would lose Luke.

Usually, working on motors took Hendrick's mind off things he couldn't fix, but not today. He'd bumbled over the telephone call to Mariah's boss. Isaacs had to suspect that she was in trouble. Hendrick sure did.

After the call, he drove back to the ranch, only to find Gillard, Mariah and Anna had left on horseback. The servants didn't know where they were heading or when they'd be back. He couldn't stand waiting around, so he returned to town to work on the motor for the fire engine. And to stew.

Gillard was doing everything in his power to win over Mariah. He'd flattered her, given her everything he thought she wanted. He had an answer for every question, and now, after their discovery last night, it seemed clear that he truly was Luke's father. Mariah was fighting a losing battle, one that he had left her to fight alone.

Hendrick's gut locked tighter than the bolt on the engine block he was trying to disassemble. He never should have left her there this morning. In frustration, he wrenched on the bolt with all his might. Compared to relationships, mechanics was easy.

Judge Weiss hadn't returned from Great Falls yet, so Hendrick and Joshua Talltree salvaged what they could from the broken motors littering the back of the filling station. With luck, they could piece together an engine that could generate thirty to forty horsepower and pump at least a hundred gallons of water per minute—if they could find that much water.

"Biggest problem I see around here is getting water," Hendrick said as he finally loosened the bolt.

"The creeks are low this year," Talltree acknowledged. The Indian had proven skilled with his hands. He kept up with Hendrick's pace and made sensible suggestions for piecing together a working motor.

"Where else can you get water?"

Talltree shrugged. "Haven't had to."

"No fires?" Hendrick eyed the hand-pumper. It looked like it hadn't been used in years.

"The usual grass fires. Sometimes wildfires. They feed on the pines in the foothills but usually burn themselves out before they get here. Fire is part of nature." He gazed off into the distance. "My ancestors understood the value of being able to move your lodging at a moment's notice."

Hendrick had seen the buffalo-skin-covered tipis set up near the train station as a tourist attraction. "Do you still live in tipis?"

Talltree shook his head. "No buffalo anymore. It takes many hides to make a covering."

Hendrick felt the deep sadness in him. Talltree's people had lost so much. Maybe at least he could give them a fire pump. "When we're finished with this pump, you'll be able to save a house. Sure would like something bigger." He saw an opportunity to turn the talk to Gillard. "Something like that twin-six in Mr. Gillard's Packard."

Hendrick eyed Talltree, who had never explained his warning from yesterday. The Indian revealed nothing.

Hendrick ran a finger around the cylinder wall. Scored pretty badly, but at least a couple of the valves looked usable. "Mariah—Miss Meeks—says Gillard was flat broke a couple years ago. Can't help wondering how someone that poor can get so rich in such a short time."

Talltree scowled as Hendrick handed him the valves one by one. "He cheats."

"Cheats at what?"

Talltree didn't answer.

Hendrick pushed. "At cards? Is he a gambler?"

"Not the way you're thinking."

Talltree's cryptic answers were driving him crazy. "Did he cheat you?"

"Not directly."

Ordinarily Hendrick would have left the matter at that. Talltree didn't want to talk, and Hendrick didn't like to stir things up, but Mariah was in Gillard's clutches. "Is he... dangerous?" The word stuck in his throat.

Talltree stared at him, the dark eyes unreadable. "If crossed."

Hendrick's blood ran cold. What if Mariah said the wrong thing? What if she refused to hand over Luke? "Would he hurt...someone?"

Talltree didn't move a muscle. "It's happened."

"A woman?" Hendrick's muscles coiled. If that man hurt Mariah or Anna, Hendrick couldn't be responsible for what he'd do.

"Perhaps," Talltree hedged.

Hendrick's heart raced. "Mariah and my sister are with him. They've been with him all day." Judging by the angle of the sun, it had to be midafternoon. "Gillard was supposed to bring them to town after showing them his property."

Talltree's silence only made the tension worse.

"Maybe they're at the Mountain View." Hendrick hoped rather than believed. He hadn't seen Gillard's car travel down the town's single street, but maybe he'd passed while Hendrick was working on the motor. "I'd better check."

"They're not at the hotel."

Fear shivered up Hendrick's spine. "How do you know?"

Talltree pointed to the building across the street. "That's the Mountain View. Gillard's car never passed."

Fear turned quickly to panic. "I've got to find them."

He didn't think, just ran out into the street. He looked left and right. No Packard.

"Where would he take them?" he asked Talltree, who'd followed.

The Indian shrugged.

Hendrick tugged a hand through his hair. Where were they? "He took them on horseback to look at his land. Where would that be?"

Talltree pointed toward the mountains and then swept his hand east.

Hendrick's jaw dropped. "He owns all that?"

"He calls it his."

"That must be the whole reservation," Hendrick stammered. He'd never find them.

Talltree shook his head, the braids rolling side to side. "The reservation is ours, but he wants to take it."

"Take it?"

Of course. Gillard was a vulture, taking everything he

could. The artwork, the fancy china. That's how Gillard made his fortune, by bilking the desperate and the less fortunate. Gillard didn't do it for wealth; he did it for power. Was Mariah just another conquest to him?

Hendrick flung open the Overland's door. "I need to get Mariah and my sister away from him. Where would Gillard take them?"

Talltree's eyes narrowed. "Only the eagle knows."

Now was not the time for cryptic answers. He got into the driver's seat of the Overland, set the spark and throttle and pressed the ignition. The engine cranked and started. "Point me in the most likely direction."

Talltree placed both hands on the door. "Where they go, there are no roads."

As Hendrick scanned the vast plains, he realized the odds of finding Mariah and Anna were infinitesimal. From what Talltree had just told him, the chances he'd find them unharmed were even less. Still, he had to try.

He revved the engine and pushed in the clutch.

"I'll go with you," said Talltree. "From Chief Firestorm hill we might see them."

Hendrick would take any help he could get.

Chapter Thirteen

Not only did Gillard have Luke's birth record, he'd answered most of her questions. Mariah's mind whirled on the car ride back to town.

He whistled while he drove, confident and secure. She stared out the window, trying to piece together some way to keep Luke from his father.

How much easier this would have been if Gillard had been rough and disreputable. Instead, he appeared respectable, prominent and well-spoken. His grief over his family seemed sincere. He'd shown her Luke's room, filled with toys a boy Luke's age would love. The schoolroom overlooked the vast plain stretching north and contained a chalkboard, books and even a globe. He took her on a tour of the stables and outbuildings. She found nothing to point to criminal activity, nothing wrong at all. He asked how tall Luke was, if his hair was still dark and curly. He wanted to see a photograph. In short, he was everything a father should be.

Her only unanswered questions were if Gillard would publicly recognize Luke's Indian heritage, how he made his money and why Luke was so afraid of him. The first was easy enough to test. Townspeople might be able to answer the second. The latter could prove impossible to discover. Luke wouldn't talk, and Gillard certainly wouldn't tell her. No one in Brunley knew about Gillard's past. The agency report didn't mention where he'd lived before Detroit, but the birth record came from Onondaga, New York. Maybe that was the avenue she needed to pursue.

"You said you came to Detroit, looking for work." She tried to make it sound like small talk. "Where did you originally live?"

He stopped whistling. "New York."

That much matched. She'd try for more. "Is that where your wife passed away?"

His jaw tightened. "Yes."

Whatever had happened, he clearly didn't want to talk about it, but she had to know. "I always wondered because Luke never speaks about his mother."

"He probably doesn't remember her that well," he said tersely. "She died when he was six."

"Six?" That didn't fit with the agency report. "I thought your wife died just before you left Luke at the orphanage. He was eight then."

Gillard fixed his gaze on the rutted road. "She died in New York, near her homeland. Her people buried her."

"Her people?" Mariah's stomach fluttered.

"Seneca, though she was part Blackfeet."

"Blackfeet? How could she be part Blackfeet and part Seneca? The two tribes are thousands of miles apart."

His mouth ticked up in one corner. "The train. Indians can travel, too."

Mariah flushed with embarrassment. "Of course. How silly of me." She'd assumed the tribes never left their reservations. What a ridiculous, stereotyped thought.

They rode in silence for some time before she dared speak again. "It took you two years to get to Detroit?"

"After my wife died, I don't remember much. The following year is a blur. I worked, existed, I guess you'd call it, and took care of Luke, but I wasn't really there for him. Then I realized I needed to pick myself up, so I came to Detroit." His Adam's apple bobbed. "I'm not proud of my actions. I know it's hard for you to understand. A woman's strongest tie is to her child. A man needs to know he can provide. I couldn't, but that doesn't mean I didn't love Luke. It means I cared enough to ensure that he has a good life. I thought I did the right thing at the time, but it didn't take long for me to realize that I'd made the biggest mistake of my life."

"By not bringing Luke here," she whispered.

He nodded. His gaze was still fixed dead ahead. His lip trembled in an attempt to quell his emotions.

Sympathy mixed with dread. He must love his son. But Gabe and Felicity loved Luke, too. Which option was best? She fought back tears.

"Thank you for caring," he said softly. "That's what drew me to you from the start—how deeply you care for people. I can tell you have Luke's best interests in mind. You would love him like your own."

Like her own. Mariah bit her lip. She did love Luke like a son, but Gabe and Felicity were his real parents. They didn't just enjoy visits. They loved him through the good times and the bad, when he was acting up and when he was sick. They tied his shoes and comforted him at night. They taught him and prayed for him. He sat at their table and in their pew at church.

A lump formed in her throat. "Luke's foster parents love him very much."

Gillard snorted. "They'd change their minds if they knew he was mixed-blood."

"No, they wouldn't. They haven't a prejudicial bone in their bodies."

"It's true," Anna piped up from the back. "Pastor Gabriel and Mrs. Meeks adore Luke."

Mariah gasped. She'd forgotten that Anna was there, listening to everything she'd asked Gillard. No wonder the girl felt compelled to contribute her support, but she'd unwittingly revealed the last of Mariah's secrets. She could only hope Gillard didn't notice.

Unfortunately, he did. "Mrs. Meeks?" Gillard applied the brake to stop the car. He then turned to her, fire in his eyes. "*You* are Mrs. Meeks?"

Mariah cringed, her cheeks hot. There was no getting out of this gracefully. "I'm *Miss* Meeks. Mrs. Meeks is my brother's wife."

"I thought you were an agent for the orphanage."

"I am." Her heart thudded hard against her ribs. *Please don't demand Luke yet. Please give me time to know deep in my soul that I'm doing the right thing.*

"And your brother is taking care of my son."

Her whitened knuckles ached. "He is."

"I see." His voice was flat, the anger latent and dangerous, like a coiled snake poised to strike. "Just how well do you know my son?"

The time for evasion was over. Though her ears rang, she must answer. "I took care of him for three months, before my brother married." That time still brought to mind joyous memories. Luke running after Gabe's dog. Playing hide-and-seek in the park. Tucking him into bed at night. Telling Bible stories and teaching him to pray before sleep, silently at first, for he would only speak to

Gabe's dog. Then one day he prayed aloud. She blinked back tears. "That's when he began to speak again."

"To speak?" Gillard shouted before lowering his voice to a more normal level. "He stopped speaking?"

His reaction gave her the answer she needed, though not the one she wanted. He was clearly shocked that Luke had gone mute. That meant the separation had been the cause, not some horrible abuse. Luke stopped talking because he'd been abandoned.

Mariah absently smoothed her skirts, trying to wipe away her disappointment. She was fast losing every hope of keeping Luke in her family.

"When did it happen?" Gillard asked.

"At the orphanage. Apparently, the moment you left."

"But he's speaking now?"

Mariah shot a glance at him. Did she just hear a tremor in his voice? Emotion or fear? His expression betrayed nothing. "Yes. He's a normal little boy."

Instead of being relieved, his jaw tensed and his brow drew low.

Mariah didn't understand. "I thought you'd be pleased that he's back to normal."

"I am," he said hastily. "I'm just wondering what he said about…my leaving?"

"He never talks about it."

This time he did sigh in relief. "That's good to hear. I was so afraid he blamed me. I can't wait to bring him home." Gillard released the brake and edged the car over a small rise. "I hope that will be soon. I want to hold him in my arms and let him know he'll never need to be away from me again. I hope you understand by now, Miss Mariah, how important this is to me."

She was fighting a losing battle. "I do."

"Then you've finished your evaluation? I've reconsidered his schooling. I'll send him to school in Cut Bank, but I also want to hire a tutor for bad weather."

"That's wise," she had to admit. He was taking every step possible to ensure Luke's welfare.

"You'll understand that I want to get him here by the end of the month so he'll have time to settle in before the school year begins."

"So soon?" she gasped. The end of the month was less than two weeks away. So little time. How would Gabe and Felicity cope?

"I've waited over two years."

"Yes, but the trains aren't running regularly."

"Often enough. Surely your brother can bring him."

She had a hundred reasons why Gabe couldn't, but none of them would make any difference to Gillard. She stared dully at the ochre-colored fields as they crested the hill. Brunley lay before them, baking in the late-afternoon heat. If she couldn't figure out something soon, this would be Luke's home.

"Mariah, is that your car?" Anna's question jolted her from her thoughts.

Mariah peered across the shimmering plain and saw a car speeding toward them. No doubt. That was her Overland.

Hendrick slowed the car the moment he spotted Mariah. She looked pale and near tears. What had Gillard done to her? He slammed on the brake and brought the vehicle to a stop in front of Gillard's Packard. If that man had laid a finger on her, he'd beat him to a pulp.

Within seconds, he'd leapt out of the Overland, run to the Packard and whipped open Mariah's door. "Come with me. You, too, Anna. I'll take you the rest of the way."

Neither woman moved. Anna stared at him, and Mariah looked dead ahead at the Overland.

"What happened?" she said softly.

"What happened? You're late. I got worried."

"Is that why you're racing my car over these hills?"

Hendrick felt like an idiot. She wasn't in any danger. Gillard was bringing her to town, just like he said he would. Hendrick had jumped to conclusions. He looked at the Overland to hide his embarrassment. The car was surrounded by clouds of dust that were just now beginning to settle. Talltree, whose head almost touched the canvas roof, hadn't budged from the passenger seat.

In the Packard, Gillard slid an arm behind Mariah's shoulders. "I don't recall giving you a specific time, Mr. Simmons, as if it's any of your business what Miss Mariah does."

But it was his business, wasn't it? He'd promised to protect Mariah, even though she didn't seem to want protecting. Reluctantly, he realized Mariah could do as she pleased. She could up and marry Frank Gillard, and he couldn't do a thing to stop her.

"I thought you were coming back earlier." The excuse sounded as lame as it was.

Anna rolled her eyes but crawled out of the backseat. "I'll go back with you."

He suspected that had more to do with Talltree's presence than any concern over her brother.

He stuck his hands in his pockets. "Well, I guess everything's under control, then. See you at the hotel." He hated to leave her with Gillard, but he had no choice.

"Oh, Hendrick," she called out before he took more than one step. "Were you able to make your telephone call?"

For a second, he didn't know what she meant, but then

he remembered the call to Mr. Isaacs. "Yes." He didn't dare say more with Gillard hanging on her every word.

"Any problems?"

He wished he knew what he could and couldn't say. He settled for a simple no.

"Good."

"I hope there's no trouble at home." Gillard smirked at him.

"No." Hendrick wasn't about to converse with the man. He turned to Mariah. "Are you sure you don't want to ride with me?"

Gillard took Mariah's hand without asking and raised it to his lips. "If you wish to go with him, I will try to endure the separation. Don't forget my offer to show you the park tomorrow."

Another day together? Hendrick couldn't let her fall prey to that man. "I can take you."

Gillard laughed. "You'll need horses, Mr. Simmons."

The man rubbed Hendrick the wrong way. Gillard took every opportunity to cut him down a peg. Not this time. If Mariah and Anna wanted to go to the park, Hendrick would find a way to take them, even if it cost every cent he had. "Then I'll rent horses."

The corner of Gillard's mouth quirked up. "Suit yourself. Miss Mariah, I am at your service."

Hendrick understood the unspoken insult, that he wasn't good enough or rich enough to entertain Mariah. Well, he didn't have to stand by and take this.

"Let's get going," he barked, grabbing the bags from the backseat of the Packard.

Mariah didn't budge. "My car looks pretty full."

Hendrick could have kicked himself. With Talltree, Anna and the bags packed into the Overland, there wasn't room for Mariah.

"It does look like a tight squeeze," Gillard noted. "I'd be glad to drive you to the Mountain View." He shot a gleaming grin at Hendrick.

That scoundrel had outwitted him again.

"That will be $4," the hotel clerk stated. Stodgy and middle-aged, she was likely the proprietress or the owner's wife. She was also chewing something. Mariah hoped it was chewing gum, not tobacco.

"For one night?" Mariah had expected to pay at most a dollar a room.

"That's right, plus fifty cents per day per person for meals." The woman resumed chewing. "More if you want tours or box lunches."

Five-fifty a day. Mariah fingered the few remaining bills in her handbag. The ride into Brunley had been painfully silent. Gillard expected her to confirm that she would have Gabe bring Luke here at once. She couldn't think of a reason to deny him except the sinking feeling in her stomach. Now, she faced a financial dilemma. At five-fifty a night, she could afford only three nights' lodging. She had to wire for funds—if that was even possible in Brunley.

"Are those your least expensive rooms?" she asked, eyeing the cluster of tourists in the lobby, their trunks piled high while the bellhop, a scrawny lad in his early teens, tried to sort out which trunk went to which room. "We don't require meals or a private bath."

"Allow me," said Gillard. Apparently he'd followed her into the lobby. Now he stood to her left, a dominating presence in the noisy room.

"Thank you, but I can take care of this."

"I'm perfectly willing." A grin snaked across his lips. "Mrs. Pollard, send me the bill."

"No, thank you," Mariah reiterated. "I cannot accept your generosity. Agency rules." That much was true.

Gillard shook his head. "That agency of yours ought to pay its agents better."

"I am well provided for," she said stiffly, though the truth was that Mr. Isaacs was barely keeping the agency afloat. She turned her best smile on Mrs. Pollard. "Perhaps you have less spacious rooms."

"That won't be necessary." Hendrick came up on her right and pulled three one-dollar bills from his pocket. "Four for two rooms? Make it one room and two for meals. I have somewhere else to sleep."

Mariah clutched her bag. Dear, wonderful Hendrick, willing to give up his comfort so she and Anna could have a room.

"Two rooms," she insisted as she shoved Hendrick's money out of Mrs. Pollard's reach. "We don't require a view."

Mrs. Pollard frowned as Mariah forced the bills into Hendrick's hand. "Three-fifty is as low as I can go." Her lips curved into a smirk. "We're busy."

"I can see that," Mariah said as she doled out the fee. "Hendrick, could you take the bags to our rooms and get Anna situated? I need to go to the telegraph office."

Gillard stuck out his arm. "Then I will escort you, Miss Mariah."

She saw Hendrick tense. When would those two understand they weren't in competition? "Thank you, but I prefer to walk."

She shut the clasp on her handbag and handed the room keys to Hendrick. After a backward glance at Gillard, he reluctantly escorted his sister upstairs.

"Shall we?" Gillard motioned her toward the front door.

"I told you I wanted to walk. Alone." Could she never shake the man?

He opened the door and held it for her.

She heaved a deliberate sigh and stepped onto the front porch. "Thank you, Mr. Gillard," she said in dismissal.

He paused beside her, not taking the hint. "Sure I can't change your…?" His voice trailed off as something caught his attention.

She followed his line of sight and saw a black Willys sedan parked at the filling station. Talltree was bent over, speaking to the driver.

"Someone you know?" she asked softly.

Gillard's jaw muscles worked. "Judge Weiss."

A judge. Mariah shivered. A judge could demand that she turn Luke over immediately. One look at the botched agency paperwork and the birth certificate, and her case was over.

Talltree returned to the station, and the judge's car started forward.

"I'm afraid I won't be able to walk you to the telegraph office," Gillard said, heading for his car. "I have some unexpected business."

Mariah didn't point out that she didn't want his escort. "What sort of business?" It was an impudent question, but she needed to know if he was pursuing legal action.

"Nothing that concerns you." Without saying goodbye or even tipping his hat, he hopped into his car.

He looked agitated. And focused. He'd honed in on something of vital importance and would let nothing stand in his way. Her niggling worry blossomed into outright fear. He wanted Luke. He'd get him—one way or another.

She pressed a hand to her queasy stomach as spots danced before her eyes. What could she do?

Gillard trailed the judge's car through town. They

both stopped in front of a small, nondescript building two blocks away and then vanished inside.

In her experience, whenever men said their business didn't concern her, it did. There was only one reason Gillard would need to see a judge that instant. He was going to press the law to get Luke. All they had to do was call New York, and Mr. Isaacs would insist that Gabe bring Luke here, even if Hendrick properly conveyed her message. Within minutes, the wheels would be set in motion. She could do only one thing to lessen the pain.

"Mariah?" Hendrick stepped onto the porch beside her. "What's wrong? You look pale." He tried to guide her to the bench, but she shook him off.

She had to place a long-distance telephone call, but not at the hotel with a lobby full of tourists and Mrs. Pollard listening to every word. "I have to go to the telegraph office."

"Now? It's almost five o'clock."

"Then I'll have to hurry." She dashed off the porch and into the dusty street.

Hendrick followed. "At least let me drive you. You'll get there faster."

"I don't have time." She pushed him away, but he grabbed her elbow and pulled her to a halt.

"We're right here, at your car." Hendrick gestured to the passenger door, not five feet away.

Maybe he was right. She gnawed her lip. The car would be faster. She let him help her into the passenger seat. "Hurry."

He then raced around to the driver's side and in seconds had the car rolling down the street. She tried to breathe, but the weight pressing on her chest wouldn't let her take more than little gasps.

"What happened?" he asked again, his expression grim. "What did Gillard say to you?"

She shook her head even as a little sob escaped. Reality was beginning to set in. Gabe and Felicity would lose Luke. They'd be devastated. The shock might send Felicity into premature labor. She could lose the baby—or worse.

"It's all over," she sobbed in shuddering breaths. "I've lost him."

Chapter Fourteen

Secretly, Hendrick was glad Mariah had lost Gillard. The man didn't deserve her. But he had no idea she would take it so hard, nor did he understand what that loss had to do with the urgent need to send a telegram.

Though he offered to go into the office with her, she insisted he wait outside. The car was too hot, so he strolled in front of the building, but the sun reflected off the windows, and he couldn't see inside. A good ten minutes later she exited, looking worn and defeated.

He hurried to open the passenger door while reassuring her. "It will be all right."

Not only didn't she answer, but she took her seat without begging to drive. He closed her door while she sat, clutching her handbag and absently opening and closing the clasp. *Click. Snap. Click. Snap.* Something was really wrong. He got into the driver's seat and reached across to still her hand.

"I'm here for you," he said.

She looked away. "I want to go back to the hotel."

He drove her there and walked with her upstairs. Anna, who'd waited in the lobby, followed. Mariah didn't say a word to her, either. She entered their room and closed the door in Anna's face.

Anna stared at the grimy wooden door that must once have been painted white. "Oh, no." She looked like she'd lost her best friend. Maybe she had.

Hendrick drew her across the hall to his room. "What happened to make Mariah so upset?" he asked. "Did Gillard hurt her?"

"Of course not."

"Then what happened? What did he do?"

"He didn't do anything." Anna sat gingerly on the end of the bed, and the springs squeaked. "I'm afraid it's my fault."

"Yours?" That didn't make any sense. Mariah had said she lost *him.* "I don't think so. She's worried that she lost Gillard."

Anna rolled her eyes. "She's not interested in him."

"She's not?"

"But he's sure trying hard to interest her."

Hendrick was only too aware of that. The man's excessive flattery and attention made him sick. "That doesn't explain why she's upset. You said you think it's your fault. Why?"

Anna colored. "I might have said something I shouldn't have."

"Like what?"

She squirmed on the bed. "I might have mentioned Pastor Gabriel."

Hendrick blinked, trying to piece together why that would upset Mariah. "Did you say he's taking care of Luke?"

"No." Anna bowed her head. "But Mr. Gillard figured it out."

"Oh, Anna." He squeezed his eyes shut. No wonder Mariah was upset. She must have cabled her brother or the agency. She'd asked if he'd called Mr. Isaacs. He ran his fingers through his hair. She hadn't lost Gillard; she'd lost Luke. Trouble was, he had no idea how to help her.

"What're we going to do?" Anna looked stricken.

He sat heavily beside her. "I don't know." He shook his head. "I just don't know."

"If Luke comes here, she might stay."

Anna's words sent a dagger through Hendrick's heart. Why hadn't he thought of that? Gillard was throwing himself at her. With Luke's happiness at stake, she might just capitulate. She *had* said she would only marry a widower.

"You have to romance her," Anna said.

Hendrick felt the heat creep up his neck. "This isn't a dime-store novel. This is real life. I need to solve the problem, not worry about romance. This is serious, Anna."

"Serious-schmerious. A woman doesn't want serious. She wants romance. If you want to stop her from marrying Mr. Gillard, you're going to have to let her know you're the better catch, and that means romancing her."

Romance her? Aside from the fact that Mariah had made it perfectly clear they could only be friends, romance was as foreign to him as a hundred-dollar bill. He supposed it meant flowers and jewelry and fancy words, none of which he could provide. He couldn't compete with Gillard in the romance department, and he sure didn't measure up when it came to money. He didn't have a nice house. He didn't have any house at all. The woman he married would have to move in with his mother and Anna. No woman of Mariah's social standing would settle for that kind of life. Romance her?

It was hopeless, but he had to try.

The telephone call had gone poorly. First, Felicity had answered, and Mariah had to say vaguely that she hadn't finished her business yet. That seemed to satisfy Felicity, and she spent precious minutes chattering about how the baby would be coming soon.

Finally, Gabe dislodged her from the receiver, though Mariah could tell by his clipped responses that Felicity hovered nearby. Mariah had spelled out her failures without naming Luke, in case Felicity could overhear her words. Gabe said he was sorry and asked if there was anything he could do. Did she need him to come west? Bless him for offering, but that was the last thing she wanted. He belonged with his family—especially since that family might be losing a member soon. She did mention her fears that the courts might get involved. He'd sighed and said that could keep her in Brunley for a long time. She had to figure on that.

Between fitful bouts of sleep, she recalled every word spoken over the past couple days, looking for one glint of hope, one fragment that would justify keeping Luke in Pearlman.

By morning she'd found just one: Mr. Sowich's warning. He must know something about Frank Gillard. Something incriminating?

"I'm going to the school this morning," she told Anna as she packed a lunch of crackers and tinned beef.

The girl wiped the sleep from her eyes. "I thought we were touring the park with Mr. Gillard."

"Maybe another day. I'll leave a note for him at the registration desk."

"Then I'm going with you. I promised I'd help in the classroom."

Mariah had forgotten Anna's promise in the hubbub of the past couple days. She'd hoped to walk alone to the school to gather her thoughts, but she couldn't keep the girl from joining her.

After Anna dressed, splashed water on her face and combed her hair, they set out.

"We aren't taking the car?" Anna asked as Mariah walked past the Overland.

At this hour, she hoped to avoid Hendrick, who hadn't yet appeared in the hotel's dining room or lobby. Starting up her automobile would bring him running.

"It's only a mile, and the exercise will do us good." At least it would do her good. She needed to draw the fresh morning air into her lungs. She needed to feel the solid earth beneath her feet. She needed the ache of muscles to go with the ache of her heart.

"But it will be hot by the time we walk back," Anna complained.

The awkward, shy little Anna that Mariah had known two years ago had not only acquired a mind of her own, she'd gotten a touch spoiled. Mariah could understand that. Mothers poured their love into only daughters. Mariah had been just as spoiled when she was young…until the surgery that had altered her future. Life's course could turn in an instant. It did for her. It had for Luke.

They trudged on in silence. Songbirds chirped in the low trees, rising in a cloud when she and Anna got too close. Little poufs of dust rose with every step. The sun angled across their path, setting the grasses afire with dewy diamonds.

The school was busy when they arrived. Children performed their chores under the supervision of the adults. Mr. Sowich hurried out to assure them that classes would begin at eight o'clock.

"I wonder if you could spare a moment to further explain your unique curriculum." Mariah needed to speak with him alone, and an educator liked nothing better than to talk about his work.

Anna yawned. "Where do you want me to help?"

"Miss Meade could use assistance with the youngest girls," Sowich said.

"Is that Constance's class?" Anna asked brightly. "My brother talks about coming to see her all the time."

Sowich frowned. "Tell your brother not to visit. Successful integration of the Indian into American society requires strict adherence to our principles. A visit would undo all our work."

Judging by Anna's scrunched forehead, she neither understood Sowich nor believed him. Mariah stifled a sigh. Mr. Sowich was helping these children to be successful later in life. It might be painful now, but in the long term, they would thank him for their education.

"I believe that's Miss Meade." Mariah pointed out the teacher, who coincidentally led little Constance by the hand. The tiny girl still looked pale and frightened, and for a second Mariah thought how Luke must have felt being left at the orphanage and then taken to a strange town. Maybe returning him to his father was the right thing to do, after all. She shook herself. Constance's case was nothing like Luke's. Luke could not be happier than he was right now. Dislodging him would only bring pain.

Anna called out to Constance, who turned her solemn dark eyes in their direction. Though she was twenty feet away, Mariah caught a glimmer of hope in the girl's eyes before Miss Meade pulled her toward the porch. Anna caught up to them in seconds and chattered away to the little girl, who stuck a dirty hand into her mouth.

Still homesick. Poor thing. Every instinct told her to take the girl home. Only intellect could overcome maternal emotion. That's what she'd have to summon for Luke.

"How long does it take them to get over their homesickness?" she asked Mr. Sowich.

He shrugged. "It's different for every child."

"Constance just got here, then?"

Sowich's expression grew more guarded. "Some months."

"Poor thing, and she's still homesick. When is their next holiday?"

"Holiday?" He stared at her blankly.

"When they go home for a visit."

His mouth twitched. "This is not a traditional boarding school, Miss Meeks. The children live here, like in your orphanages, until they graduate."

A wave of dismay washed through her. "But they're not orphans. And even in the case of orphans, we strive to place our children with foster families as quickly as possible."

Sowich extended an arm, waving her toward his office. "This is an Indian school, Miss Meeks. Our mission is quite different from any other institution."

They mounted the stairs and entered the school building, oppressively hot even at this hour. Sowich guided her through the entry hall and into his office. "Beson Creek School was built in 1884, after the starvation winter. The government knew we had to do something to help the Indians learn a new way of life." He launched into the same soliloquy he'd told her the other day, but this time she observed things she hadn't noticed before.

The paint was cracked and peeling off the interior walls. The floors could use a good sweeping. The stink of the latrines permeated the thick air. The windows were open but didn't have screens, so flies buzzed inside unhindered. She hadn't spied any fans to help move the air, and the children wore dark-colored cotton uniforms that had to make them hot in the summer and cold in the winter. So much more could be done for these children.

"Why haven't any modern conveniences been brought in?" she asked when he finished the history of the school.

Sowich leaned back in his chair, his desktop polished to a high gloss. "Insufficient funding, plain and simple. The school doesn't get much notice in Congress, not when business ventures catch their eye," he said with evident distaste.

"Business ventures?"

"Such as the five-year plan, proposed by reservation superintendent, Frank Campbell, to introduce industrialized agriculture. Or the previous idea to provide each family with cattle. All failures. The latest fad is oil leases."

Mariah sat up a little straighter. "What about oil leases? Mr. Gillard says they will lead to prosperity."

At the mention of Gillard's name, Sowich fidgeted with his fountain pen. "Yes, well, he's correct, in a manner of speaking."

"What exactly do you mean, Mr. Sowich?"

"Not a thing. Not a thing."

He apparently didn't want to talk about Gillard, but she had to find something incriminating about him today. She decided to get straight to the point. "You warned me about Mr. Gillard the day we met. Why?"

He wiped the perspiration from his round face with a handkerchief. "You said you came on personal business. I wondered if perhaps you might be—um, how shall I put this—participating in a business venture."

"Business venture? What sort of business venture?"

Sowich breathed out. "That's a relief. I can tell by your response that you're not involved with him."

Involved? Mariah lifted her eyebrows. "Why are you relieved? He seems quite nice."

Sowich paused, as if contemplating what he should tell her. "He does know how to charm the ladies."

Mariah thought of the lingerie in the bedroom. "What ladies, Mr. Sowich?"

Sowich smiled thinly. "There are always women for men with money."

She could barely spit the word out. "A brothel?"

"I didn't say that. Not at all." He held up his hands.

Frustration set in. Sowich would tell her nothing useful, and if she returned to search the house, all evidence would be gone. Like the wine, Gillard would have disposed of anything incriminating.

"Don't look so disappointed, Miss Meeks."

Mariah forced a smile. "You mistake my expression. I was horrified to think such a thing could exist and pleased to learn it doesn't." But she needed some proof of wrong-doing. "Then if I understand you correctly, you were warning me that Mr. Gillard is not to be trusted in business matters."

He nodded. "But you're obviously not here on business, so what does it matter?"

She couldn't set her concerns aside so easily. "He mentioned something about oil leases. Is that a good business venture?"

Sowich steepled his fingers. "No one has made money off oil leases yet."

"No one? That doesn't make sense. I thought…that is, Mr. Gillard says oil is the means to prosperity. Surely the Blackfeet stand to gain."

"Perhaps, but the lessees will be the real winners."

"Lessees?" The papers on Gillard's desk flashed into her mind. Was that what he was after?

"Entrepreneurs like Hill and Lambert and Sherburne."

"Oh." She didn't know these men, but couldn't help being relieved that he didn't mention Gillard. "I thought the leases would give the Indians financial independence."

Sowich leaned forward. "How many altruistic entrepreneurs have you met?"

"A few." Some of her parents' friends gave freely of their wealth.

"Far more are out to line their own pockets or the wallets of their friends. Unfortunately, it's hard to tell which are which until it's too late."

"Which is Mr. Gillard?" she asked softly.

Rather than answer, Sowich rolled his chair back and hunted in his filing cabinet until he located an old newspaper. He spread the yellowed newsprint in front of her. The headline jumped out at her: Tribal Council to Issue Leases.

She scanned the article, but didn't see Gillard's name mentioned. The names Sowich had mentioned were listed as potential buyers, but most of the article focused on limitations placed by Indian Affairs on the size of the lease and the tribal council's desire to ease the restrictions.

She looked up. "I don't understand."

"It's war, Miss Meeks. No guns or arrows, but it's war all the same. Sides have been chosen. Between the federal government and the tribe as well as inside the tribe. Full-bloods resist white interference. Some mixed-bloods agree with them, but most have teamed with white settlers to oppose the full-bloods. Oil leases are the flashpoint."

That didn't answer her question. "Forgive me, Mr. Sowich, but what does this have to do with Mr. Gillard?"

The director reveled in his superior knowledge. "An unscheduled meeting of the tribal business council was held late yesterday. Apparently, Mr. Gillard was the crux of the discussion."

That's why Gillard had suddenly left her, why he raced after the judge—not to file legal action to get Luke. He didn't mistrust her at all. It was nothing more than a business transaction. Those papers on his desk were probably his application for an oil lease, and the meeting must have been called to grant or deny that lease. But why was it unscheduled?

"Do you know what the discussion was about?" she asked.

He shrugged. "How would I know? I wasn't there."

Sowich might have his guesses, but he apparently wasn't going to tell her what they were. She fidgeted when he drifted back to discussing the curriculum. She needed to talk to someone who was at the meeting, someone like Judge Weiss. Maybe that's what the judge had been discussing with Talltree when Gillard took off after him. If so, Hendrick could get the answer from Talltree.

"Thank you, Mr. Sowich." She stood without waiting for him to finish. "I've taken enough of your time."

If he was shocked at her breach of etiquette, he didn't mention it. The director walked her out and bid her farewell. She barely heard a word. She had her nugget.

By the end of this day, she would have the upper hand on Frank Gillard.

Hendrick could not believe Mariah and Anna had left this morning without telling him where they were going. He learned from Mrs. Pollard they'd taken off on foot. She divulged the information only after he paid for the next night's lodging. That left his pockets empty, and his mind whirling as he went to the garage to work off his frustration. What were they up to?

He had only one answer—Gillard. The man had invited them to tour the national park today. They'd accepted and didn't tell him because they knew he'd object.

They were right. Just thinking about Mariah with Gillard made Hendrick's blood boil. The man was getting to her. After yesterday, she'd stopped talking. She'd slammed the door in Anna's face. And now she was off with Gillard again. Gillard. Even the name tasted rotten. The man had everything Hendrick didn't. He could give her a fancy home, nice clothes and Luke.

Hendrick shook his head as he got to work on the engine. Mariah would never hurt her brother. She adored Gabriel, even mothered him a bit. She'd never take Luke away…unless she had no choice.

Was that why she'd been upset last night? Had she cabled Gabriel that all was lost? Hendrick's gut clenched. Impossible. Yet Anna had hinted that might happen. She'd also said that Mariah might be more interested in Gillard's courtship if Luke was part of the package. She'd insisted he romance Mariah before it was too late. After considering his options, he'd bought a little cake from Mrs. Pollard to share with her at breakfast, but instead it sat on the workbench, its icing drooping in the heat. No doubt Talltree wondered why they didn't eat it, but Hendrick still hoped Mariah would return.

With a groan of frustration, he resumed piecing together the fire pump motor. Motors were simple. They either worked or they didn't. Unfortunately, this one didn't.

He reached for the three-eighths wrench. It was gone.

"Joshua?" Hendrick still felt uncomfortable calling the Indian by his first name.

Not hearing a reply, he looked around and spied a black Willys in front of the building. He'd seen that car yesterday, next to Gillard's Packard across from the telegraph office. Hendrick wondered who owned it and what business its owner had with Frank Gillard.

He stood and spotted Talltree and four other Indians carrying a heavy wooden pallet covered in oilskin. They strained under the weight, so he rushed to open the doors before they got there. The hot midday sun streamed in as the Indians hefted the pallet inside, supervised by a stocky white man in a suit and waistcoat. Though the man's clothing was dusty and his hat well used, he carried himself with the assurance that only money and power brought.

"You must be Hendrick Simmons," the man said, extending a hand. "I'm Judge Weiss, Judge Oscar T. Weiss."

Hendrick grabbed a rag and managed to wipe off most of the grease before shaking the judge's hand. "Pleased to meet you, sir."

A judge. Gillard had met with a judge. Why? Was he pursuing legal action to get Luke? Hendrick gulped. Or was Gillard pressing charges against Mariah and him for trespassing in his office? The judge already knew his name.

Judge Weiss got straight to business. "Talltree here told me you're putting together a pumper motor and needed something with more oomph. Will this work?"

Hendrick's concerns melted away as the men removed the oilskin tarp. Judge Weiss had brought him a straight-six. Hendrick examined the motor. From what he could see, it was in excellent condition. Of course, the cylinders might be scored or the valves frozen. "I'll have to check it over thoroughly, but it looks good. Much better than anything we have here."

"Can you make it work, son?"

Hendrick nodded. "If we can get even eighty percent of this engine's horsepower, we should be able to pump a few hundred gallons per minute."

Satisfied, the judge peeled two fifty-dollar bills from his money clip. "The first fifty's for parts, and the second's for your time. How soon can you have her running? This place is tinder dry. Haven't had a gully-washer in months.

All it'll take is one stroke of lightning, and this town'll go up in a blaze."

Hendrick could see that. The field grass was the color and texture of straw, even at Gillard's house. Gillard. Just thinking of the man made him angry. "Do you know Frank Gillard?"

"Ain't a soul in Brunley outside my acquaintance. 'Course I know Frank Gillard, though I can't say I'm glad I do. Why do you ask?"

Hendrick breathed a sigh of relief. The two men weren't friends. Gillard couldn't have gone to him to try some legal shenanigans. He cast a sideways glance at Talltree and hoped he wasn't betraying a confidence. "Some people don't like him."

The judge grunted. "Most people don't like him."

"But he seems pleasant."

"So does a wolf, son, until he bites your hand off." Judge Weiss patted his pockets until he found his pipe. "If you're the type to take advice, steer clear of him."

"Why?" Hendrick's pulse hammered. That director at the Indian school had said the same thing. "What do you know about him? My, uh, friend is with him."

The judge looked him square in the eye. "Tell your friend to watch his back. Gillard's your best friend as long as you're doing things his way. Challenge him?" Weiss clucked his tongue and shook his head. "It ain't purty, son."

Hendrick's blood ran cold. As soon as Gillard figured out that Mariah wanted to keep him from his son, he'd turn against her. Men who hated to lose would stop at nothing to win. Even murder. Or compromising her.

Hendrick clenched his fists. "I need to find her."

"Her?" Weiss peered at him in surprise. "Your friend's a woman?"

"What woman?" said the familiar voice of the very woman in question.

Mariah stood in the open doorway, as calm and collected as always. Perhaps her cheeks were a bit flushed, but she certainly hadn't been harmed.

Judge Weiss tipped his hat and begged his leave. Talltree vanished into the station office. That left Hendrick alone with her.

"What woman?" she asked again.

"Uh, no one," he hedged. "I wondered where Anna disappeared to."

"She's helping Miss Meade at Beson Creek School. We both had a fulfilling morning."

Hendrick did not want to know what Gillard had done to fulfill Mariah's morning, especially since they'd apparently been alone together on the tour.

"Me, too," he said sullenly.

"So I see." She glanced at the jumble of disassembled motors.

"I'm making a pump motor," he started to explain before noticing she'd braced her hands on her hips. She didn't care what he was doing. She'd come here because she needed something. "What happened?"

"I need your help." Her wide hazel eyes glistened in the afternoon light.

When she looked at him like that, he couldn't resist. "With what?"

"I need you to ask your friend here at the filling station—Mr. Talltree, is it?—about the tribal business council meeting yesterday afternoon."

"The tribal council? Why?"

"I need to find out what they said about Frank Gillard at that meeting."

The buzzing sensation started in his fingers and moved

through the rest of his body. Talltree was a private man, especially wary when it came to talking about his fellow Indians. Hendrick couldn't ask the man to reveal tribal business. "That's prying where we don't belong."

"Just ask. He can always refuse to answer."

Some things he couldn't do—even for her. They were interlopers in Talltree's world. They did not belong here. He certainly wasn't going to pry, especially to find out something about Frank Gillard. "Did Gillard ask you to do this?"

Her hopeful expression collapsed into shock. "What? Why would he do that?"

"Because you two are so close now."

Her jaw tightened. "Is that what you think? All this time together, all we've gone through, and you think I'm falling for him? Honestly, I don't know you anymore, Hendrick Simmons." She trembled, fists clenched, mouth working.

Hendrick's gut double-clutched. He'd made a stupid mistake. He'd let jealousy get the best of him. "I'm sorry."

"Sorry isn't going to help," she cried, "and apparently you aren't going to, either." With that, she stormed out.

In her wake came painful silence. Hendrick stood alone in the garage, his hands stained with engine grease. On the worktable, the last of the icing dripped off the cake.

Chapter Fifteen

Mariah stormed across the street to the hotel. The nerve of that man. One little thing. That's all she wanted. She'd gone to him looking for help, and he'd refused. Refused. Hendrick had never refused her before. What would she do? She had to find out what had happened at that meeting.

By the time she reached the empty hotel lobby, her irritation had eased, but not her restlessness. She couldn't just sit around. Anna wouldn't be back from the school for a couple more hours, and she hadn't spotted Gillard's car in town.

Mrs. Pollard peered at her over her reading spectacles. "Anything I can help you with?"

"Um, no." Mariah scanned the list of tours posted at the desk. All cost money, which she didn't have, but she had to do something, anything. "Is there a library in town?"

"I'm sorry, there isn't."

"Anything else?"

"We got a hiking tour leaving at one," Mrs. Pollard offered.

"No, thank you." Even if she could afford the fee, she didn't need a bunch of chattering tourists with Brownie cameras. She needed…answers.

What had come over Hendrick Simmons? He'd always helped her before. He wasn't acting like himself. First, the jealousy. Second, saying she had no right to know what had happened at the meeting. Why, business council meetings must be public events, reported in the newspapers.

Her eyes widened. The newspaper. That was it.

"Do you have today's paper?" she asked Mrs. Pollard. The woman pointed to a single copy at the end of the registration desk before turning her attention to the leader of the tour. The group thundered down the stairs in their hard-soled boots and pith helmets, clutching binoculars and cameras.

Mariah scanned the headline, but quickly saw that the paper was two days old and from Great Falls. That wouldn't tell her about yesterday's meeting. She needed the local paper. Alas, Mrs. Pollard was surrounded by tourists asking about box lunches and canteens.

She surveyed the lobby, hoping someone had discarded a copy of the local newspaper. By the time she'd finished, empty-handed, the tour had left, so she approached Mrs. Pollard again.

"Do you happen to have the local newspaper?"

Mrs. Pollard didn't look up from her ledger. "Next one comes out Friday. It's a weekly."

Mariah's hopes flagged. Even if she could find a copy of last week's paper, it wouldn't cover yesterday's meeting. She needed another plan. Judge Weiss had been there. If she couldn't get any information from the tribal council or the newspaper, perhaps he could help.

She headed down the dusty street, working off her irritation at one Hendrick Simmons with every determined stride. If he'd asked his friend, she wouldn't have to do this herself.

"Imagine the nerve," she huffed when she reached the building where Gillard had entered with the judge.

No one seemed to be there. She tested the door, which was unlocked, and poked her head inside. The dark room contained rows of chairs and a large table at the front, clearly a meeting room. This must have been where the tribal business council meeting had been held. She let the door slip shut. It could tell her nothing today.

She headed back toward the hotel, hot and sticky but with Sowich's words still ringing in her head. If she could just learn what had happened at that meeting, all her worries would be erased.

"Imagine seeing you here," drawled none other than Frank Gillard, who fell in step with her.

"Not as unusual as seeing you." She tried to hide her displeasure. "Your house, after all, is seventeen miles from town, whereas I'm staying at the Mountain View."

He doffed his hat. "Right you are. I had business in town and happened to see you. I had to say hello."

"Business?" His words made her wonder if she dare ask him about that vital meeting. If she took care to hide her emotions, maybe she could pull it off. "Do you have an office in town?"

If he guessed the reason behind the question, he didn't let it stop him from answering. "My office is at the ranch. I come to town to send telegrams, collect the post and place telephone calls. When I get wire laid to my ranch, even that won't be necessary. But surely you don't want to hear the boring details of my business."

"Actually, I'd love to learn more about your business. I know nothing about ranching other than what I've read in novels. Cattle drives and cowboys and riding the fences."

He laughed. "As you've seen, there aren't any fences on

the reservation. The cattle range free, and we round them up before we take them to slaughter."

"Just as in the novels?"

He nodded. "But times are changing for the better."

"Oh? Is that what your meeting yesterday was about?"

He didn't even flinch. "Exactly. If my bid goes through, things will change around here." He leaned closer. "We'll have schools and hospitals and libraries. Every convenience of modern society. Progress is coming to Brunley." He smiled with satisfaction. "It'll be the perfect place for Luke to grow up."

"But you live so far from town," she pointed out, unwilling to accept that she'd lost.

"Is that what's holding up your decision? If it is, I'll build a house in town. I'll do whatever you require to bring Luke home."

She couldn't look at him, lest he see how disappointed she was. The meeting had been nothing. It wouldn't help her keep Luke in Pearlman, and she had no other options.

"Forgive me." She hurried her step. Heartache threatened to overflow into tears. "I need to return to the hotel."

He caught her hand and pulled her to a stop. "You love Luke, don't you?"

She couldn't look at him. "I need to go." She tugged away and stumbled backward into the dusty street.

"Watch your step." He caught and steadied her, but his touch didn't send that electric feeling zinging through her as Hendrick's did. "You do love Luke. It all makes sense now. The time you spent with my son made you feel like his mother." He ran a finger down her chin. "What a fine mother you'd make."

Oh, he was cruel, tempting her with the deepest, most selfish desires of her heart. She tried to pull away, tears on the brink now, but he didn't let go.

"I had a thought last night," he said. "It might be a crazy idea, but knowing the way you love Luke, maybe you'd consider it. Stay here. Help him adjust. There's no reason you have to leave."

She gasped, hand to her mouth. Stay? Be with Luke? It was horribly tempting, but that would mean the end of Gabe and Felicity's dream. "I—I can't."

"Luke will need someone he trusts, someone who loves him."

She ducked her face, torn by conflicting emotions. "It wouldn't be proper for me to stay in your house," she protested weakly.

He barked a short laugh. "That might be a problem in New York, but out here, we do what we have to. You've seen my staff. You wouldn't be alone."

True, but it was still improper. "I shouldn't."

"I'll hire you, then. You can be his teacher, tutor, governess, nanny, whatever you want to call it."

At a glance, it seemed like that might be the best solution to a terrible situation. If Luke had to come to Brunley and stay with a man like Gillard, he'd need someone he trusted to look out for him and protect him. Maybe her involvement would even help Gabe and Felicity accept their loss.

He waited with his hat in his hand. "You don't need to give me an answer now. Think about it overnight, and let me know tomorrow when we tour the park. I'll pick you up at eight in the morning." He didn't ask if she wanted to tour the park with him, but she was too overwrought to argue.

"Tomorrow." She had the rest of the day to figure out what she was going to do.

Hendrick saw Mariah with *him*. Gillard watched her poke her head into the tribal council building and then joined her the moment she headed back this way. She was clearly agitated, but that man would not let her go. He hounded her and even blocked her path. Any decent man would know when to quit, but then, Gillard wasn't decent, was he?

Hendrick's stomach churned as he strode out the filling station door. With the Indians' help, he'd gotten the pump mounted on the old fire engine, and they'd taken it to the creek to test it. He should be following, but he couldn't let Mariah fall victim to that snake.

He saw Gillard glance briefly in his direction before touching a finger to her chin. Then Mariah stopped trying to get away. Her hands pressed to her cheeks as her mouth dropped open. Gillard must have promised her the moon, but his promises were fool's gold. Why couldn't she see he was deceiving her?

"Think about it overnight, and let me know tomorrow..."

Hendrick froze. The only time a man was willing to let a woman think over a proposition was when that proposition was for marriage. No! The revulsion tore through him with the force of a tornado. She couldn't marry Gillard.

"Tomorrow," she said, giving that snake such a vulnerable smile that it cracked Hendrick's heart in two.

He had to prevent this, not just because he loved her but for her own sake. A life with Gillard would break her spirit. That man didn't want a lively filly; he wanted a broken mare. He'd tether Mariah to that ranch until she went mad. She'd be little more than a servant. A person only had to look at how a man treated the less fortunate to know his true character. Gillard didn't even call his housekeeper by name. His staff cowered before him. If Mariah married him, soon she would, too.

Fists clenched, Hendrick hurried toward her. Gillard flashed him a confident grin and sauntered to his car. She hadn't said yes, had she? Hendrick hadn't heard it, but then he couldn't see her face.

He quickly closed the gap. "Mariah. I'm sorry for earlier."

She shot him an indecipherable look before hurrying toward the hotel.

"Mariah, wait."

She walked faster.

He matched her stride. "There's something you need to know about Frank Gillard. He's not what he claims to be."

"What do you mean?"

He caught his breath. She was going to listen. "He got his ranch by bilking the Indians out of their land."

Her hopeful look disappeared, and she wiped a tear from beneath her eye. "That won't help. It's not enough."

"But don't you want to know who he really is?"

"I know who he is. He's Luke's father." She gripped his shirt, her voice low and desperate. "Hearsay won't help. I need something more, something that would disqualify him for claiming Luke."

"That wouldn't? It's a crime, isn't it?"

She dropped her hands. "If it was, he'd already be charged, wouldn't he?"

He grasped at straws. "Wouldn't character references count for anything? Can't you use that to deny placement?"

She shook her head, eyes hollow with despair. "I have no real power to keep Luke away. Gillard has all the rights.

He c-can take him anytime." Her voice broke, and she ran into the hotel.

Hendrick crushed his cap in his hands. He had to help, but how?

The hotel room was deathly quiet, but Mariah's heart still pounded as loud as a sledgehammer against stone. Everyone was pulling her every which way. Gillard wanted one thing, and Hendrick wanted another. Gabe and Felicity loved Luke. Did Gillard? According to the law, it didn't matter. Gillard was Luke's father. He had the birth certificate. Luke must come west.

Her head ached.

She went to the washroom and splashed water on her face to cleanse the dust from her skin. If only she could wash away the layers of deception so easily. What should she do?

She patted her face dry and looked in the mirror. A little redness puffed her eyes, but not enough to notice.

"Should I?" She sighed, thinking of Frank's idea.

Working with Luke would help him as well as Gabe and Felicity, but she'd be bringing both Luke and herself into a situation that just felt wrong. They didn't belong here. For all Gillard's wealth and fine manners, something wasn't right about the man.

"What should I do, Lord?"

The best place to find answers, in her experience, was the Bible. She pulled out her worn copy and leafed through the annotated and dog-eared pages.

Normally, Mariah read from her Bible every day, but on this trip she'd fallen out of the habit. Perhaps if she'd been reading faithfully and lifting her concerns to God each day, she would have heard His direction clearly, instead of wallowing in this muddled confusion.

A passage in Matthew caught her eye. *You will know them by their fruits.* She'd always understood that passage to mean that people's actions spoke louder than their words, that the works of their hands meant more than idle promises. Christians bore fruit or were cut from the vine. But how did that verse apply to this situation? What fruits? And whose?

She shut her eyes and lifted her confusion to God in prayer. "Please tell me what to do, Lord," she whispered, knowing she must give the situation over to Him, yet afraid of His answer.

Mrs. Pollard turned out to be a romantic. When Anna insisted that a picnic supper was the ideal way to capture Mariah's heart, Mrs. Pollard supplied a small folding table and chairs as well as a white tablecloth, china and silverware. Two dollars bought a full chicken dinner, packed into a basket so Hendrick could drive to the perfect location, which she also supplied.

"She said that it's next to a pretty stream," Anna relayed, "not far from the road about five miles that way." She pointed toward the mountains.

Hendrick was skeptical. The nearby creek was low, certainly not a full-fledged stream, and the blazing sun would make a picnic torturous.

"Even if it is nice," he said, "how do I get her to go?"

"Simple. We'll all go together, and then after we eat, I'll make some excuse to go off somewhere while you and Mariah talk." She shoved a book into his hands. "I suggest you read poetry to her."

"Aloud?"

"She's not going to hear you if you read to yourself, is she? Of course, aloud."

If only he could impress her with something more comfortable, like fixing her car or driving her somewhere, but apparently women found none of that the slightest bit romantic.

"All right," he grudgingly agreed. If humiliating himself would save her from Gillard, he'd do it.

Mariah tried to beg off with a headache, but she was hungry. When Anna insisted that food would help clear her head and Mariah smelled the fried chicken, she accepted. They'd all be together, after all.

Hendrick solemnly took off his cap when she approached and clutched it to his chest. "I'm sorry. I was wrong."

His boyish abashed smile melted her heart. "Me, too. Friends?" She stuck out a hand.

He hesitated but shook it.

With that out of the way, he helped her into the Overland. The whole thing was awkward, from the way he hovered over her to his apologies for slamming the door too hard. Then, before starting the car, mortification colored his face. "I should have asked if you wanted to drive."

She could have echoed Anna's groans, but settled for a polite response. "I don't know where we're going."

His oversolicitous awkwardness crumbled into a shy smile. "Mrs. Pollard says it's pretty there."

"Mrs. Pollard, eh? I imagine she knows the area inside and out." She settled back in the seat. "Where are we going, or is it a surprise?"

Anna bounced in the backseat. "Joshua says it's where all the Indian guys take their gals."

"Joshua?" Mariah turned to Anna. "You have a guy?"

Anna blushed. "He's just a friend."

"Joshua Talltree," Hendrick explained. "From the filling station. Good man." Though he shot his sister a warning glance.

Mariah smiled to herself. Hendrick couldn't help being the protective older brother. She supposed it was natural, since he'd practically raised Anna. The eight-year age difference meant she was just seven when their father died. At fifteen, he'd taken charge of the business and the family.

Hendrick drove the car out of town toward the mountains. A thrill ran through Mariah at the sight of the tall peaks. A few still had traces of snow near the top. They couldn't possibly be going into the mountains. Gillard said no roads ran west through the park. The nearest way to get across the Continental Divide was to take the Great Northern Railway over Marias Pass.

Before long, the dry hills grew steeper. After a particularly long ascent, they descended into a fertile valley shaded by trees. Mariah breathed in the cooler air, relishing the relief from the heat.

"It must be near here." Hendrick slowed the car, and everyone hunted for the famed picnic spot.

Undergrowth made picnicking impossible almost everywhere. When Anna pointed out a passable location, Hendrick vetoed it.

"That can't be it," he said.

"What if it was?" she countered.

Mariah laughed at their sibling rivalry. "We'll be in Canada before long."

"Not heading in this direction," he groused.

"There it is." Anna pointed to their right, where a lazy river wound past, its surface dappled by sunlight.

Mariah drew in her breath. Compared to the hot town and prairie, this was blissful, serene and almost like...

"It looks like Pearlman," she said.

"No, it doesn't," Anna contradicted at once.

But Hendrick said nothing. His experienced eyes must

have seen what she did, a river so similar to Pearlman's that it felt like home.

He pulled off the road and stopped the car. Anna immediately flung open her door and hopped out.

"It's beautiful," Mariah breathed.

Anna ran to the water where she yanked off her shoes and stockings and dipped her feet. "Yikes, it's freezing." But she didn't get out of the water.

"Youngsters." Hendrick sighed, sounding so much more mature than his years. Though a few years younger than Mariah was, Hendrick was so worldly-wise that he seemed older.

She closed her eyes and listened to the birds chirp and the wind rustle the leaves. After all the frustration and confusion, she needed this peace, this sense that God had created the trees around her, that He could be felt in every leaf and blade of grass and drop of water.

"I could stay here forever." She sighed as she heard her door latch click and felt the breeze against her arm. Hendrick must have swung open the door.

"No hurry," he said softly, his voice thick with emotion. "I'll set up the table."

She shook her head and opened her eyes. The peaceful moment had passed.

"May I?" He extended his hand to help her from the car.

Though he was trying too hard, she gave him her hand. It looked so small and white against his.

"I scrubbed as hard as I could," he apologized.

Only then did she notice the stains of his profession. From her own tinkering, she knew that engine grease was impossible to wash off completely. Truly, that didn't matter. She smiled, and he looked at her so hopefully that her heart broke. How he must care for her. Yet he did not push for her to feel the same way. Unconditional, yet impossible.

"Thank you." She hazarded a glance at his eyes, warm and soft in the sunlight. It was a fatal mistake, for she saw in them the love he'd harbored for her these past two years. As far as he knew, that love was unrequited. It had to stay that way.

She withdrew her hand. "I think I'll soak my feet, too." Without waiting for a response, she headed for the river.

The excuse was easy. Seeing his hopes dashed wasn't. She wanted to say she was sorry. She wanted to rest in his strong arms and create that future he so desired, but it couldn't be.

Here, by this peaceful river, she knew what she must do. Luke's needs mattered most. She must stay.

Hendrick caught Mariah smiling at him so often that he was sure she'd forgiven him for that jealous outburst. Now that the heat of anger had died, he recognized his reaction for what it was. Gillard was trying to win Mariah's heart, a heart Hendrick desperately wanted. But it wasn't Hendrick's to claim. Mariah could bestow it on whomever she chose, even Gillard.

She didn't tell him if she planned to accept the man's proposal, and he didn't bring it up. Better to enjoy one last meal together. So he sat across the folding table from her and memorized every curve of her face, the way the light danced off her curls, the strength of her jaw and the brightness of her light hazel eyes.

"Mrs. Pollard is a good cook," Mariah said after they'd finished the berry pie and sat drinking coffee from real china cups. They didn't match exactly and the rims were chipped, but it was better than a tin cup or straight out of the vacuum bottle.

Anna excused herself and returned to the river.

Hendrick watched her wade into the water. "Not too far," he cautioned. This was probably her way of leaving him and Mariah alone, which didn't seem like such a good idea anymore.

Mariah glanced at Anna. "Oh, she's fine. The stream's no more than knee-deep."

That wasn't the problem, but he couldn't very well tell Mariah that he was nervous being alone with her. Too many times over the past two years he'd dreamt of this moment. He always wondered if he'd have another chance, but he didn't expect it to be a last chance. If he didn't win her today, he'd truly lose her.

The moment had arrived, and he had no idea what to do. What would capture her heart? A brilliant thought? Wit? Humor? He wasn't good at any of those.

He lifted the vacuum bottle and swished the remaining liquid. Perhaps one cup remained. "Want some more coffee?" What a stupid thing to say.

Still, she smiled at him. "Oh, no, I couldn't eat or drink another thing." Her eyes softened, and she placed her hand lightly on his. "Thank you, Hendrick. This must have cost a lot. I'll pay you back."

Though her hand sent a hum of electricity through him, her words snapped it off. Why did it always come back to money? Yes, compared to her, he was poor, but that didn't make him any less of a man. He'd made his own way in this world, and he could pay for a picnic dinner if he wanted to.

"That's not necessary. Judge Weiss paid for my work on the fire pump." He omitted that it was fifty dollars. To her, that would be nothing.

Her eyes widened. "You've been working on a fire pump?"

He'd told her that earlier, but she hadn't been listening. Still, she looked interested now.

"All they had was an old hand-pumper," he explained, relieved to talk about something familiar and impersonal. "It wouldn't put out a grass fire. Joshua Talltree and some of his pals have been helping me motorize it." He shrugged. "I just wanted to keep busy."

Her smile could melt the hardest heart. "Oh, Hendrick, that's so thoughtful."

"It needed to be done." He stared into his cup of coffee, not sure what to say next.

She didn't speak, either.

He glanced at the river. Anna had wandered downstream a little, but she was still within sight—and earshot. Probably waiting for him to embarrass himself reading poetry. The little book weighed down his trouser pocket. He supposed he'd have to take a stab at it, if only to please Anna.

He slipped the slim volume from his pocket. "I, uh, thought I'd read a little from this book." He didn't dare look up. No doubt she was laughing.

"That would be wonderful." She didn't sound like she was laughing. In fact, she sounded delighted.

His eyes met hers, and for an instant he forgot what he intended to do. The sun brought out the green in the hazel, making her eyes sparkle like drops of morning dew.

"Who is the author?" she asked softly, waking him from his reverie.

He glanced at the spine. "Oh, uh, Tennyson."

"I love Tennyson. Perfect for a day like this."

She leaned back in her chair, and he struggled to turn the little pages. His fingers were rough, and the pages stuck together and then flipped back before he could get them separated. At this rate, he wouldn't get a word out before nightfall.

Finally, he found the opening page and stammered out the first line. Poetry. He had no idea how to read poetry. No doubt he sounded like a fool, but Mariah didn't stop him. He plodded through line after torturous line until at last the thing was done.

"Bravo!" she exclaimed and clapped far too loudly.

He felt the heat rise to his face. "That wasn't very good."

She leaned toward him, a gentle smile curving her lips. "It was wonderful and totally unexpected." Tears welled in her eyes. "I am so honored." Her lips were full and red and so beautiful he could hardly stand it.

"Thank you."

He wanted to kiss her, to hold her close and smell her hair and feel her soft skin. He wanted to gaze at the stars like that night at Gillard's ranch and know without a doubt that they were meant for each other. He wanted above all to tell her how he really felt, that he would go to the ends of the earth for her, that he would do anything for her.

But she'd set her heart on Gillard.

Unless she hadn't given her answer yet. The man said something about tomorrow morning. Maybe Hendrick still had one last chance. Well, he'd take it. No holding back. Even if she chose Gillard, she deserved to know how he felt.

Hendrick Simmons didn't speak of love through poetry. He said it straight, clear and unmistakable. "I love you, Mariah."

Her eyelids flickered in panic. "Hendrick—"

He wouldn't let her cut him off this time. "I've always loved you, from the moment I first saw you drive into town in your Overland. So confident and certain of what you wanted. I've never met anyone like you." Though her expression grew more stricken with every word, he pressed on. "I would love you forever. I don't have a fancy car or a big house like other men, and I can't give you everything you deserve—"

"Stop, please." She pushed away from the table. When she stood, her chair toppled over and her napkin fell to the ground. "It can never be." She clutched a hand to her throat, her chest rising and falling rapidly.

He stood. "Mariah. I love you."

"Stop, oh, stop," she cried, flailing her arms though he hadn't even touched her. "I told you we could never be more than friends." Her voice came out ragged, and it killed him not to hold her.

"I know I'm not wealthy or educated."

"It has nothing to do with money or education." She hugged her arms, shaking.

"Then why?"

She sobbed once, a quick heave before regaining her composure. But when she looked up at him, his heart sank. "Because I can't have children." The words fell like bricks. "Ever."

No children? His mind reeled. He'd always hoped for a family, dreamed of raising children. Boys or girls. It didn't matter, as long as there were lots of them. A houseful. Children had been the most important thing to Pa. How often he'd told Hendrick that he was glad he'd had a son to carry on the family name. No children?

"Are you sure?"

She nodded, unable to look at him. "The doctors… confirmed it. I had surgery when I was Anna's age. They found tumors…and took everything." Her shoulders shook as she forced out the last painful words. "It's impossible."

She was hurting, and he knew he should hold her, but

his world had just shattered. She couldn't give him the one thing he most wanted. No wonder she'd said she wanted to marry a widower. No wonder she'd brushed him aside over and over.

"I knew I should tell you," she whispered, "but I..." Her voice trailed off.

He reached out to comfort her, but his hand trembled. He let it drop. He shouldn't hold her if he couldn't promise her a lifetime together. And now they both knew that was impossible.

He had to go somewhere. He had to take it all in, not here, far from all he knew and loved. He had to leave.

"I'm sorry," he whispered, backing away. "I have to go."

Only this time, it would be forever.

Chapter Sixteen

Mariah pressed a hand to her mouth to stifle the sob that threatened to break loose. Hendrick had reacted exactly the way she'd thought he would, but she'd never imagined it would hurt so much.

Any hope of a life together was over, and she realized now that she had clung to that hope more than she wanted to believe. She did love him, and that meant breaking it off now, before she gave her answer to Gillard, before Hendrick learned she was staying. At least he would have a chance to love again.

The drive home was painful. Only Anna spoke, chattering away about fish and birds and whatnot. Mariah barely heard a word she said. Hendrick kept up a stoic facade, but she could tell he was hurting. Oh, he acted the gentleman, but not one word of substantial conversation passed his lips.

Once they arrived at the hotel, Mariah excused herself, claiming she needed to rest. In truth, she needed to get away before she fell apart. Only when she reached the sanctuary of her room did she allow the sobs to wring out. She would never forget his expression. Surprise followed by disbelief and then resignation as the truth sank in. He didn't bother to brush aside the curl that drooped across his brow. His warm brown eyes grew cold. His hope shriveled.

She'd done it. Over and over she stabbed herself with the memory, weeping for all that had been lost and all that would never be.

Suddenly the door burst open.

Mariah lifted her tear-dampened face to see Anna.

"He's taking the first train home," Anna announced, oblivious to Mariah's distress. She slammed the door shut. "How could you?"

He'd told her. Mariah traced the squares on the checked coverlet. "Nothing has changed since two years ago."

"You have. You're cold and unfeeling and, and...I hate you." With the black certainty of youth, Anna flung open the door. The knob banged against the wall. "I can't believe I wanted you to be my sister." A sob escaped. "I used to look up to you. I thought you were so smart, but you're as bad as the rest of those snobs."

Mariah flinched. She'd never considered herself arrogant. Was that how Anna saw her? "I'm sorry I hurt your brother."

"No, you're not. You're not sorry about anything. It's all about what you want. You think you know what's best for everyone. You think you're helping Luke, but you never even asked what he wants."

"He's a child."

"He's ten years old. He knows what he wants. He remembers his father, and he remembers being left at the orphanage."

"How do you know?" Mariah asked. "Luke never talks about his past."

"He talks to Peter. He tells him everything, even how scared he was that that man would hurt him. If you'd just asked, you'd know how Luke felt, but you didn't, did you? You just assumed that what you wanted was best for him."

Two words burrowed into Mariah's brain. "What man is he afraid of? His father?"

Anna shook her head. "He loved his father. No, someone else who hurt him."

"Who, Anna?" Mariah wanted to shake her. "This is important."

"He doesn't know the man's name, but he'd know him if he saw him."

Mariah squeezed her eyes shut. Another dead end. Her fate was sealed. If Luke had feared his father, she might have been able to bring that to the courts, but an anonymous man? That didn't help one bit.

"Please tell your brother that I'm sorry I hurt him," she said softly, "and that I won't be returning to Pearlman."

"Good. We don't want you there. We're tired of being at your beck and call." Anna tossed her head, but her quivering lips betrayed her. "Hendrick is checking the train schedule, and I'm going with him." She spun out of the room, slamming the door behind her.

The reverberations echoed deep into Mariah's soul. She hadn't used Hendrick and Anna, had she? They'd wanted to join her. Gabe had insisted they go. She would have driven to Montana by herself. They were in no way obligated to come along. She'd paid their way.

No, she hadn't used them. But if she was truthful with herself, she had to admit that she'd let Hendrick believe she cared for him. She'd let him kiss her.

Of that, she was guilty.

"First train heading east is Friday at twelve-thirty," the Great Northern Railway agent stated. "You'll need to change at Shelby and Slayton, where, if you're lucky, you can catch the Chicago, Milwaukee and St. Paul east-bound."

Hendrick heard the details, but he couldn't concentrate on them. Mariah couldn't have children. No wonder she'd devoted her life to the orphans. They were her children, but that wasn't enough for him. He wanted little ones of his own, babies in his arms. He wanted to experience the miracle of creation and know he'd been part of it. From the moment he'd first seen Mariah, he'd imagined them together, holding their first child, touching the tiny toes and marveling over a new life. He couldn't give that up.

"Do you want to purchase tickets now?" the agent asked.

"Huh?" Hendrick shook his head. "Friday, you said? Are you sure that's the first train?"

The man grumbled, "Of course I'm sure. It's my job."

"Sorry. It's just that I'm anxious to get home." He'd say goodbye to Ma and head east to Curtiss Aeroplane. He couldn't stay in Pearlman where everyone would whisper that Mariah had rejected him again. He needed a new city and a new start as an aviation engineer.

"I told her how I felt." Anna bounded to his side while he pulled out the bills to pay the fare. "I'm going with you."

That would leave Mariah alone in Brunley, but Hendrick had a feeling that's exactly where she intended to stay.

"Tickets for two, then." He handed the agent the fare before asking his sister what Mariah had said.

Anna shrugged. "What could she say? That she was sorry she hurt you, blah, blah, blah. But she didn't mean it. She wouldn't even look at me."

Hendrick thought he couldn't hurt anymore, but Anna's words drove the last spike into his heart. If Mariah wouldn't look at his sister, then her mind was settled on Gillard. He felt like vomiting.

"She still thinks she's doing the right thing, that she's the almighty judge of everyone's life," Anna continued.

Hendrick squeezed his eyes shut. "Stop, please."

"Why?"

He steeled his jaw. "I won't hear anything bad about Mariah. She's a good and honorable woman. It just didn't work out between us. That's not her fault." He breathed out, hoping to expel a little of the pain. "It's my fault for pushing even after she told me to stop."

He clutched the train tickets. Soon he'd leave Mariah behind forever, but not the pain. No, that wouldn't disappear for a long, long time.

Mariah pretended to sleep when Anna returned to the room after dark, but her mind wouldn't rest. She had to accept the position with Frank Gillard, didn't she? It made sense. She couldn't keep Luke from his father. He'd need her to make the transition.

Then why did she feel so awful? Hendrick Simmons stirred her soul. This decision would be much easier if she didn't love him. But she did. She did.

Though she tossed and turned all night, when morning dawned clear and warm, she acted decisively. She dressed for touring, in a simple split skirt and blouse. Breakfast being out of the question, she packed crackers for later and stepped out of the hotel to meet Frank Gillard.

Anna had slept through her preparations, but Hendrick was already at the garage. She could see him with a handful of locals gathered around the fire engine. His sleeves were rolled up and his hands dirty, the hands of a workingman who would provide for his family. A good, honest man of the highest integrity. She choked back a sob as Frank Gillard's blue Packard approached.

The time had arrived.

Hendrick glanced up, spotted her and Gillard's car and looked down just as quickly. She bit the inside of her lip until it bled, but the pain could never rival his. She wished above all that she could have done this without hurting him again.

Gillard jumped out of the car. "Ready?"

She dragged her attention away from Hendrick. Gillard held the passenger door open. "I thought we had to travel by horse to get into the park."

"We'll drive to East Glacier and take horses from there." He helped her into the passenger seat before hopping behind the wheel. "I keep a pair in a stable near the big hotel. Have you seen it? The beams are made out of huge trees."

Her mind wandered while he talked about the hotel and the park. She'd half expected him to demand an answer the moment he picked her up, but he smiled and talked as if he already knew what she would say.

Still, her stomach knotted tighter and tighter as they got closer to the mountains. She squeezed her eyes shut when they reached the switchbacks so she wouldn't see how close they came to the precipitous drop-offs.

"You can open your eyes now," he finally announced, gliding the car to a stop before a large stable. "We're here."

She gladly got out of the car. A hot wind swirled through the dusty stable yard, raising clouds of fine silt. Two horses awaited them, a bay and a painted mare. Though a groom stood by, Gillard helped her onto the paint before mounting the bay. He tipped the groom, and they took off.

"It's a short ride to my favorite spot," he said. "About an hour."

For the first part of the trip, they rode side by side while Gillard pointed out the peaks of the Continental Divide and the cut where the Great Northern Railway went through Marias Pass.

"Only way across the Rockies for a couple hundred miles," he said, "unless you cross on horseback. One day they'll build the road through, but now, you have to put your car on the train to get across."

She pretended to be interested, but all she could think about was if Hendrick and Anna had boarded the train yet. Would she return tonight to find them gone? The cowardly part of her hoped she would, and the aching part of her hoped she'd have one more chance to make amends.

Gillard didn't notice her distraction and continued to talk about the park. "The Great Northern Railway built the lodges and chalets a day's ride apart, so tourists can travel deep into the park. The most stunning peaks are north, but we don't have enough time for that today." He smiled at her beneath the wide brim of his cowboy hat. "Luke needs to see this. It's his heritage and his inheritance."

Again, Mariah recalled the birth record she'd seen on Gillard's desk. Luke was half-Indian, mixed-blood. Did Luke know? Is that why he'd been so ashamed by the racial slurs flung at him two years ago? She still cringed at the rancor of that day. Thank God Gabe had taken Luke into his home. Thank God Luke responded to Gabe's love. She'd been Gabe's housekeeper at the time and had scolded her brother for taking on the added responsibility when he was just starting his ministry, but within days the boy had won her heart. Over the following weeks, she'd watched him blossom from a mute, terrified orphan into an outgoing, beloved son. Now he would have to go through that process all over again.

For the next fifteen minutes, they ascended single file up a narrow trail through a spruce forest. Mariah had to squeeze her knees into the mare's sides to keep her seat. She hadn't ridden a horse in years, and it showed.

"Are we almost there?" she wheezed, breathing harder.

"Take long, slow breaths," he said. "The air is thinner up here."

"Also cooler." She was glad she had a sweater with her.

After more switchbacks than she could count, they at last came into a field strewn with wildflowers in every imaginable hue. Before them rose the mountains, their peaks lightly dusted with the remnants of last winter's snow. Far below, a turquoise-colored lake glistened like a gemstone. The sheer beauty left her speechless. God's creation spread before her in all its majesty. Inspired, she sang a couple lines of "For the Beauty of the Earth."

"What's that tune?" Gillard asked as he helped her dismount.

Who didn't know that cherished hymn? "Surely you've heard it in church before."

He lifted an eyebrow. "In case you didn't notice, there aren't many churches in these parts."

"There's a very nice one in town."

He shrugged. "I'm not much of a singer."

"You said you'd bring Luke to church."

His mouth curved. "Of course. Do you want to eat our lunch or sightsee?"

Though he'd answered her in the affirmative, Mariah couldn't shake the sense of dread. Something was wrong, off-kilter. It must be fatigue. She hadn't slept much last night. She was overwrought. Nothing a little rest—or a good meal—wouldn't cure.

"Let's eat," she decided.

Compared to her paltry crackers, Gillard laid out a feast on the flat rock overlooking the valley. Roast-beef sandwiches with mustard on fresh bread. On any other day, she would have savored the flavors, but today everything tasted like paste. Must be nerves. Once she gave Gillard her answer, she'd feel better.

"I thought over your proposal," she began, shifting to a flatter spot on the rock. Flies buzzed around them, drawn by the food.

He lifted a hand. "Let me speak first."

Though he sat close, the sun from behind cast his face in shadow. She had to squint and pull her hat low to make out his features.

"Do you believe in fate?" he asked.

"I believe in God's plan."

"Same thing. Over the last few days, I couldn't help thinking that fate had intervened. At first I was annoyed at the delay." He laughed. "I thought you were trying to keep my son from me."

She smiled wanly.

"Then I got to really know you, and I realized you were perfect."

"Perfect for what?" Mariah tensed. This was beginning to sound like a repeat of yesterday, except this time she felt nothing for the man. If Frank Gillard had fallen in love, it definitely was not reciprocal.

"Perfect for me, we're perfect for each other. Surely you feel it, too. Our lives have been intertwined for years, even though we didn't know it. We both love Luke. We both want what's best for him."

Did they? Anna's accusations rang in her ears. Before yesterday, Mariah had been so sure of herself. Not now. Neither one of them had asked Luke what he wanted.

"What *is* best for Luke?" she asked softly.

"A family," he said without hesitation. "A mother and a father."

"He has that," she pointed out. "My brother and his wife adore Luke."

"I'm sure they do, but your brother is not Luke's father."

Mariah thought back two years to when Felicity discovered that she'd been adopted. The news had shocked her deeply, but in the end she'd realized that her true father was the man who had loved her and raised her. If that was the measure of fatherhood, then Gabe was much more of a father to Luke than Gillard was.

"Fathers come in many forms," she said.

He ignored her. "This will all be Luke's one day." He spread his arms wide. "He will inherit my ranch and its three thousand acres. He will grow up free as the wind. He will look to the mountains and know their power. He will *be* someone."

"He already is someone."

"Of course, but with the love of a mother and father and the inheritance I'll leave him, he will become all he's meant to be." Gillard took her hand. "He needs you." His voice had grown thick, and she instinctively recoiled.

"I will be his nanny," she blurted out. "I'll help him make the transition to his new life. It's the least I can do."

"But not the most. I love you, Mariah."

She shuddered.

"I know it's only been a short time," he said, his smile too practiced, "but life moves quickly on the frontier. You would be the perfect mother for my son. Just think. You'd never have to leave him."

He ran his lips down her hand to her wrist, and a cold chill shook her. This was wrong, terribly wrong. Her chest tightened so she could barely take a breath. She tugged her hand away.

"I'm sorry, Mr. Gillard, but I don't feel the same way." To be safe, she slid a short distance away from him.

"I don't understand. Why settle for being a nanny when you can be a wife?" His proprietary air did nothing to settle her nerves.

Gillard collected whatever caught his eye, and that now included her. He saw her as a conquest, a trophy to capture. Was that how all the staff had come to his ranch? Were they lured there, bought, forced? If she married him, she would be forced to submit. Her breath caught in her throat.

"I can't have children," she cried when he reached for her.

He laughed. "Is that what's stopping you from accepting? I have Luke. I don't care about any other children."

Shocked, she backed away. What man didn't want children, especially when he was so desperate to get his son? "A-are you sure?"

He tipped up her chin, as if to kiss her. "Yes, I'm sure."

She felt ill. This had to stop now. She shook away. "I'm sorry. I'll work for you as nanny, but that's all. Please understand. I can't marry without love, and I don't love you."

He watched her, considering. The man betrayed no emotion. Hendrick had been devastated when she turned him down, but Gillard seemed to feel nothing.

At last he shrugged. "Fair enough." Then he grinned. "I had to try, though. No hard feelings?"

He'd recovered awfully fast. Though relieved, Mariah also grew more concerned. What had she gotten herself into? Nonetheless, she nodded. "No hard feelings."

"Wonderful. How soon until Luke arrives?"

What could she say? After rejecting his proposal,

should she dare to ask for more concessions? Though he might refuse, she had to try. "Could we wait a couple of weeks?"

His gaze narrowed. "A couple of weeks? Why?"

"My sister-in-law is due to deliver around the end of the month. She's having a difficult pregnancy and she doesn't know yet that you want Luke back. The news will shock her and might send her into premature labor."

His steely eyes bored into her. "That isn't my problem. Your brother should have told her. I don't see why I need to wait for a situation that isn't my fault."

She was aghast. "But what if something happens?"

"She's almost due. What's going to happen? I assume there are doctors where they live."

Mariah's mind whirled at his cruel words. She'd always insisted that Gillard didn't deserve Luke. If he didn't care about the welfare of an expectant mother, he shouldn't be raising a child. Yet he was Luke's father. She could do nothing to keep them apart. Now it seemed that she couldn't even postpone it for the sake of Gabe and Felicity.

"I'm sorry to sound harsh," he admitted, "but I'm so anxious to see my son. You can't imagine what it's been like to wonder how he's been, and to hope he still remembers me. Please, Miss Meeks? Mariah."

She licked her lips. "I understand, but Luke's too young to travel alone on the train. Someone would need to come here with him. My brother can't come until after the delivery. It's just a couple of weeks."

"I've waited more than two years. I don't want to wait a minute longer than I have to."

She sighed, beaten. Gillard could send anyone to fetch Luke. Best it be someone Luke knew. "Then I'll take the first train east and get him."

She stood, thinking their conversation was over, but he grabbed her by the shoulders.

"It will take too long for you to travel back and forth. Surely there's someone who can bring him, a friend or relative? Someone from your agency?"

Her mouth got dry. Of course there was someone. Pearlman was small. An entire congregation would rally around their pastor. "I'll ask," she conceded.

He beamed. "Good, we'll head back to town so you can call your brother right away to make arrangements."

Thunder rumbled in the distance, signaling danger. To the west, dark clouds poured over the shrouded mountain peaks. How fitting.

She'd just failed.

Chapter Seventeen

Hendrick started the new fire engine pump.

"Ready with the intake?" he asked the man who'd dragged the hose down to Beson Creek.

"Ready," came the shout from below.

"Nozzle open?" Hendrick asked Talltree and his friends who manned the fire hose.

"Ready," they chimed in unison.

Hendrick opened the valve and heard the growl of water getting sucked from the creek. The intake hose filled and stiffened like a sausage. So far, so good.

He trained his attention on the nozzle as the pump roared, all six cylinders firing perfectly. Any moment now. He tensed in preparation for the spray of water. Air bubbles exploded out the nozzle as the water pushed from behind. This time it had to work.

"It's coming," Talltree yelled.

It was. The hose had fattened its entire hundred-yard length.

Hendrick waited, tense with anticipation.

Water trickled out the nozzle. Then air popped and sizzled, interrupting the flow. Finally, with a gurgle, came the full stream of water.

"Tighten the nozzle," he barked. "Try to get some distance out of it."

Talltree did as directed and the men aimed the stream into the air. It went twenty yards up in an arc and twenty yards down, creating a rainbow in the sunlight.

"Is that the best you can do?" he called out.

"That's all it's got," Talltree yelled back.

"All right. Let's shut it down." Hendrick cut the motor, and the stream of water piddled out.

He scrubbed his head. "That's good, but I was hoping for more." He'd tinkered and tweaked, trying to get the most horsepower out of the motor. Maybe he should have taken apart the water pump. Now there wasn't enough time.

Talltree coiled the hose back on the engine. "It's a hundred times better than before. Now we stand a chance of putting out a fire. Thank you."

Hendrick wasn't satisfied. "I wanted to get it running better before I left."

Talltree grinned. "Don't worry, chief. I can handle it. Go home where you're needed."

"Home?" Judge Weiss had apparently noticed the test and came over to supervise. "You planning on leaving, son?"

Hendrick looked the judge square in the eye. "I have to, sir."

Weiss assessed him quietly. "Woman trouble, eh?"

How would he know? Hendrick bristled. "I don't go back on my word, sir. I'll do all I can to improve the engine before I leave. You can count on it."

"I know I can," Weiss said quietly. "Talltree here says that you've got integrity, and he doesn't trust white men without good reason." He squinted at the mountains.

"Looks like weather coming, boys. Let's get this pumper back to the station."

Everyone, Judge Weiss included, coiled up the hose and helped drag the fire engine back to the filling station. Ordinarily, horses pulled the old pumper, but for this short of distance, Hendrick hadn't bothered to ask for a team.

"We need another way to get this around," the judge huffed, wiping his brow. "Last time we had a blaze, it took fifteen minutes to get a horse team here. Can it be hooked up to a vehicle?"

"It could," Hendrick said slowly, "but I need to install a hitch on the vehicle you plan to use." He'd seen only a handful of cars in Brunley, and the only ones capable of pulling the weight belonged to rich men.

"Use my Bessie," Weiss said. "I'll back her up to the garage door."

Hendrick looked at Talltree. "Bessie?"

"His car."

The judge continued to surprise Hendrick. Apparently, he cared more for the community than for his belongings. Unlike Gillard.

"He'd let me weld a hitch onto his Willys?"

Talltree nodded. "He'd do that—and more—to help this town. That's why the tribal business council favors his proposal."

The tribal business council. Mariah had wanted him to ask about their meeting the other day, to find out what they said about Gillard. If he'd done what she asked, maybe they wouldn't have come to this crossroads. Maybe she wouldn't be with Gillard right now.

"What proposal is that?" he hazarded, not really expecting an answer.

"For oil."

The paperwork that had been on Frank Gillard's desk

said something about oil leases. "Did Gillard want a lease?" Hendrick pressed.

"What do you think?"

"I think he does." Hendrick worked it through his mind. Gillard wanted an oil lease that only the tribe could grant. "Then he's going up against the judge."

Talltree nodded. "The council doesn't trust Gillard, but he claims he has tribal blood in his family through his son."

Luke. The tingling started in Hendrick's fingers and moved through to his toes. That's why Gillard wanted Luke so badly.

"But the council still favors Judge Weiss."

Talltree's expression was grave. "We can't ignore blood."

"Then Gillard will get the lease?"

"If he can produce his son by the end of the month."

Hendrick felt sick. No wonder Gillard was pressuring Mariah. No wonder he flattered her, led her to believe he loved her and proposed marriage. He had to have Luke—and soon. "Are these leases valuable?"

"There are rumors of oil near Sunburst, east of the reservation land that's up for lease."

If exploration paid off and oil was found, this lease could make Gillard as rich as a Rockefeller. No wonder he wanted it so badly, but just how far would he go to ensure that he got it? Hendrick recalled Weiss's warning that Gillard wasn't someone to be crossed. If Mariah didn't go along with his plan, what would he do to her?

A low rumble followed by an earsplitting crack made him jump. Lightning had struck very close.

"Sounds like the storm's here," Talltree said before heading outside to look.

Through the open garage door, Hendrick saw that daylight had turned to night. The wind howled down from the mountains, bending the grass flat and sending the dirt through the air in a dust blizzard.

Mariah was out in that with only Gillard to protect her. Hendrick wished he could fill that role, but Mariah had made it clear that everything was over between them. She'd chosen Gillard. He'd seen it in her look of determination this morning. She'd marched toward the man and let him seat her in his car. But, come to think of it, she hadn't embraced him or even smiled at him. No, she'd looked more like a woman headed to a funeral. Well, that was her choice, and he'd better find a way to accept it and stop worrying about her all the time.

He shivered as more lightning crackled outside. Letting go of Mariah wasn't going to be easy.

Thankfully, he didn't have time to dwell on it. Weiss pulled his car across the open door and hopped out.

"Let's go, boys," the judge said. "I'll get Straight Arrow's mule team. We've got a fire on our hands."

Mariah felt exposed on the mountaintop. Thunder crackled around her, and lightning streaked across the sky. The wind rushed upon them all at once, rattling the bushes and scrub trees. Gillard rode by her side, but that was little comfort. She urged her mare to hurry down the trail toward the spruce forest where they had to travel single file.

Rain hadn't fallen yet, but the wind whipped the branches into a clattering frenzy. Needles and pinecones showered down. Cold air sliced through the heat, turning summer to fall in an instant.

"Hurry," she urged the mare, anxious to get away from both Gillard and the storm.

"She's going as quickly as she dares," he snapped.

"Horses don't like storms any more than we do. Just make sure you let her know you're in control so she doesn't get spooked."

Mariah was *not* in control—of her horse or the situation. Gillard expected her to have Luke sent immediately. He wouldn't listen to reason. Why? Why was he so adamant that Luke come now? She could understand a father's longing to see his son, but a couple of weeks didn't matter. It would take days to get here by train anyway. She shook her head. It didn't make sense.

"When we get out of the forest, we'll ride side by side again," Gillard said. "That way I can take the reins if your mare gets spooked by the storm."

Those were not calming words. Mariah gripped her reins against the saddle horn, dreading the moment they got back into the open. At least when they rode single file, Gillard couldn't see her expression. She could think freely, without worrying about inadvertently frowning, which would prompt a question.

The trek through the forest seemed to take longer than it had going up. The trees all looked the same, and Mariah began to wonder if she'd taken a wrong turn. Then they reached an impasse. A downed tree blocked the trail.

"I must have missed a turn," she said. "There wasn't a tree blocking the trail on the way up."

Gillard dismounted and examined the tree. "This is fresh. See the soil? The split where lightning struck? We're lucky it didn't catch fire."

A shiver ran down Mariah's spine. Fire. The last thing they needed in the midst of this tinder-dry forest.

"Can we get around it?" she asked.

He pointed to the left. "Dismount and lead your horse around the base of the tree. I'll be right behind you."

That gave her little comfort. More and more she felt

trapped, as if an oppressive blanket had been cast over her. Luke was just ten. She would be here eight more years, making her nearly forty by the time Luke became an adult. She could never love Gillard. She didn't even trust him. In time, he might strike her or worse. She shuddered. But she had to protect Luke. Someone had to protect Luke.

"How much farther?" she asked as she mounted again.

"No more than a mile to the meadows." His smirk sent shivers through her. "Don't worry, Miss Meeks. Soon we'll be safe."

Mariah doubted she'd ever feel safe again. She prayed she could somehow keep Luke safe.

They left the forest and entered the open meadow, where the wind whipped the grasses flat. Lightning crashed all around, and her horse pranced, anxious. Mariah had visions of the horse rearing and throwing her to the ground, but then Gillard grabbed her reins.

"Take charge," he barked, "or she'll run on you."

Mariah had long since lost control. Trembling, she realized that she'd never really had it. Oh, she thought she could control things, but in the end, she was the one who'd been manipulated. She'd placed herself in Gillard's hands and now found herself in the midst of a storm on a jittery horse. Death might release her, but not Gillard. All she had left to trust was God. He never failed. He gave His followers the power to defeat the enemy. On Him could she rely. At that moment, clinging to a horse, she finally did what she should have done from the start. She let go and commended everything into His care.

A sense of calm came over her at once, followed by bitter regret. Despite the wind and lightning, she saw herself with terrible clarity. How wrong she'd been during this whole trip. She had treated Hendrick without the consideration he deserved. She'd taken him for granted, had misled him by accepting his kiss and then tossed him aside. She was no better than Frank Gillard. The truth stabbed through her with painful precision.

With a sob, she prayed that God would give her the chance to right her mistakes.

"Please forgive me, Lord," she wept. "How I have sinned, how horribly I have sinned."

As the tears flowed, she felt His healing grace and forgiveness.

"Why are you blubbering?" Gillard snapped. "We're almost there."

Mariah's eyes flew open. She'd forgotten that he was beside her. But so was God. She knew that now.

"Where is the fire?" Hendrick asked Judge Weiss.

The judge nodded to the south. "Out by the school." He put the car in gear and started to roll away from the station.

Hendrick's gut clenched. The children. Anna. She'd gone to the school to help one of the teachers. He raced forward and grabbed onto Weiss's car. "My sister is there," he panted. "No time for mules. Hitch to car."

Miraculously, the judge understood what he meant. He applied the brake, and Hendrick bent to gather his breath.

Weiss got out and came around to the back of his Willys. "You telling me you can hitch that fire wagon to my car?"

Hendrick took a deep draught of air. "Not hitch, but we've got enough men here to set up your car to pull it."

"You lost me, son."

Hendrick explained how they could use a towrope or chain to drag the fire engine behind the Willys. It would take some strong men in the car and on the engine, but it would be faster than waiting for a horse team to arrive. "But it might scratch your paint job."

Weiss laughed. "You think I don't have any dings on that car? It's a car, son, not family. We got a fire on our hands. Let's hop to it, boys."

In no time, Hendrick, Talltree and his friends attached a chain to the fire pump. Meanwhile, Weiss pumped several cans of fuel for the motor and stashed them inside his car. Three strong men got in the back of the car.

"Don't drive too fast," Hendrick cautioned, "or the wagon'll sway and tip over."

"I'll ride it," one of the remaining Indians volunteered.

The others followed alongside, ready to hop on or steady it if necessary. Hendrick motioned for Talltree to join them, but the Indian waved him on.

"I'll get help," he said, backing toward the hotel.

Hendrick didn't know if Talltree intended to recruit the tourists or if he had some other idea, but they needed all the help they could get.

When Mariah and Gillard reached the Glacier hotel, he suggested she call Gabe from there. Mariah tensed. What would she tell him? What if Felicity picked up the telephone? She rapidly calculated the hour.

"He wouldn't be home from church yet," she said triumphantly, "and there's no telephone there."

"Then you can talk to your sister-in-law." He winked. "Break the news to her."

Mariah couldn't do that. "We'll just wait."

He frowned. "Why put it off? An hour isn't going to make any difference." Without waiting for her to reply, he pulled her into the lobby and asked to use their telephone.

Her heart pounded. What would she tell Felicity? How could she warn her without alarming her? She pondered running, but Gillard would catch up to her before she reached the car.

"Hello, operator. Hello?" Gillard tried unsuccessfully to make the connection. After several failed attempts, he replaced the receiver. "The line's dead," he said to the clerk. "Do you know why?"

The clerk picked up the receiver, tested the connection and replaced it. "No, sir, I don't, but we do have periodic outages."

Praise God.

Gillard wasn't that easily dissuaded. "We'll head back to Brunley. We'll go all the way to Cut Bank if we have to."

Mariah's nerves went on alert. He desperately needed her to make that call today. Why? It didn't make sense. There was something he wasn't telling her, some reason he had to have Luke here. More and more she worried that wasn't for any of the reasons he'd stated. That niggling fear returned full force. Something evil lurked in Frank Gillard, and she was at its mercy.

The sky grew more lurid the closer they got to Brunley. It had to be late afternoon now, but the sky was darkened by the rainless storm. Back in Pearlman, Gabe and Felicity would be resting after supper. Perhaps Gabe worked on his sermon while Felicity embroidered clothes for the baby. Luke would be playing in the backyard.

Mariah squeezed her eyes shut, though this time not because of the hairpin turns. Then she smelled something. She sniffed.

"Is that smoke?" She looked ahead, but the wind had tossed so much dust in the air that she couldn't possibly tell it apart from smoke.

"Wildfire," he said tersely.

They'd left the foothills and were entering the rolling

plain. That's when she saw the flames shooting high into the air. She gasped. No wonder the telephone line had been dead. "Brunley's on fire."

The mile-long drive to the Indian school took forever. Hendrick watched the flames leap into the sky, clouds of smoke climbing high. Rain would help, but only one or two drops splattered against his face.

"Keep Anna safe," he prayed. Mariah would probably be with Gillard at his ranch by now. The thought still made him sick.

When they finally rounded the turn that took them to the school, the heat knocked his breath out. His skin sizzled, and his eyes itched and burned. This fire was hot and getting hotter. Trees burst into flames like fireworks, huge torches in the gloomy afternoon. The smoke made him hack and cough, so he pulled out his handkerchief and covered his mouth and nose.

Even before Weiss stopped the car, Hendrick saw the horror that faced them. Flames shot skyward in a wall of fire not twenty yards from the back of the schoolhouse. Screaming and crying children ran around the yard like chickens on the loose, their teachers trying desperately to round them up.

Hendrick looked for Anna and spotted her consoling several of the youngest children. Relief gave way to a welling pride. She was a good girl, a strong girl, a loving girl. She'd make Ma and Pa—God rest his soul—proud.

"Where do you want the fire engine?" the judge asked, drawing Hendrick back to the task at hand.

"We'll draw water from the creek. The men know what to do."

Thank God he'd finished the motor before leaving. Thank God he hadn't been able to catch a train until Friday. As it was, they might be able to keep the blaze at bay until everyone was safe. But he knew they stood little chance of saving the school with the pumper's single stream of water. They needed more.

He looked around and spotted the hand pump in the yard. "I want every adult not watching children to grab a bucket," he yelled, cupping his hands as a megaphone.

The frantic people actually listened. Mr. Sowich ran toward the pump. "There are more buckets in the laundry."

Gradually, order came to the chaos. A brigade formed, and buckets of water were tossed on the fire. The new pumper motor fired up, and water began to flow. But it wasn't enough. They could never beat back a fire this big. The water merely hissed and turned to steam while the fire marched on. Maybe they could save just the schoolhouse.

"Throw the water on the building," he yelled.

In the confusion, no one seemed to hear him, so he grabbed the nozzle and directed it toward the building. The squat but muscular Indian manning it nodded with understanding and began sweeping the water across the face of the building. Soon the others understood what he wanted, and the bucket brigade began dousing the building.

"We need to help with the fire," Mariah insisted when they reached Brunley. The town wasn't on fire, but it soon would be. In this wind, it wouldn't be long before the flames rolled across the mile or two that separated the fire from the dry and dusty town.

Gillard continued to drive down the main street. "Not until you make that telephone call."

"Why?" Mariah had been wary before. Now she knew something was odd in his behavior. "I can call tomorrow or the next day. Why is it so important for me to call right now?"

His jaw had tensed. "Because I need my son."

She didn't believe his excuse. He pulled in front of the telegraph office and stopped the car. She shot out. She'd get away from him, go help with the fire.

He grabbed her. "Where do you think you're going?" The smile had long since vanished, replaced by steely determination.

"What are you doing?" She tugged her arm. "You're hurting me."

He gripped harder. "You are going to call your brother and you are going to tell him to send Luke on the next train, understand?"

This Frank Gillard terrified her. No one was on the streets or in the shops, presumably because of the fire. No one would come to her rescue if he struck her.

"You can't make me say anything," she fired back.

His grin was cruel. "Yes, I can. If you don't do as I say, I'll file legal action against your Society."

He would win. She had obstructed his right to his son. The agency would fold. Mr. Isaacs would be crushed, but he'd understand if she told him it was to save a child. He'd understand.

"I won't do it."

He gripped her jaw with his other hand and forced her to look at him. "You won't do it for me or for your agency. Maybe you'll do it for Luke."

She paled.

"Every hour you delay will be taken out on his back."

She gasped. "You're the one he's afraid of." Anna's words came back to her, that Luke had told Peter he was afraid of a man, but that man wasn't his father. "You're not Luke's father."

Gillard's lips curled in a sneer. "I have the birth certificate to prove I am. Now I know who has him. Trust me, Miss Meeks, I can find your precious Luke."

Her legs lost all strength, and she stumbled as he dragged her to the telegraph office. He rattled the knob.

Locked. Praise God.

"It's too late. They're all at the fire."

"You're not getting out of this that easily." He grabbed her by the elbow, forced her into the car and drove to the Mountain View Hotel.

Through the windshield she could see fire shoot above the trees that edged the narrow road to the Indian school.

"The school," she gasped. She unlatched the door before the car came to a stop at the hotel.

Gillard grabbed her arm. "You're not going anywhere."

He dragged her up the steps, and she felt something cold and hard press into her back. A gun? She nearly collapsed. Surely she looked terrified. Surely Mrs. Pollard would notice.

The woman looked up when they approached. "Oh, good. I need you to pack in case the fire heads in this direction. I just pray Mr. Hendrick's fire pump works. I'm heading to the church to set up for those poor children."

Mariah braced herself on the edge of the counter since her legs were about to give away. "Are the children all safe?"

"Don't know, Miss. All we can do is pray."

Gillard slapped twenty dollars on the counter. "Can you give us a minute, Mrs. Pollard?" He used that oily-smooth tone that had fooled her for so long. "We have a private telephone call to place."

Mrs. Pollard looked from him to her with surprise. "Are you sure there's time?"

Gillard's smile fooled so many. It fooled Mrs. Pollard, too. "It won't take long."

The woman hesitated a moment before picking up the money. "Five minutes. Then you're out."

Noooo. Mariah wanted to cry out to her, to beg her to stay, anything to stop this telephone call. Instead, she must hope the lines were down or no operator answered.

Gillard walked her to the telephone and placed the receiver in her hand. He cranked to make the connection. Alas, an operator answered. She had no choice but to proceed.

"I'd like to place a long-distance call to Pearlman, Michigan." Then Mariah gave her the exchange and number. During the intervening wait, she prayed that no one would answer, that Felicity would not be home, that the call wouldn't go through. Instead, after a single ring, Gabe's voice crackled over the line, barely audible.

Her mouth was dry. No words came to mind. The hard barrel of the gun pressed into her back.

"Gabriel," she croaked out.

"Mariah? Is that you?"

She had to concentrate to hear him.

The gun pressed harder. She had a choice: tell Gabe to bring Luke west or die.

"He, uh." She swallowed hard, but there was nothing to swallow. Her throat ached. Her limbs had gone numb. Her ears rang.

Gillard's left hand circled her neck.

She could barely breathe.

"Mariah?" came Gabe's faint voice on the other end. "What's wrong?"

"N-nothing," she stammered. "It's Gillard—Mr. Gillard. H-he has Luke's birth certificate. It shows he's the father."

After a long pause on the other end, Gabe quietly asked, "Do you want me to bring him?"

Had Gillard heard? He stood within inches of her, but Gabe had spoken softly and the connection was very bad. Maybe he couldn't hear. Her mind raced to find an answer that would satisfy Gillard while warning Gabe.

"Do it," Gillard hissed in her opposite ear.

Of course. The opposite.

"No, don't," she said with exaggerated urgency, as if Gabe had just asked if he could wait to bring Luke. "He insists on seeing Luke at once."

That should make no sense to Gabe. It certainly had the desired effect on Gillard. He took his hand from her throat and broke the connection.

After holstering his gun, he said, "Now, that wasn't that difficult, was it?"

The firefighters' efforts couldn't halt the wind-driven flames. They advanced with unrelenting fury, consuming everything in their path. Sparks landed on the schoolhouse roof. Hendrick directed the pumper's spray upward, but in the stiff wind it couldn't reach above the second-story windows.

He ran from the creek to the engine to the bucket brigades, coordinating the effort. More and more people appeared every minute, and three bucket brigades had formed. The whole town must be there. Still, it wasn't enough.

Before long, the shingles caught fire, and then the flames crept down the walls to the windows, which shattered with terrifying explosions.

"Hendrick." The cry came from a familiar voice.

He turned to see Mariah running toward him, her face ashen. He had no time to comfort her. The battle with the fire required his full attention. The pump needed more fuel. The stream of water ebbed and flowed as the hose picked up debris in the creek and the valve had to be stopped momentarily so they could unplug the intake.

The fire was gaining strength. He could use more people. Where was Talltree? Questions flew from every direction. He barked orders to get the children away from the building, to direct the water on the lower level, to refuel the pump.

He ran from place to place, shouting directions. That's why he didn't notice the tap on his shoulder the first time. The second time Anna punched him in the chest.

"What?" he snapped. He didn't have time for his sister's questions.

"They're not all out," she cried, her soot-streaked face drawn with terror.

"Who's not out? The children?"

She nodded, her eyes wide.

Adrenaline shot through him. Why hadn't he asked that first thing? Didn't each teacher count her students?

"How many?" He grabbed Anna by the shoulders. "How many are missing?" There was still time to save them if he moved fast.

"Three from my class. They were going to the latrine but never got there."

He sprinted toward the schoolhouse, the enormity of the task smacking him hard. The building was huge, encompassing two stories. It would have numerous classrooms. Where would the missing children be? With the smoke and the flickering light, he'd have a hard time finding them, but he had to try.

As he ran toward the building, he calculated the most likely location. Fear drove children to the place they felt most secure. That wouldn't be the director's office. It might be the classroom, where they would have expected to find their teacher. He'd forgotten to ask Anna where her classroom was located, but time had just about run out. Flames licked the walls. The roof looked ready to collapse. The heat scorched, so hot it was like being in a closed oven. He could barely breathe.

He'd nearly reached the porch when a woman darted past him. Mariah. He grabbed her arm and pulled her back before she set foot on the first step.

"The children," she cried, struggling against him.

She must have overheard Anna.

He wasn't about to let her run into a burning building. "I'm going in, not you." Then he recalled that she knew where Anna's classroom was located. "Where would the children go?"

Mariah looked pale as death as she pointed to the upper floor. There, framed by the broken window, stood Constance with two smaller children clinging to her.

His heart nearly stopped. *Not Constance.*

Chapter Eighteen

Mariah stood paralyzed as Hendrick raced up the stairs and bashed open the front door with his shoulder. The back of the building was enveloped in flame, the interior dense with smoke. He waved toward his firefighters, and they directed the stream of water at the front door, wetting him to the bone.

"Hendrick," Mariah gasped as he vanished into the flames.

A car horn honked. She knew that sound. It was her car, the Overland, and it stopped next to the fire engine. The doors opened, and Joshua Talltree and Gillard's entire staff piled out.

Then, to her horror, she saw Gillard's Packard drive up.

He jumped out and yelled at his staff, "What do you think you're doing here?"

Not one of them answered. Mrs. Eagle stepped next to Mariah.

"Get back to the ranch," Gillard barked, "now." He wheeled on Mrs. Eagle. "You, too."

Then Mariah saw the gun. He aimed it at the housekeeper.

"No," she gasped, darting in front of the woman, "don't shoot."

"You heard the lady." Judge Weiss tossed a bucket of water at Gillard, knocking the revolver to the ground.

Gillard scrambled after it, but Talltree got there first. Mrs. Eagle held tightly to Mariah, but her grip relaxed once Talltree had the gun.

The Indian casually pointed the gun toward Gillard. "How does this work, Judge?"

"I wouldn't know. Care to try it out?" The judge stared down Gillard. "I'd suggest you either make yourself useful or leave."

Gillard's lips curled into a sneer even as he backed away. "I'm not risking my life like some other fools around here."

Mariah grabbed the bucket from the judge. "Hendrick is a hero, and I'm not sitting here doing nothing when I can help."

She turned her back on Gillard and joined the closest brigade, hoping her little bit would help bring Hendrick and the children out alive. Flames shot high, and her skin sizzled from the heat. The dense smoke made her cough. It would suffocate them. With a crash, a section of the roof collapsed into the upper floor. She cried out. How could they survive?

The answer was clear: with God's protection.

Mrs. Eagle joined her, and as the hymns rang out, the brigades increased their pace. She saw all of Gillard's staff and Talltree, too. Everyone pitched in.

"Mr. Gillard will hold this against you," Mariah warned Mrs. Eagle.

"No work for Mister Lawd anymore," said the house-keeper. "Get Constance and go home."

"Constance?" That was the girl Hendrick had gone to rescue. "Constance is your daughter?"

"Mister Lawd take her from me, put her in school, not let me see her. Mister Lawd evil."

Mariah couldn't agree more.

"Where is Constance?" the housekeeper asked, looking around.

The fire still raged, and neither Hendrick nor the children had come out of the building yet.

Mariah handed off the next bucket and drew Mrs. Eagle out of the line. "Hendrick is fetching her."

The housekeeper's sharp intake of breath meant she understood that Constance was in danger. The woman closed her eyes, and then chanted in a language Mariah could not understand. The haunting words needed no translation. She was praying. In any language, God understood.

The rest of the roof collapsed, still without any sign of Hendrick or the children. The lump in Mariah's throat thickened as she wept for them.

Dear, wonderful Hendrick always gave of himself without asking for anything in return. How clearly she now saw his life of sacrifice. Instead of pursuing his dreams, he'd left school to support his widowed mother and sister. Even the journey here had been a sacrifice. He'd left behind an opportunity with Curtiss Aeroplane. And now he'd likely given his life to save children he didn't even know.

As the blaze continued without a sign of Hendrick or the children, hope dwindled. No one could survive that inferno. Anna joined them, and the three women clung to each other, alternately closing their eyes against the terrible spectacle and scanning the building in hopes they'd spot a survivor.

Anna was the first to cry out. "Children!"

Mariah peered in the direction Anna indicated while

the housekeeper gripped her arm even tighter. Eventually, she saw them, the two youngest, walking out from the far side of the building where the fire wasn't as hot. Teachers rushed to gather them up.

"No Constance." The Indian woman bit her quivering lip.

"There's still time," Mariah said hopefully. "They have to make it out. They have to."

But time was running out. All but one corner of the building had collapsed. The fire engine pumped water on that corner, but the fire could not be stopped or even slowed now. It would burn until it had consumed everything.

Mariah leaned heavily against the Overland's fender, too numb and tired to feel more than emptiness. No one could have survived. All sense told her they couldn't have. She closed her eyes and let the tears bubble up.

Hendrick had died never knowing she loved him.

As the chill of night descended, she knew that nothing else mattered. Love was indeed the greatest gift of all. Hendrick had given it to her, and she'd withheld it from him. If given another chance... No, it was over.

Exhausted, she knelt beside the Indian woman and hugged her tight. No words could quiet the grief. They could only weep.

"Hendrick!" Anna cried in disbelief.

Mariah's eyelids shot open. He'd survived? She soon spotted him walking from behind the smoking ruins. He was black, singed, his clothing charred. And in his arms, he carried a child.

"Constance," the housekeeper cried, running toward them.

The little girl held out her arms, and joy flooded both the mother's and the daughter's cries. Hendrick set Constance down, and she ran into her mother's arms. The two became one, sobbing and caressing each other to be sure they weren't dreaming.

Then he walked toward Anna and her. Mariah held her breath, anxious to wrap her arms around him, to tell him that she loved him.

But Hendrick walked right past her to hug his sobbing sister. "It's all right now. Everyone is all right."

Mariah let the pain sink deep. She'd gotten what she wanted. He no longer cared for her.

The church opened its doors to the fire victims, but by the time the fire backed onto itself and Hendrick and his crew suppressed the blaze into a smoldering pile of embers, most of the children had been taken into local homes.

He scanned the sanctuary-turned-relief center. A couple of children remained, surrounded by adults who gave them food, water and blankets. The teachers assisted, and Sowich sat in the front pew, staring blankly at the altar. Mariah was not there. Probably with Gillard, Hendrick thought bitterly.

"The students aren't Blackfeet," Judge Weiss explained as they downed cups of coffee.

"Then where are they from?" The hot liquid scalded Hendrick's already raw throat. He coughed. The smoke had taken its toll, no doubt, but at least everyone was safe.

"Some from across the Divide, others from as far as the Dakotas. Indian Affairs, in its infinite wisdom, decided the children needed to go to school far from their tribes so their parents and elders wouldn't influence them. They want to assimilate and civilize the Indians. No one ever stops to question why. These people have a rich heritage." He shook his head. "It doesn't deserve to die."

Apparently, Judge Weiss agreed with Hendrick when it came to government policy. "Bad idea."

The judge nodded. "But the school's gone now, so we can do the right thing. We'll take 'em in, get 'em settled down and then send 'em home."

Hendrick was glad to hear that. "There's a little girl, Constance, the last one I brought out of the fire. I promised to take her back to her parents."

"Constance Eagle." The judge nodded toward the far pew where Gillard's housekeeper stroked Constance's hair. "Talltree said she's Salish, what we call Flathead, from over on the other side of the Divide. She's one of the ones Gillard brought to the school."

"Gillard brought her? Why would he do that? Certainly not to get a housekeeper."

"For the bounty, son. When parents refused to send their children to the school and the police wouldn't yank them out by force, Sowich offered cash to anyone who could bring in a child."

Hendrick felt sick. "Gillard took her from her home?"

"He wasn't alone. There are a lot of unscrupulous characters out here who'll do anything for money. Gillard's just one of the worst."

Hendrick fingered the bills in his pocket. "I'm going to make sure Constance and her mother get home. Can I drive to their reservation?"

The judge chuckled. "No, son. You'll have to send them on the train."

"Then that's what I'm going to do." He went to Mrs. Eagle, who looked up when he approached. Tears shimmered in her eyes.

"Thank you," she whispered.

Constance lifted her eyes to him. She didn't need to say a thing. Her smile told him everything.

Hendrick sat beside Mrs. Eagle. "I promised your daughter I'd get her home." He pulled a twenty-dollar bill from his pocket. "This is for train tickets and whatever else you need. Leave on the next train."

"But Mister Lawd will stop me." She trembled and did not take the money.

With a start, Hendrick realized that the Mr. Lord that Constance so feared was Gillard. Anger surged within him. "I'll make sure he doesn't. I'll go with you if I have to."

"You can count on it, ma'am," the judge said from behind him. "Mr. Simmons is a man of his word. I'd take the morning train, though. Get out of town before Gillard realizes you're gone."

Mrs. Eagle gratefully accepted Hendrick's money. "You're a good man," she whispered. "No white man so good." She raised defiant eyes. "I help you. Keep boy from Mister Lawd."

"What boy?" Hendrick sucked in his breath. "Do you mean Luke?"

She nodded.

"But Luke is Gillard's son. I saw the birth certificate."

She shook her head. "False. He have lawyer make up paper."

Hendrick's pulse thrummed loudly. "But Mariah, Miss Meeks, said everything checked out. He changed his name from Francesco Guillardo to Frank Gillard."

The woman smiled triumphantly. "His real name Corliss."

"Corliss?" Hendrick repeated, not sure he understood.

"How do you know this?" The judge squatted before her.

"Hear him tell lawyer. He need Indian boy to make tribe give him oil lease. Make up name. Make up paper."

This was beginning to make sense. "Talltree said he claimed to the tribal council that he had an Indian son."

Weiss nodded. "That was his advantage to get the lease."

"But he made it up. He's not really Luke's father." Hendrick's heart pounded, hoping he understood correctly. This would save Luke a lifetime of misery.

"Mister Lawd tell lawyer he know orphan boy who look Indian. Son of man he kill in fight."

"Dear God," gasped a voice that tore through Hendrick. Mariah.

She stood behind the judge, a tray of cinnamon rolls in her hand. Judging from the horror on her face, she'd heard everything. The tray wavered, and Hendrick took it while Judge Weiss helped her sit down. Constance reached for a roll, and he absently let her take one in each hand before handing the tray to another woman.

If he weren't in a house of God... Well, what he had to say about Gillard couldn't be said in a house of worship. Gillard wasn't Luke's father; he'd murdered the man. No wonder the boy was terrified of him. Peter had said that Luke confided in him. That must be why Peter defended him so staunchly. The boys from the orphanage had formed a tight bond that even loving families couldn't break.

"That's a mighty serious accusation," the judge was saying, "though I wouldn't put it past him. The trouble is, we only have your word, ma'am. Sorry to say, but no jury in these parts'll take the word of an Indian woman. We need proof."

Hendrick sat down heavily. He didn't relish searching Gillard's house again. "If he's not really Luke's father, he doesn't have the real birth certificate. Maybe if we could get the real one—"

"We don't need it." Mariah's eyes flashed with excitement. "All Gillard wants is the oil lease. Remove that, and he has no need for Luke."

"True." The judge tapped his lips with his finger. "Mrs. Eagle, would you be willing to tell the tribal business council what you just told me? A local jury might not believe you, but the tribal council will. I think that will put an end to Mr. Gillard's application and therefore his interest in the boy."

Mrs. Eagle nodded her assent.

"And to make sure Gillard doesn't cry foul," the judge continued, "I'll withdraw my application and suggest the tribe reopen the application period."

"Thank you," Mariah said. "Thank you all. I pray it's enough."

"Oh, it'll be enough." The judge slapped his thigh. "Once Gillard realizes we know his real name, he'll slither off into whatever hole he crawled out of. Corliss, eh? If I had the rest of his name and an idea where this killing took place, I could see if there's a warrant out for his arrest."

"Desmond," Mariah said, her eyes glassy. "Desmond Corliss, and it probably happened in Detroit."

Hendrick wondered how she knew that. "Is that what he told the agency?"

"A Desmond Corliss signed the paperwork when he dropped off Luke at the Detroit mission. We thought it was an agency mistake." She sighed and rubbed her sooty face.

"That should be enough," the judge said.

"I hope you're right," she whispered.

Judge Weiss patted her shoulder reassuringly. "Mrs. Eagle, the head of the council lives next door. If you could take a few minutes to tell him your story, we'll have this settled before you catch your train." He nodded toward the open doors, through which night was giving way to early dawn.

Judging by the pale gray, it was probably no later than five-thirty in the morning. Hendrick stretched his limbs, eager for a bath and a hot meal, both of which would have to wait until he'd seen Constance and her mother safely onto the morning train.

"Thank you, Judge," Mariah said quietly, shaking his hand.

"Don't you worry, miss, we'll skin that skunk." The judge sauntered to the doorway, put on his hat and waited for Mrs. Eagle.

Hendrick turned to the Indian woman and Constance, who was asleep, a half-eaten cinnamon roll still clutched in her hand. "I'll carry her, if you'd like."

The woman nodded, and he lifted Constance's tiny frame, scarcely heavier than a basket of apples. Her head lolled against his shoulder, and she sighed and cuddled closer, secure in his arms. Nothing had ever felt better.

Constance would go home. So would he. Hendrick knew Mariah waited behind him. He sensed that she wanted to talk, but he couldn't, not yet, not while the wounds of rejection were still raw. Without looking back, he strode out into the shimmering gray of dawn, carrying the one person who trusted him implicitly.

He'd walked away without saying goodbye. During those horrible minutes when Mariah thought he would never get out of the fire alive, she'd regretted never telling him that she loved him—only him—but of course nothing she said could change the barrier between them. She'd watched how tenderly he held Constance, the look of joy on his face. Mariah could never give him the child he so desperately wanted.

She could make sure that Luke stayed home, though. Even if Gabe didn't understand her garbled message, he couldn't have gotten on a train yet. The first train wouldn't leave Pearlman for an hour. She had time to reach him.

"Is there anything I can do for you?" the pastor's wife gently asked. Short and plain, she nonetheless radiated beauty, a beauty that reflected a pure soul.

"No, thank you. I just need to place a telephone call." Mariah clasped her hands. "Thank you so much for all you did tonight. It was an answer to prayer."

The woman smiled softly. "God always answers prayer, though sometimes not the way we imagine."

Not the way we imagine. As Mariah took her leave, she wondered if God would answer her prayer and show her a way into Hendrick's heart. She didn't deserve it. But then no one deserved the great gift God had given mankind. No one deserved the gift of His Son.

As the cool morning air brushed against her face, Mariah felt renewed. The northerly breeze blew the last traces of smoke and grime from her, cleansing her with God's healing touch. The heaviness lifted from her soul and hope returned. God had brought good people to help Luke, people she could never have expected. He would answer her prayers.

She laughed and caught a hand to her mouth. It was too early to make such noise, but she wanted to skip and giggle like a little girl. After calling Gabe and stealing a nap, she'd tell Hendrick that she loved him.

Maybe he'd give her one more chance.

When Mariah awoke hours later, she breathed in the sweet lavender scent of the pillowcase. Why hadn't she noticed that before? Probably because, for the first time in weeks, she wasn't worried about Luke. Yes, yes, worry was sinful. Worriers didn't trust God, and that's exactly where she'd erred, but He'd forgiven her, granted her a fresh start and saved Luke.

She smiled at the news she'd received earlier. Gabe hadn't left. He hadn't even told Luke or Felicity. The telephone connection had cut off before she delivered her confused message, so he waited for her to call back. Later that night Felicity went into labor and gave birth to a healthy little girl. A girl. Mariah could hardly wait to see her. The pastor's wife was right. God did answer prayers, though not always the way people imagined.

Mariah rolled over and noticed that Anna was gone. She sat up with a start. The girl's bag was missing, along with every article of clothing, even the souvenir hat from South Dakota. If she was gone, then so was Hendrick.

The train.

She dressed as quickly as possible, but her fingers fumbled over the buttons and stockings. Her wildly curled hair still smelled smoky, but she didn't have time to bathe.

She raced downstairs and found Mrs. Pollard alone at the desk. "Where is Anna Simmons?"

The woman didn't look up from her ledger. "Checked out."

Mariah's pulse raced. "When is the eastbound train?" The lobby's flocked rose-striped wallpaper spun wildly.

"Six tonight."

Thank goodness. She still had time.

"Have yourself a cinnamon roll, dearie," Mrs. Pollard said, shoving a small plate under her nose.

The plate reminded her of the tray of Mrs. Pollard's rolls she'd taken to the church last night and how Hendrick had taken it from her hands. Then she thought of the gentle way he'd lifted Constance, and the look on his face. He had risked his life to save her. A lump formed in her throat as the mournful cry of a train whistle reverberated through the open lobby doors.

Mariah clutched Mrs. Pollard's hand. "I thought you said the eastbound train leaves at six."

Mrs. Pollard shrugged. "Could take the twelve-thirty to Shelby and change trains."

"Twelve-thirty!" Mariah pushed aside the plate of rolls. "I only have fifteen minutes."

She dashed out onto the porch and nearly ran into Judge Weiss.

"Miss Meeks." He tipped his hat. "I was hoping you were awake. Wanted to let you know the results of my investigation."

This was important, but catching Hendrick rated higher. "Can this wait? I need to see Hendrick before he leaves."

The judge waved. "Yes, yes, go ahead. Catch your young man. And let him know that we have Mr. Gillard in custody."

That was nearly the best news she could imagine. Nearly. She jumped into her car and tried to start it. Nothing. She hadn't set the throttle and spark controls. She tried again. This time the engine turned over, and she was on her way.

Mariah generally prided herself on driving cautiously. Not today. She pressed the accelerator pedal to the floor and spun around the corner onto the main street. The train could leave at any moment. She could see its puff of smoke rising into the wide blue sky.

Hendrick. Hendrick. His name pounded in time with the engine.

She couldn't let him leave without telling him how she really felt, that she did love him, that she would give up her job with the Society, whatever he wanted. She'd seen him with Constance. Surely he realized that adopted children were just as wonderful as having his own. He had to.

The locomotive's brakes shrieked as the engineer let off steam.

Don't go. Please, Lord, don't let him go.

The depot got closer, a hundred yards away. The small unpainted building was within reach. She braked, and as soon as the car stopped, she jumped out, not even taking time to close the door.

Anna stood on the platform, waiting to board. Hendrick must be just out of sight. The whistle blew, and Anna moved toward the train.

"No! Wait!" she yelled, running toward the platform.

Anna spotted her and quickly turned away. Mariah's heart sank. Surely, after all they'd been through, Anna would forgive her.

Mariah climbed the steps to the platform, where Hendrick and Anna stood together, their bags at their feet. Neither seemed to notice.

"Please don't go," she said.

Anna didn't respond. It cut Mariah to the quick, but then Hendrick turned and walked toward her, and hope returned.

She hadn't the nerve or time to say more than a few words. The little she could get out had to count.

"I love you," she said, choking on a rush of tears.

He halted, just out of reach.

With heaving gasps, she got out the rest, "I always loved you."

His brown eyes regarded her somberly, the errant lock of hair securely tucked under his cap.

She clutched her hands to her chest, which hurt so badly that she feared her heart would shatter. "I—I was wrong.

About so many things. I treated you badly. I'm so sorry. Can you ever forgive me?"

Slowly he nodded.

"Oh, thank you," she gushed, praying he would take her in his arms and tell her they could start over.

But he didn't. He licked his lips, looked over her head. "I'm sorry to leave you without a mechanic for the drive home."

The drive home? How could he think about something so unimportant at a time like this? She bit her lip, trying to stop its trembling.

"It's all right," she tried to joke, "but the job is still available."

He shook his head.

She pressed her lips together to hide her disappointment. Nothing was going the way she wanted. She forced a laugh. "What's a car? I'll ship it home."

He nodded solemnly. "That's probably wise."

He started to back away, but she couldn't let go.

"Did Constance and her mother make the early train?" she asked hastily.

Again he nodded, but at least he stopped.

She swallowed hard. He examined his shoes. They stood in awkward silence until the warning whistle sounded.

"We have to go," Anna called out.

Hendrick hesitated, and for a moment Mariah thought he was going to change his mind.

"I wish you well, Mariah," he said, sounding tired.

No words could have pummeled her harder, but they didn't stop coming.

"I need time," he said softly. "I need to think, to figure out who I am and what I want. My whole life I've done what others needed and expected. This is my chance to try for more."

She knew what that meant. "You're taking the job with Curtiss Aeroplane."

"I have to. Do you understand?"

She shook her head. No, she didn't understand, but the choice wasn't hers. She swiped at her eyes. "It's because I can't have children."

"No." At last he took her hand. "Well, maybe a little, but I understand now why the orphans are so important to you."

"I'll give up my job."

He touched a finger to her lips. "Don't do that. It's where you belong. I just need to find where I belong. Can you accept that?"

Though her heart was breaking, she had no choice. She nodded, and then bowed her head to hide the welling tears.

"Thank you," he said. "I'll always remember you." Then he let go of her hand.

His words sounded too much like goodbye forever. She wanted to reach out to him, to beg him to reconsider. Instead, she clutched her arms around her midsection and watched him walk Anna to the train. He helped his sister board and then, with the briefest glance back, disappeared inside.

The whistle blew, and the locomotive released its brakes. Slowly the train inched forward.

Desperation gathered steam inside her, but she recognized it for the selfish impulse it was. She wanted him to remember her as the strong, independent woman he'd once loved, so she walked to the edge of the platform and raised a single hand as the train rolled out of sight.

Chapter Nineteen

Two months later

Hendrick strolled the Coney Island boardwalk with a gal, but his mind wandered elsewhere. He didn't feel the sea breeze. He didn't hear the crash of the waves or the excited cries of the children. He tried not to notice that nearly everyone walked in pairs.

"Puh-leaze?" pouted the blonde whose name he couldn't recall. "I want to ride the Wonder Wheel. I hope we get one of the sliding cars. I've been dreaming of it for weeks and weeks. Dickie said you'd take me on it."

Dick Burrows, the aeronautical engineer who'd gotten him into Curtiss Aeroplane, had talked him into going to Coney Island. He hadn't mentioned that he'd invited girls to join them.

Hendrick felt nothing for the platinum blonde with the cherry-red lips. Oh, she was pretty, but she couldn't compare to the dark-haired, hazel-eyed beauty from New York who'd settled in Pearlman.

"Well?" The blonde leaned into him, batting her eyelashes and pursing her lips in an attempt to generate interest.

In that instant, he knew he'd taken a wrong turn. His

road didn't lead to fame at Curtiss Aeroplane. It didn't include empty-headed women or casual encounters, and it sure didn't end on Long Island. He didn't want to run from responsibility. He wanted to embrace it. Pearlman was home. He could build his engines there. He'd be part of the community he loved. He could try to mend things with Mariah.

The thing that had seemed so important two months ago—having children of his own—no longer mattered. Blood ties didn't mean a thing when it came to putting together a family. Pastor Gabriel and Felicity were proof of that. They loved Luke as much as their new baby girl. And Peter had become a real brother to Hendrick.

"The three of you go ahead without me," he said, the idea taking hold so strongly that his fingers itched.

"Without you?" the blonde protested. "You're no fun."

Dick reined his girl to a stop. "Are you sure?"

He looked as though he was about to needle him, so Hendrick answered while backing away. "I saw a telephone back there. I need to make a call."

Dick grinned. "Go get her."

"Her?" the blonde cried.

Hendrick didn't bother to explain. The blonde would find someone else. She was already linking arms with her girlfriend.

He raced back to the telephone and placed the long-distance call. Long minutes passed before the call was put through and he heard his sister's voice on the other end.

"Anna, it's Hendrick. I'm coming home."

Her shocked silence didn't dampen his excitement.

"It's where I belong," he explained. "Tell Ma I should be there by Tuesday, on the afternoon train."

"What happened?"

"Nothing happened. I just figured out that everything I love is in Pearlman."

She paused, and he thought for a moment that he'd lost the connection.

"What do you want me to say to Mariah?" she finally asked.

That was the big question. Once he'd explained to Anna why he and Mariah had parted, his sister had taken Mariah's side. She was even volunteering at Mariah's new orphanage, and, according to Ma, the two women had become close friends. It made sense that Anna would think of Mariah first. She was certainly the first person on his mind. Had she forgiven him for the dressing-down he'd given her at the Brunley train station? He couldn't get her crestfallen expression from his mind. She'd poured out her heart, and he'd walked away.

"Do you think she's still upset with me?" he asked.

He heard Anna suck in her breath. "You'll have to find out for yourself. When you get here, go straight to the trees west of town. If she's still interested, she'll meet you there."

Hendrick's stomach churned, but he wouldn't change his mind. Nothing had ever felt so right. Even if it took a lifetime, he'd win back Mariah's trust.

"Sorry, Miss Meeks, you need a new pump." The repairman from Belvidere wiped his hands on his overalls as he delivered the bad news about the well pump. "I can get it installed in a couple weeks."

Mariah sighed. "And what am I supposed to do for water in the meantime? We have four children living here."

He shrugged. "Maybe a neighbor can spare some?"

Mariah tried to hide her exasperation. Hendrick could have fixed it. He could fix anything. Unfortunately, he was in New York, working for Curtiss Aeroplane. He'd left Pearlman before she returned from Montana. He'd stayed long enough to see Gabe and Felicity's new baby girl and then he'd taken the train east. She supposed it was better they didn't meet, for she had decided to accept Felicity's job offer and settle in Pearlman.

Mr. Isaacs had closed the Orphaned Children's Society, perfectly meshing with Felicity's plans. Mariah now headed the newly founded home for orphaned children and unwanted cats and dogs. At present they had equal amounts of each in residence.

"Gotta get going, Miss." The man picked up his toolbox. "The train's here."

"Fine, fine." She sighed, waving him off. "We'll make do somehow."

One more repair. The old parsonage had seemed like the perfect location once the church bought the Elder house for the new parsonage, but the building had its share of problems. Electrical, the furnace and now the plumbing.

"I could sure use a handyman," she sighed from the broad front porch as she watched the repairman hustle toward the train depot.

Anna wrapped her arms around one of the porch's white pillars. "I think I know the perfect candidate for the job."

"Oh?" Mariah lifted an eyebrow. "I thought Peter wanted to continue at the garage."

"Not Peter," Anna said slyly. "Someone else. I hear he's arriving on the train today."

Mariah tried to ignore the suggestive glint in Anna's eye. "Very well, have him stop by after he's settled, and I'll talk to him."

"You can't wait that long. He has other opportunities."

Mariah lifted an eyebrow. "Other opportunities? Just who is this handyman?"

"Oh, no one in particular, but I'm sure he could fix the pump."

Mariah knew full well that Anna was setting her up with the one person she most wanted to see, but she wasn't about to let the girl know how eager she was.

"All right." She heaved a big sigh. "I'll fetch my hand-bag, and we can head to the train depot."

"I think you'd better go alone." Anna handed Mariah her bag. "The children will be getting out of school soon. I should be here for them."

School didn't end for another hour. "You're not going to help me through this, are you?"

Anna smiled coyly. "If he's not at the depot, look for him on the road west of town."

A thrill ran through her. Hendrick's favorite spot. Would he want to see her? "Are you sure I should?"

Anna gave her a hug. "Just tell him again that you love him."

Tears rose in Mariah's eyes. It was the truth. She not only loved Hendrick, she'd looked for him every single day, hoped for a letter and prayed for his happiness.

She hugged Anna tight. "Will it be enough?"

Anna half laughed and half sobbed. "If he's not stupid."

Hendrick arrived on the afternoon train and, after step-ping off, left his bag at the depot and walked to his favor-ite spot, where Anna told him to wait.

The maples lining the road were starting to turn. Hints of red and orange peeked from the fringe of the ancient trees, brilliant against the deep blue of early autumn.

He breathed deeply. This was home, and he'd never leave it again.

"Anna said I'd find you here."

The soft, throaty voice quickened a spot deep inside.

"Mariah." Even saying her name made his heart race. He'd thought of her every day. Wondered how she had taken their parting. She didn't write, didn't call his boardinghouse, though Ma had given her the telephone number on more than one occasion. No, she'd left him alone, and he respected her for that, but it didn't tell him if she still cared.

He summoned the courage to look at her. The dark, curly, bobbed hair, the mossy scent, the clearness of her hazel eyes. The stupid idea that he'd be strong went right out the window.

"You look…" He searched for a word. Beyond beautiful. Her face glowed with a serenity and grace he'd never seen before. "You look happy," he finally said. "Ma wrote that you're running Felicity's orphan school."

"Constance House. I couldn't think of a better name."

He had felt a rush of warmth when he'd learned the name. A note from Joshua Talltree told him Constance and her mother had reached home safely.

"Many orphans?" he asked, watching the horizon rather than her, too afraid that if he looked at her, his emotions would overflow. Overhead, the geese were already forming their vees to fly home.

"The last four at the Society. Mr. Isaacs closed the doors last month, and they arrived shortly afterward."

"Good, good." He cleared his throat and, not knowing what to say next, drew patterns in the dirt with the toe of his boot.

A long pause ensued. He looked up at the migrating birds. "Did you know geese mate for life?"

"I think I heard that once."

Though he couldn't bear to look at her, he could feel

her presence, could smell the mossy scent that surrounded her. How right she'd felt in his arms at the beach in July. How badly he'd wanted to keep her there.

"I won't leave Pearlman," she said softly. "Is that a problem?"

Yes or no. He still loved her with every fiber of his being. He dreamed about her at night. He thought about her all day. Every time he saw an Overland, he looked to see if she was driving. He'd committed to staying here regardless of her feelings, but now that he was near her, he wasn't so sure he could do it.

"No problem," he said gruffly.

"That's good, because this is home now."

He nodded, toed the dirt again.

"I love my work," she said a little too brightly.

He sneaked a glance and saw her blinking back tears. Did she still feel something for him?

"The children are wonderful, and the pets…" She pulled a handkerchief from her handbag and pretended to dab at her forehead, but he could tell she was wiping her eyes.

His pulse quickened. Was it possible? He'd dismissed her so thoroughly. She should have been crushed. She should have wanted to have nothing to do with him.

She took a deep, ragged breath. "We could use a handyman. And a father figure, especially for the boys."

"What about your brother?"

"Gabe is busy with the church and the baby." Her voice hitched.

Her pain and longing drove a spike into Hendrick's heart. How she must have ached when she learned she could never have a baby of her own. He searched for the right words. There weren't any.

"It's all right." He took her hand. Her fingers were icy, so he wrapped his other hand around hers.

She stared at the ground to hide her tears, but she couldn't hide the tremble of her shoulders.

He swallowed hard against the emotion. "God gives us children in different ways," he said slowly, feeling out each word. "You're meant to help the orphans."

She sobbed, a hiccup really, and he couldn't wait any longer. He pulled her into his arms.

"Sometimes I wonder…" She broke down and wept against his shoulder.

He ran a hand over her springy hair, reveling in the feel and scent of it. She felt so good, so right, so perfect. He breathed deeply and wiped the tears from her cheek. "I am, too."

"You're what?" Her head shot up.

"I'm meant to help the orphans."

Her brow crunched as she tried to understand.

He smiled. "What I'm saying is I'd like to take that handyman job, if you think I meet the qualifications."

She drew in a shaky breath, still looking uncertain. "Of course. Yes, I'd love to have you work at Constance House."

But he could see the disappointment in her eyes and had to work hard not to rush things. "I suppose that'd mean I should live there, so I can be around when something breaks. Plus, you did say something about a father figure."

"Yes, of course." She wiped her eyes. "Though it might be a bit awkward since I live there, too."

He pulled her hands from her face and held them the way he'd always wanted to hold them. She didn't pull away, and he looked into her glistening hazel eyes. "It wouldn't be awkward if we were married."

Her jaw dropped. She stammered something unintelligible, and then she started shaking. "Are you? Did you? Do you mean what I think you mean?"

He nodded. "I'd like to make a life with you, Mariah Meeks, if you'll have me. I love you. I always have."

"But the children—"

"Are at Constance House."

And then, for no reason at all, she started sobbing and crying and he had no choice but to take her in his arms and hope he hadn't said the wrong thing.

"I'm sorry I upset you," he said when she finally calmed down.

She shook her head violently and took a ragged breath. "I'm not upset," she wailed. "I'm the happiest woman in the world."

"Then you accept?"

"Yes, yes." Then she threw her arms around his neck and cried some more until he had to kiss her just to stop the tears.

* * * * *

Dear Reader,

Thank you for joining Mariah and Hendrick on their journey to Montana and beyond. In 1922, it was still a feat to make such a lengthy trip. The roads were narrow and poor, nothing like today's paved highways!

My grandfather, first in a long line of mechanics, drove from Michigan to Oregon and back in 1926. He brought his brother along and suffered many breakdowns during the twelve-day trip each way. I'm grateful that he kept a journal of his travels.

These days, I hop on a plane and get there in a day. Glacier National Park and the adjacent Blackfeet Reservation are dear to my heart. My husband and I have made four trips there, including one for our twentieth wedding anniversary. The beauty of the mountains continues to awe me.

It's easy to see why the land is sacred to area tribes. If you visit, take a moment to listen to the whisper of the wind, the cries of the eagles and the rush of glacial melt—and to praise God for His marvelous creation.

I love to hear from readers. You can contact me through Love Inspired Books or my website at http://christineelizabethjohnson.com.

Many blessings,
Christine Johnson

Questions for Discussion

1. At the beginning of the story, Luke's father asks for his return. Why does Mariah feel this is such a problem? Have you ever acted on a strong hunch? How did it affect the outcome?

2. Does Mariah's quest to save Luke from his biological father go too far? If so, why?

3. Taken to an extreme, good intentions can turn into an obsession that impacts others. How does Mariah's quest affect her brother Gabe? Hendrick? Anna?

4. Early in the story, Hendrick turns down the chance to promote his engine design to a major aviation manufacturer. Why? Deep down, what holds him back? Have you ever faced a similar decision? If so, how did your choice affect the course of your life?

5. What qualities does Hendrick admire in Mariah? Why? How do those qualities feed into Mariah's goals? How do they affect her relationship with Hendrick?

6. Mariah has formed a mental image of Frank Gillard that doesn't match reality. Have you ever done that? How did it affect your initial reaction?

7. Frank Gillard is handsome, well dressed and charming. Hendrick recognizes that that's all su-

perficial. What tips him off? Why doesn't Mariah spot that?

8. Joshua Talltree is reluctant to talk with strangers. What might have happened in his past to inspire such distrust? Have you ever been reluctant to talk to someone? What happened that made you lose trust? How could your trust be regained?

9. Constance is also reluctant to speak with Hendrick and Mariah. What changes her mind? How could you reach out to people who are shy or afraid?

10. Why does Frank Gillard's housekeeper urge Mariah and Hendrick to leave the ranch after she catches them snooping? What else could she have done?

11. Why doesn't Mariah tell Hendrick much sooner how she really feels about him? Do you agree with her decision? Why or why not?

12. Under duress, Frank Gillard finally reveals his true self. Though Mariah's instincts told her not to trust him, she ignored those gentle nudges. Why? Have you ever ignored a gut feeling? What happened, and how did you handle it?

13. The community and tribe rally to help the schoolchildren after the fire. Crises tend to bring out both the best and the worst in people. Think of examples of each in this book and in real life. What might explain why people react so differently?

14. Though Hendrick forgives Mariah, he rejects a relationship with her. Why? What needed to happen to change his mind and heart?

15. How did Mariah's and Hendrick's faith help them to overcome the obstacles they faced?

INSPIRATIONAL

Wholesome romances that touch the heart and soul.

COMING NEXT MONTH
AVAILABLE FEBRUARY 14, 2012

THE COWBOY FATHER
Three Brides for Three Cowboys
Linda Ford

HOMETOWN CINDERELLA
Ruth Axtell Morren

THE ROGUE'S REFORM
The Everard Legacy
Regina Scott

CAPTAIN OF HER HEART
Lily George

REQUEST YOUR FREE BOOKS!

2 FREE INSPIRATIONAL NOVELS
PLUS 2
FREE
MYSTERY GIFTS

Love Inspired.

HISTORICAL
INSPIRATIONAL HISTORICAL ROMANCE

YES! Please send me 2 FREE Love Inspired® Historical novels and my 2 FREE mystery gifts (gifts are worth about $10). After receiving them, if I don't wish to receive any more books, I can return the shipping statement marked "cancel". If I don't cancel, I will receive 4 brand-new novels every month and be billed just $4.49 per book in the U.S. or $4.99 per book in Canada. That's a saving of at least 22% off the cover price. It's quite a bargain! Shipping and handling is just 50¢ per book in the U.S. and 75¢ per book in Canada.* I understand that accepting the 2 free books and gifts places me under no obligation to buy anything. I can always return a shipment and cancel at any time. Even if I never buy another book, the two free books and gifts are mine to keep forever.

102/302 IDN FEHF

Name	(PLEASE PRINT)

Address	Apt. #

City	State/Prov.	Zip/Postal Code

Signature (if under 18, a parent or guardian must sign)

Mail to the **Reader Service:**
IN U.S.A.: P.O. Box 1867, Buffalo, NY 14240-1867
IN CANADA: P.O. Box 609, Fort Erie, Ontario L2A 5X3
Not valid for current subscribers to Love Inspired Historical books.

Want to try two free books from another series?
Call 1-800-873-8635 or visit www.ReaderService.com.

* Terms and prices subject to change without notice. Prices do not include applicable taxes. Sales tax applicable in N.Y. Canadian residents will be charged applicable taxes. Offer not valid in Quebec. This offer is limited to one order per household. All orders subject to credit approval. Credit or debit balances in a customer's account(s) may be offset by any other outstanding balance owed by or to the customer. Please allow 4 to 6 weeks for delivery. Offer available while quantities last.

Your Privacy—The Reader Service is committed to protecting your privacy. Our Privacy Policy is available online at www.ReaderService.com or upon request from the Reader Service.

We make a portion of our mailing list available to reputable third parties that offer products we believe may interest you. If you prefer that we not exchange your name with third parties, or if you wish to clarify or modify your communication preferences, please visit us at www.ReaderService.com/consumerschoice or write to us at Reader Service Preference Service, P.O. Box 9062, Buffalo, NY 14269. Include your complete name and address.

LIH11B